D0983660

SHOLEM ASCH

TALES OF
MY PEOPLE

Translated by Meyer Levin

Short Story Index Reprint Series

 BOOKS FOR LIBRARIES PRESS
FREEPORT, NEW YORK

present American Jew. Greater than the physical legacy is the spiritual heritage that the new American Jew has received from his forefathers, and it is this spiritual heritage that is presented in this volume.

SHOLEM ASCH

The Little Town

Reb Yechezkiel's Place

The door of the house is open day and night. People are forever coming in and out, just as if it were an inn. Actually, this is Reb Yechezkiel Gumbiner's house, but at the same time it is a gathering place open to one and all. If a complete stranger were to come in and sit down, the villagers might not even ask him what he had to say for himself. For here everyone is at home.

If a man leaves his house in the morning without having swallowed something to warm his insides, he simply walks into Reb Yechezkiel's, still wrapped in his praying shawl and phylacteries, and just as if he were one of the family, he calls to the servant to fetch him a glass of tea. Or, more frequently, it's a cup of borsch for which people are indebted to the house. For not long after breakfast, on a wintry morning in a cracking frost, one feels the need for something warm again, and word soon gets around that Reb Yechezkiel's wife Malka is brewing a garlic borsch in her kitchen. There's nothing evil about taking a sip of something there—actually it's the custom—a cup of borsch, a glass of water. . . .

If a village housewife is too lazy to build a fire in her oven, she takes up her pot and carries it over to Malka's kitchen. And in that kitchen, the cooking pots of the entire town may be found. Sometimes the good housewives become confused as to whose pot is whose. Then things are lively.

And if a lad has trouble at home, he betakes himself to Reb Yechezkiel's stable. He has nothing to worry about. Bread and rolls are never locked up in Reb Yechezkiel's house. In the kitchen everything is as free as water, and butter and radishes are always

4

to be found in the cellar. The key to the cellar hangs by the stove in the care of Yente, the servant girl. But she's a good enough girl, and if she doesn't do as she's told—a little beating helps. Reb Yechezkiel says so himself.

Night takes the village under her wing, and within the night all the surrounding world is hidden. In the midst of the night the noisy beat of horses' hoofs and the rattle of wagon wheels on stone is heard. The noise ceases as a light shines forth from a window; then people are heard getting down from a wagon.

Heavy manly steps make themselves heard down the corridor. These must be habitual guests for they find the lock immediately, open it, and come into the big room.

There is no one in the long wide chamber; it is filled with shadows. Only one light burns among the shadows—the great winter lamp, with its wide shining arc like a grandmother's broad apron.

The Jews coming into the room wear long full sheepskin coats with broad collars that hang halfway down their backs and have red shawls wrapped around their throats. In the dark folds of their coats there still seem to linger the dark secrets of the night, which they have carried in with them from outdoors. On their heads they wear sheepskin caps with earlaps, and there are icicles on their hats and collars. The icicles melt in the warmth of the room, and drops of water fall from their sheepskin caps and coats so that they leave little trails of water behind them as they move about the room.

They approach the great stove that stands in a corner of the room. A blast of heat from the stove keeps them from coming too close. The warmth embraces them. They remove their sheepskins and remain standing in their thick red-belted jackets, and only now their beards appear. Some white, some black, some short, some long.

5

The younger men leave the places near the stove to the elders and seek out havens for themselves. One stretches out on a bench, another on a table. They are soon asleep. The old ones sit quietly around the stove, and occasionally one asks a question of another, about business, and after a long while the other gives him an excuse for an answer.

Now the night comes through the window as though peering through gray glasses. One may imagine that a few barrels of light have been emptied into the black ocean of night, making it just a shade grayer. From somewhere the long-drawn-out crowing of a waking rooster is heard. Wheels rattle over stones, making a forlorn sound in the quiet night.

With ever grayer spectacles the night peers through the window. More and more barrels of light are stirred into the sea of darkness. From another house a rattling is heard and the sound of water pouring. Then there are steps moving about and away. And soon from the other house one hears an old man's voice repeating the morning prayer in a tearful singsong. The voice carries a long way. Then a bold young voice mingles with it. The young voice is hurried, joining almost pretentiously in the ancient, tearful chant. *"Thus saith the Lord ..."* It rattles against the elder voice, but the aged one continues solemnly, as though for itself alone, avoiding and disdaining the bright young intrusion and pouring forth its lamentation into the world.

The Jews huddled around Reb Yechezkiel's oven hear the voice of prayer as they awake, rubbing their eyes. One washes his hands by rubbing them against the window. Each soon draws a prayer from his pocket, and they repeat the responses with a sharp, half-Litvak accent. *"Why hast Thou forsaken us? ..."*

One might imagine that the voices are merely exchanging greetings with each other in the dim light, before the men can see each other.

And through the window the night peers, a paler gray, until one cannot tell whether this is the hour of daybreak or of nightfall.

Wood chopping is heard from the kitchen, and the crackling of fire. Someone pours something from one pail into another. The door opens; people move about; people come in; somebody puts something down and goes on his way. A child's cry is heard from a house nearby. Now all of the sounds seem to merge—the mournful praying of the old man, the high-pitched singsong of the young boy at his devotions, the servant's wood chopping, the crackling of the fire, and the scattered voices greeting each other and saluting the newborn day that peers in through the windows.

It is already half light in the room. On the great table, there lies a heap of fur coats, greatcoats, and shawls. A tall young man is stretched on the sofa with his long legs extending into space. Doors and gates are open. People are coming in and going out; Jews of all sorts and all ages are arriving. They are tall and they are short; they have long beards and short beards. They say good morning to one another, and without wasting a word they are in the midst of bargaining. They talk and argue. To some questions there is no answer, and to other questions there are too many answers. Already one sees a good Jew taking another by the arm, steering him into a corner where he buzzes something into his ear. A third person stands by a table with his little prayer book open while his eye wanders to that corner, and suddenly he too seizes someone by the arm and walks him to another corner, showing that he too has a secret business—and let his competitor's eyes pop out of his head!

Meanwhile there is yet another who wakes, and winding himself in his prayer shawl and his phylacteries, he stands and prays, and there is even another who is already off on his way. At the table two businessmen are adding up their account with a bit of chalk. One of them wets his finger and rubs out what the other writes, and the other writes again what the first has rubbed out. In another corner stand two good Jews occupied in a further stage of business. One of them, with a little yellow beard and a round little belly, counts out money on the table. He counts solemnly, like someone piously praying—seventy-four, seventy-five, seventy-six—and as though he wishes to emphasize to the other, "You see what money means?"

Now the door opens, and in bursts a huge fellow, blind in one eye and with a long reddish beard. Without a why or wherefore he begins to curse the yellow beard who is counting out money. "You yellow dog! Paying two hundred and fifty rubles! Have you gone crazy?" The yellow beard keeps on counting out the money, one hundred and one, one hundred and two.... "What are you doing with my money?" the one eye shouts. Yet scarcely has the recipient picked up the money before the red beard and the yellow beard are off whispering together, and all is peaceful between them.

On the table there are samples of grain heaped in red handkerchiefs, and every Jew who comes into the room picks up a few kernels and examines them; he pops one into his mouth and asks of no one in particular, "What's the market today?" He gets no answer, so he cracks the kernel in his teeth and creases his brow as though he would discover by himself the answer that no one has offered.

This room is the village market place. Little merchants go around buying grain from the peasants, and they sell it here in "Reb Yechezkiel's granary." In this room all sorts of affairs are arranged, not only matters of business with Reb Yechezkiel but all sorts of side affairs between one customer and another. For if a Jew has a little private business to negotiate, or if a young man wants to take his first step away from the study table and get into business, he will come and pass his time in this room.

In the house there is a special little room known as the office—for Reb Yechezkiel himself. In front of a square desk sits Reb Yechezkiel—a short, thickset patriarch, with a round white beard, holding his glasses on his nose with one hand. A lens is always falling out, and Reb Yechezkiel picks it up, cleans it with his kerchief, and sets it back in place on his nose while he's asking something or answering something in his endless discussions with his man, Reb Toby. Reb Toby, a tall fellow with a thin face, replies to Reb Yechezkiel with alacrity, and with a little cackle as if to say, "Everything is fine; everything is going fine."

Wrapped in his long, ample sleeping coat, with his four-pointed hat on his head, Reb Yechezkiel sits there rolling a bit of bread dough between his fingers, giving ear to his man. For a moment he frowns, then he smiles again, as one who is ready to advise his helper. He pulls open a drawer, takes out a document, and instructs Reb Toby, "Wolf had better write to Danzig that the first transport has gone off."

A door opens, and at first a head appears, saying, "Good morning," then it disappears, and then a tall peasant comes into the room, his high muddy boots leaving a distinct track behind him. His face is red with heat, drops of sweat run from his damp hair, and without a word he flings open his coat, and then his vest, pulling out a letter, which he hands to Reb Yechezkiel. While Reb Yechezkiel is reading, Reb Toby goes over to the messenger, plying him with questions. But the peasant stands dumbly. He keeps his eyes on Reb Yechezkiel as though waiting for a signal.

"Hitch up the wagon! I'll go myself to Trisk!"

"I said from the first—you can't trust the water! Even then. Two weeks before the holiday—who knows what can happen! If the first frosts are strong..." Reb Toby drums to Reb Yechezkiel with a sort of soft insistence, for he already understands what has happened.

"It's lost! I had to have the lumber in readiness there. The rafts were strongly tied. The rope was thick. And the weather was good. How can you know what will happen? What is there to do? It's an act of God. How could anyone predict that before Hanukkah the river Vistula would break and—"

"We have to take along Antek and Sokolofsky—and axes and plenty of rope," Reb Toby advises.

"That goes without saying. They write to me that God should

9

only grant that the storm may not be too violent. And Trisk, it seems to me, is a sheltered spot. It's not windy. And with God's help, if only there shouldn't be a sudden storm, we may yet be able to save the logs," Reb Yechezkiel concludes. "With God's help."

"We have to send two hundred rubles to the squire. And Reb Abraham Plotsker had better buy what he needs in Shaminitz. I am afraid the Shaminitzers will buy up all the sheep before we know it. We can't let them do that to us." And still talking, they go into the other room.

About half of the dealers were already in the yard, clustered around the scales where the grain was being weighed. In the house there remained only a few of the last arrivals who had brought their wagons of grain during the night. There were also two traders from the city—one fine Jew in a goyish hat, wearing a collar and a short coat and carrying a stick in his hand. This was Kazak, the trader for the big landlord, the Paaritz. He had been sent from the big landlord's sugar refinery to Reb Yechezkiel. With every second word, he brought in the landlord and his sugar refinery. The other was Reb Zekiel Epstein, a Chassid, who had himself once been a grain dealer, buying produce directly from the farms. Now he was above all that. He had become a broker in his own name. He wore a long imitation-silk coat always torn and spotted; however, it had not yet lost the silken shimmer of its earlier days.

Reb Yechezkiel greeted all the good Jews with a hearty *"sholem aleichem"* and herded them over to the washbasin before they could utter a word, so they could wash before eating. Then a tall heavy woman in a broad apron came into the room. Her heavy rattling bunch of keys heralded her arrival; her diamond earrings flashed. She placed a clean white tablecloth upon the chalked-up table, and in a solid housewifely voice, she commanded the men, "Reb Toby, wash your hands. Reb Nota, go wash." Then she set the table.

10

The guests permitted themselves to be hustled to the washroom. Epstein, the broker, was the last. Malka set bread on the table, and everyone sat down. From the kitchen came the odor of frying onions and the steaming aroma of red borsch, which brought memories of Passover and awakened everyone's appetite. Epstein sat at the table in full equality with the other guests; he traded witticisms from the Torah as he ate. The other broker, Kazak, sat in a corner on the edge of the bench and twirled his whiskers. He sat in such a way that if one wished one could believe that he was sitting at the table, and if one wished one could believe that he was not sitting at the table. He looked down upon Epstein from his height. But the serving girl, it seemed, made a little error and counted him as a guest at the table, for she put a plate before him. He too, it seemed, made an error and turned toward the table, partaking of the food in such a way that if one wished one could consider that he was eating, and if one wished one might consider that he was merely tasting.

In the yard, there was altogether a new life. Just before Purim, winter still lies on the earth, but spring already smiles down from heaven and approaches from all four corners of the world. The long-frozen snow, which formed a second surface over the earth during the winter, now melts and dissolves. The sun's bright daughters, the warm rays, flicker in the mud. Pigeons fly back and forth over the yard. They descend and light on the ground, snatch up a kernel of oats, proudly spread their white wings, and are off. Grains of oats are scattered over the yard. Hens wander about, pick up the grains, and get underfoot. Chained in the stable to his kennel lies Borak, a large shepherd dog. He sticks out his thick head and waits his chance. As if in fulfillment of the prophecies, a white goat with twisted horns wanders around the yard with a little sheep. They have formed a partnership and sport together in the bundles of hay lying on a wagon in the middle of the yard. On the other side of the yard frozen boards and planks lie half buried in the snow. Children swarm along the boards, heading for the granary. The doors of the granary are open; in front of them stands a huge scale. One man piles sacks on the scales, and the record keeper, a young man in a fur-collared coat, holds a notebook in his hand and writes down the weight. Through the open gates one team after another drives into the yard. The drivers unload their sacks, weigh them off, and carry them into the granary. Nutta, the young stableman, a tall broad-boned fellow from Reb Yechezkiel's establishment, with a dark sunburned face and large bright eyes that look from the distance like two storm lanterns, leads a pair of tall horses out of their stalls. One of the horses has a round black mark on his forehead that shines like a dark eye out of his chocolate-colored coat. The manes of both horses are combed and braided. This pair is the favorite treasure of Reb Yechezkiel. They understand him and they know when his journey is urgent. The whip is carried only for show. There has never yet been a time when these horses have left him stranded on the road over Sabbath. They seemed to sense the coming of evening on Fridays so as to race home before Sabbath fell. He could rely on them. And when they showed their mettle, he stroked them with his own hands.

It was said that Reb Yechezkiel's horses were the souls of one-time debtors whose signatures still lay in his keeping and who could not rest in their graves until they had worked out their debts to him.

Nutta was dressed in his short winter jacket with high leather boots. On his head he wore a round military fur hat; only the insignia was missing. And with a friendly air he led his companions in labor to the wagon, placed the halters around their necks, and hooked them up in their new harness. Then he tied the blue reins to the whip and took his place on the driver's seat. Antek picked up the weight and the rope from the ground and shoved them under the seat.

While going into the stables, Nutta threw a glance into the window of the kitchen. It was successful, for he was almost immediately followed by Yente, the serving girl. The glow of her healthy red blood in her thick fleshy arms was visible through her torn smock. Black locks framed her sooty young face, and her black eyes under the sharp black brows spoke fire and flame. She slipped into the stable after Nutta, and without saying a word, she brought a half a roast chicken from under her smock and handed it to him. Nutta accepted it as a matter of course. She waited. He knew what she was waiting for. And contrariwise, since she wanted, he didn't. He picked up a bit of straw and seemed to be on his way out. And now he wanted. He seized her and imprisoned her in both his arms, still holding the whip in his hand. He paid her with a fat kiss on the cheek.

"You think I believe you'll marry me? You should live so!" she said, pulling away.

"Quick, the mistress is coming. Run!" He gave her a little push. She became frightened and started away, but in a moment she realized he was teasing her. The girl paused at the stable door. "I hope you break your arms and legs on the way!" she flung at him with a laugh as she ran off.

"You witch!" he called after her. The weighman, seeing her running out of the stables, winked to Antek, the yardmaster. "Goddam!" Antek called after her. She stuck out her tongue to him and disappeared in the cooking shed.

The snap of Nutta's whip and the growl of whirling wheels announced to the world that the wagon was waiting in front of the gate. Immediately a procession of people, carrying all sorts of packages, moved from the house to the wagon. For Reb Yechezkiel never started on the way without a few items to sustain him on his journey.

Then Reb Yechezkiel appeared, carrying his ample sheepskin. The wide-sleeved winter coat was spread over the seat since it was

13

a nice day and the frost was melting and the sun was laughing in heaven. After him came his wife, Malka, with a blessing on her lips, and a flock of children, small and large. Some of the children had their study books in their hands as they had already been in the schoolroom—and there were toddlers clutching buttered bagels, whom a servant was still urging toward the schoolroom. But the children—most of them in their fur jackets—clustered around the wagon.

"Grandpa!" they called. "Have a good trip. Go in the best of health."

"Good health to you, children. Study well!" their grandfather called, giving his hand to one after another. Then he pulled a huge purse out of his trouser pocket and handed out spending money to the children.

From a window between two open shutters, a young woman's face peered out. One could see part of a tender blooming cheek and a black silken braid tied with a blue ribbon, the whole making a delicate picture in the distance, as she called out, shaking her head to her father, "Good health, Papa!"

Reb Yechezkiel mounted the wagon. Sitting there, he gave last-minute instructions to his man, Reb Toby. He said his farewells and called out to Malka, "The best of health, the best of health!" And then called to his sweet-faced daughter, "The best of health, Leabeh!" and to his grandchildren he called out from the wagon, "Don't forget, study well!"

Yente was standing to one side. She held her hand over her heart and peered out after Nutta as he sat proud and powerful on the driver's seat. There he was in his short coat, with his rascally cap, winking down at her. He held the reins in his hands, ready to go forth into the world with the same impatience as his team of horses, who were rattling their hoofs on the stones. Yente smiled. The snap of Nutta's whip was a greeting for her. "In the best of health, Yente." The team turned out of the little lane into

14

the early morning quiet of the village and went forth into the world, and Nutta with his military cap disappeared in the distance.

In Reb Yechezkiel's house all is now peaceful. Business has been finished. The guests who came during the night have sold their wares, hitched up their horses, and left their places to other merchants who will arrive in the coming night. Only now can one see the old-fashioned leather cover of the big sofa, with all of its hills and vales. The long table in the middle of the room is scribbled over with chalk reckonings. The black stove is bescribbled, the high cupboard is bescribbled, and every chair and bench is covered with calculations. And the calculations on tables and benches, on the cupboard and on the walls, look like weapons left by soldiers who have fled from the field of battle. The calculations confront each other, contradict each other, glare across at each other.

Soon there enter two short, pot-bellied, fat young men, Chezkel and Berel. One may see by the family characteristic, the creases beside their nostrils, that they are brothers. They are, indeed, the nephews of Reb Yechezkiel.

Not long ago they were only two young students given their keep by the family, according to custom. And even today they are really still only guests of the family, but they are already in the habit of busying themselves in the big room. Since they are part of the family, they come in after breakfast to stretch out on the big couch. They stretch out on the couch together, as is appropriate for two brothers. First they take off their coats and fold them and place them for pillows under their heads. They do all this in silence as though it would be a pity to waste a word. They shove each other a little, kick each other a little, as they stretch out in opposite directions. Each would have liked the headpiece for himself. But just as they have conducted their struggle in silence, so they now silently make peace. One takes the headpiece, and the other

15

arranges himself against his feet. Chezkel, the older brother, scratches his little yellow beard and falls into thought over an account that stares at him from across the wall. "Seven times thirty-eight. How much does that make us, huh, Berel?" Berel answers only with a snore. So Chezkel gives up the question, turns to the wall, and, as though in imitation of Berel, he too begins to snore.

The River

All by itself there stands a little house in the gap between two high hills that rise into the world, tall and far, near the edge of the river Vistula. It is winter. God's world is entirely drowned in snow. Our cottage, like an old family man in his white sacramental undervest, stands at the riverbank, peering down at his frozen old neighbor, the river, and everything is still, awaiting the resurrection of the river. In the meantime the river lies there frozen and dead, wrapped in a white winding sheet. Ravens fly along the length and breadth of the river, alighting and picking little holes in its back. Occasionally a man passes over the river, leaving tracks in the deep white snow.

On both sides of the house the hills look like the broken wings of a fallen eagle, folded one over the other. Scrubby little snow-covered trees creep up along the shoulders of the hills, and one little tree, covered from head to foot with snow, has managed to scramble up to the top of the hill. It stands all by itself on the sum-mit and looks out far and wide over the white world. At the edge of the river, along the foot of the hill, stands a row of trees, one beside the other, snow-covered, looking like a row of white-clad attendants standing watch over a patient who is in danger of death —the river.

In the house, the same family has lived year after year. They live by themselves and with their neighbor, the river. Today the house is called Chaim the Ferryman's. About thirty years ago, it was called Mosheh the Ferryman's, and perhaps, in about twenty years from now, it will be called Daavid the Ferryman's. But this is no sign of change. Only the name may change with the years.

But the house, the river, and the name Ferryman's remain forever. The eldest ferryman, named Chaim, is a Jew of some fifty years. He is tall and thin, with a drawn-out face and a drawn-out beard and a high, creased, drawn-out forehead. He is a child of the water, brought up along the water's edge, and—who can tell—his grave will probably be in the water. And if not actually in the water, in any case alongside the water. And if a great storm comes, the roaring river will tear him out of his grave and carry him off to Danzig, as it did with his father and his grandfather. And in the end, what difference does it make whether one is mingled with the earth or dissolved in the sea? The earth is dead. She is forever silent and forever motionless. But the water at least is in continual movement, rushing, hurrying into the world, bubbling with life. For a long time he has been kin with the sea. Every year the river demands a human sacrifice, and it is already a long time since his little son Mosheleh became one with the river. And if the ferryman drowses by the shore sometime of a Sabbath afternoon, and a wave comes along with a roar, he might well imagine that the waves are Mosheleh and his playmates, who have come to wake him.

In the summer, he earns his living from the river. All week long he is in his little boat with the sail that cuts the sky in two. On the Sabbath, the river behaves like a good Jew. The river observes the Sabbath and the holy days. She is quiet. One wave gently kisses the other, and the ferryman and his wife sit by their door. He recites the Sabbath prayer, and his wife reads from the women's portion, and they speak of God's wonders to the waves. And each wave picks up a word and says amen.

In winter the river is frozen under her blanket of snow. The little house is covered with snow, poured over it from head to feet. From the flower-frosted windowpane, the eye of the ferryman peers out at his neighbor the river, all covered over and frozen. The ferryman studies the river, groaning. Both are frozen in, the river under the ice and the ferryman in his cottage. And when the water

18

shows again, coming to life from under the winter cover, then the ferryman also crawls out from his wintry grave, taking joy in the resurrection of his neighbor. And he smears his boat with tar.

At night all the surroundings are quiet. The moon gazes lovingly down upon the earth, like a father upon his household. The fields are covered with snow, and the hills are like corpses, peaceful in their shrouds. Then a strand of light shines out from the frosted window of the ferryman's house, blinking to the world. Somewhere, far away, a wayfarer wanders. He catches sight of the strand of light, and it draws him directly to the window of the little house wherein he may pass the night.

It is still winter. And all around everything is still covered with snow. But God already looks down from above with clear eyes. The sun falls upon the gray wintry clouds, and her rays pierce the earth's wintry grave. On the naked hills the snow melts clear and clean. Their pure whiteness has remained unsullied by a human foot, and now entire walls of melting snow slide from the hill and fall into the half-frozen river. The ice over the water is clean and transparent; the water may be seen as through a clean window. Occasionally, a fish leaps up; breaking through the window with his tail, he glances at God's free world and realizes with joy that his mother, the river, will soon uncover the window from herself; the fish dives back deep into the water to tell the good news to his comrades. Clear, clean, and white, the world of snow is marred by only one dark spot, the cabin that stands isolated in the vale.

Chaim's wife goes out to the well behind the house with a pail, and all at once she notices Reb Yechezkiel's wagon in the distance. She recognizes the horses immediately and taps on the window to her husband. "Chaim, the owner of the log rafts is coming."

"There is a wise one! In another few hours there wouldn't be a stick left of his timber!" Chaim answers, coming out to the threshold of the cabin.

19

The black line of the road lay over the white fields, and on the road two horses galloped, coming ever closer. Soon Nutta arrived before the cabin, drawing up with a flourish of his whip. The horses were steaming.

Reb Yechezkiel, wearing his heavy sheepskin, jumped from the wagon, asking, "Well, how are my logs back there?"

"We did what we could. We roped them up again. We nailed the rafts together with boards. And then we tied them to the shore with heavy ropes. But who knows; when you are dealing with her—" Chaim waved his hand, as though he would indicate the power of his neighbor, the river Vistula.

Reb Chaim approached Reb Yechezkiel, gave him his hand in welcome, and led him into the cabin. Reb Yechezkiel followed, his head hanging disconsolately.

In the quiet little room there were two high beds covered halfway to the ceiling with comforters that were stuffed with the feathers of all the geese and ducks that Chaim's wife had roasted on the eve of every Sabbath since her marriage day. These comforters were to be part of the dowry for her niece's wedding. From the little cupboard that stood in the corner of the house, red apples peered out, spreading their fresh scent through the little farmhouse.

Reb Yechezkiel seated himself at the table. In sheer agony of soul he neglected to remove his sheepskin and just sat gazing out of the window. All around was quiet. Only from far away one heard a sound of flowing water. This was a bad sign. And out of habit, a gusty "God in Heaven!" burst out from Reb Yechezkiel's chest.

Nutta came into the house, looking for something by the door. Chaim's wife began to argue with him about chopping wood. Soon a fire was snapping in the stove and a pot of soup was cooking for the merchant. Seeing that the merchant sat lost in thought by the table, Chaim's wife began to cheer him up. "Don't worry, sir, about the rafts. With God's help, you will rescue them from the water."

Reb Yechezkiel looked around and beheld Chaim's wife. That he should have to receive courage from her—from a woman— made him ashamed of himself. He arose and went out into the yard. "Reb Chaim, take me to the woods," he said as he came upon Chaim carrying two pails of water. "Nutta, come along."

Chaim carried the pails to the door. All three went down to the woods behind the house.

If one had not known that there were logs lying there, one would never have noticed them. The rafts were frozen in the ice and covered over with snow. Only the longest logs showed at all. The rafts were attached by long heavy ropes to the thick trees that stood along the riverbank.

"A terrible, terrible business," Reb Yechezkiel murmured to himself as he held up his walking stick, glancing at its length in order to guess the number of yards that remained between his logs and the edge of the river. "We must get some men from Yamo-shok. All the peasants we can get—and as soon as the ice breaks, we must drag the logs out of the water, no matter how much it costs. What's lost is lost."

"It's the only thing to do. As soon as the ice begins to break, it will drag the logs along like a bunch of feathers," Reb Chaim agreed, glancing with a sort of secret pride toward his river.

"It's not far from the edge. Five or six yards, maybe eight."

"We had better hurry; when the ice comes down from above, it's a matter of minutes," Reb Chaim said, already on his way.

Reb Yechezkiel handed him a five-ruble note for brandy to be bought in the village and himself went back into Reb Chaim's house.

The cottage was already filled with an aroma of beans and potatoes, for Chaim's wife was well aware that passing merchants licked their fingers over her beans. The woman was fully occupied in the kitchen. Nutta sat there in a corner, with his boots off, drying his leggings and palavering with Chaim's wife about a bride. Chaim's wife had the ideal match for him—her niece, the daughter of Arya of Yanosham, a very pretty, healthy girl, with a dowry of a few hundred gulden—and if it should so happen that his master remained over Sabbath, she would bring her little niece here for him to see. Nutta sat listening solemnly to her talk, nodding his head in agreement. What he really hoped to get out of the old woman was a good dinner. And he knew how to go about his affair. The old woman began to treat him like one of the family.

When Reb Yechezkiel came in, the discussion was cut off. Reb Yechezkiel found the table already covered—with an odd sort of cloth that might have been a blanket taken off the bed. And there was an old pewter spoon, a knife blade without a handle, and a fork. On the table were homebaked bread and a salt shaker. Reb Yechezkiel washed himself, recited the blessing, and Chaim's wife served him with a plate whose aroma filled the entire room.

Reb Yechezkiel scarcely tasted the food; he pushed away the plate. What was left was for Nutta. Reb Yechezkiel hastily recited the blessing after food and went out to the woods. He stood by the riverbank, waiting, casting his eye over the length and breadth of the white world. The water flowed down from the hills, pouring over the ice. Then a distant cracking was heard. A sheet of ice, large as half a lake, rushed toward them and tore onward. Water gushed up from between two chunks of ice, then broke with a roar out of a crack in the ice. Instantly, there was a huge hole. The surface was flooded. A wave of water came rushing, pouring over the ice. And immediately afterward, a crack was heard, like an explosion! The ice split, and a huge block rose on end, to be smashed to bits in the same instant. With even greater force, the water burst out of its prison of ice, sweeping along jagged, broken portions of its winter jail, toying with the ice, whirling great chunks, tossing them from one wave to another. Now the river

22

was free. The waves raced on as though chasing one another. Already, there was a break in the ice along the river's edge where the logs lay. Reb Yechezkiel heard the crack. A sheet of ice had broken but still did not move. The mass was too large and too heavy to be jarred loose all at once. The water battled the ice, sending wave after wave against the shore. The mass remained unmoved. Bits of ice broke from it, to be ground up and swallowed. For another moment the block remained in place, but a rumbling began underneath the ice, and slowly the block began to disintegrate.

Now the rafts became clearly visible. The logs had been tied together, but under the terrible upheaval they were torn apart.

Reb Yechezkiel stared at his property. He was in danger of losing all the lumber. The blocks of ice bumped and tore at the rafts. The ropes tugged and rubbed against the trees, pulling to get free. The last moment seemed to have arrived.

Reb Yechezkiel stepped closer to the water. He stretched out his hand as though to hold it back, and he looked desperately around, hoping to see the peasants arriving. No one was in sight. The water rushed on. All around, the ice groaned, cracked, burst. How could he save his fortune? O Lord in Heaven! If there were only a way to save his fortune!

Just then, Reb Chaim came running with a whole army of peasants. Reb Yechezkiel saw them in the distance and waved to them to hurry. The men approached, some carrying axes, iron bars, chains, and rope. Reb Yechezkiel's hope revived. He ran forward, paying no attention to the ice. He was ankle-deep in water. Reb Yechezkiel scarcely noticed. With God's help and the peasants behind him, he had no thought for danger. All that mattered was to save the lumber.

They leaped on the logs with their axes. They cut through the ropes. They separated one log from another. They chopped away the ties, they hauled on the ropes. There was no time to worry

23

about small matters. They jumped from one log to another, slashing, dragging. What logs they could save were hauled up from the river's edge to higher ground. The loose logs were securely tied and fastened to trees near the edge of the river.

And still the water raged and churned, battling the ice until the eye could scarcely tell whether the surface was composed more of ice or of water. The current hurled one block against another; they smashed head on and were instantly shattered to pieces. Suddenly a block of ice rose up, blocking the path of the others that swarmed around it, climbing one on top of another until a mountain of ice formed in the middle of the river. At first, the river was respectful of this mountain, flowing carefully around it. But soon the waves linked arms, made a united assault against the mountain of ice, and smashed it, destroying it completely. Then the river flowed on victoriously into the world.

The raging torrent smashed everything before it, and the peasants flew, leaping from one block of ice to another. Meanwhile night was coming on. The heavens above became frozen over in a mass of clouds. But the river kept on its own way, and the peasants kept on with their struggle. They dipped chunks of wood in pitch and set torches ablaze to light up the night. Under the leadership of old, experienced hands they labored, dragging one log after another to the banks. And the water stormed and roared, trying to drag the logs to itself.

After some hours when more than half of the lumber was already safe on the shore, Reb Yechezkiel sent his wagon to town for brandy, while he himself went into Reb Chaim's cabin. By the table sat an old Jew in a long fur coat, with a long black beard. He was half reclining on a bench and conversing with a boy of about fifteen. In the clever face of the boy, his father's worldliness could be seen more clearly than in the face of the old man himself. The boy wore a velvet skullcap over his little ear curls, and a silk kerchief. He was a little man of the world, self-possessed, neat, well mannered. Reb Yechezkiel was immediately taken by the boy, who came forward and stretched out his hand. Reb Yechezkiel greeted the boy and his father. *"Sholem aleichem.* Peace unto you," and they responded, *"Aleichem sholem.* And unto you, peace."

Then both parties asked at the same time, "From here?"

"I am from Konskavola, the village on the other side of the river," responded the good Jew with the black beard.

"I am from Kasner. My logs are in the river," Reb Yechezkiel said in turn.

"Who? Are you then Reb Yechezkiel Gumbiner of Kasner?"

"Yes. And you, how might you call yourself, in Konskavola?"

"Indeed! Reb Yechezkiel Gumbiner!" the other repeated happily as he rose from the bench, "I am Mordecai Konskar."

"Reb Mordecai Konskar of Konskavola!" Reb Yechezkiel repeated in awe. "Well!" He approached, stretched forth his hand. "Well, well!"

"The logs are still frozen in the water?"

"Yes, the logs were frozen during the winter. Nothing could be done. They were covered with snow. Now, praise be God, as much as we can—"

"A pretty business. May God watch over us and protect us. Father in Heaven!"

"Half are already taken out, with God's help. The peasants are working well."

For a moment they both remained quiet, leaning against the table. They looked thoughtful. The room was quiet. From outside one could hear the roar of the water, pouring down upon the ice with relentless anger. From a distance, there came a long-drawn-out sound, as from an empty barrel. The workers were sending some sort of signal to each other; the cry mingled with the roar of the water tearing itself away from all that was real in the world.

Reb Yechezkiel quietly took his place in a corner and began the evening prayers. Soon Reb Mordecai and his young son did likewise. All three began to walk up and down in the room. From time to time Reb Yechezkiel groaned out, "Lord in Heaven," and after a moment, they placed themselves in front of the wall, swaying and praying in silence. All became quiet in the room. Only Nutta's snoring rose from an obscure corner, echoing up and down the room.

Chaim's wife sat by the stove putting bits of wood into the fire. The kindling crackled in the stove. The woman permitted herself a respectful glance at the merchants. To behold such important men praying in her little cabin! Truly God must be present in her house! And she, an accursed fool, all she knew how to do was to put bits of wood into the fire. She pushed a few stray wisps of hair back under the marriage wig.

Suddenly, all was quiet as the men stood, each reciting to himself the silent prayer of the eighteen passages. Everything around them was as silent as the silent prayer of the eighteen. Into the midst of this, there came a terrible sinking sound from outdoors, as though an ocean were sinking within an ocean. And then there was silence again.

"Hold on, hold on!" someone shouted. The voice broke off abruptly, like a window smashed in by a fist. Chaim's wife was already outside. Nutta leaped up from his sleep. He looked around for an instant, making sure that the house was not on fire. Then he remembered something and ran out.

The three remained standing and praying. The boy, however, could not restrain himself; he broke off before reaching the eighteenth passage. He started to go out of the house, but as he saw that the two old men stood without budging from the spot, he became ashamed of what he had done. He wanted to begin the prayer all over again, but now he was abashed before God and did not know what to do.

The door opened, and Chaim burst in, breathless. "Master, the third raft has floated away."

The old Jews remained at their prayer. The boy and Reb Chaim exchanged glances without speaking. The old men completed their eighteenth passage.

Only then, Reb Yechezkiel asked, "What is it?

"*Shagetz!* Infidel!" A resounding slap was heard as Reb Mordecai paid off his son. "To break out in the midst of the eighteen!"

"It was carried away, floating."

"Carried away?"

"We had just begun to get into the third float when a huge block of ice came along like a beast and upf! It was on the way to Danzig."

"Did you save much out of it?"

"Forty or fifty small ones."

"Praised be God for that." He thought of something suddenly and walked up and down the room, repeating a prayer of thanks. As he finished, his hand was already searching in his vest pocket for his notebook. In the same moment, he put on his coat and went out.

The night was so dark that it was hard to believe that there was a heaven above and a God in heaven. The water roared. Nothing could be seen. One could hear only the force of wrath, as though some utterly unknown violence had come to swallow the world.

Reb Yechezkiel was frightened. He ordered the work to be halted. Let no more rafts be taken apart. No, let everything depend on God's mercy for the rest of the night. The rafts would remain where they were, roped together at the river's edge. He was certain that God would not forsake him.

And with a tranquil heart, with faith in the mercy of God, he went back to Chaim's place to make an offering with his blessing and to eat his supper.

The merchants were sitting at their meal, each completely occupied with his calculations. From outside one could hear the crying of the wind and the roar of the water. Reb Yechezkiel was unconcerned. "How is the grain in your village?" he asked Reb Mordecai in order to distract his thoughts.

"Our grain? Not a bit to be seen. Who has grain?" And after a moment of silence, "I've got a little for myself."

"How much does it cost?"

"Thirty-two guilder, two hundred and forty Polish."

"Two hundred and forty! Expensive. Around us it's much cheaper." And as though they had already come to an agreement, Reb Mordecai took out a little bag and opened it. Reb Yechezkiel, still talking, reached his hand into the bag, took out a few kernels, snapped one into his mouth, split it open, took it out between his two fingers and rolled it, then licked it.

"The quality isn't bad. The flour?" He wrinkled his nose. "Far from water?"

"A mile. A few hundred sacks alongside the water."

"Too much, take off five per cent."

Reb Mordecai wrinkled his forehead to indicate that this was impossible.

Reb Yechezkiel cut himself a slice of bread, not that he was hungry but simply to be doing something.

From where he sat by the stove, Nutta coughed, as though to suggest that they had altogether forgotten him and that he wished to remind them of his existence.

Chaim's wife served them with water for washing after the meal.

For a moment they were quiet. Then they began to nod one to the other.

"Well, Reb Yechezkiel? You will say the blessing?"

"No, Reb Mordecai, the honor should be yours."

Finally one took it upon himself, saying, "Enough. It's time for the blessing." They repeated the thanksgiving after food.

Reb Yechezkiel was the first to rise from the table. With a

chuckle he asked of the boy, "Well, young man, can you recite anything?"

"Why not?" the boy answered.

His father smiled proudly. "He's just coming from the Yeshiva."

"How far are you in the Talmud?" The boy named it. "Oh, that, that's a fine passage. Are there any commentaries?" And without waiting for the boy to answer, he whispered to the father, "The boy pleases me."

"He's got a fine head," Reb Mordecai answered, winking solemnly.

"Well, I would like to buy the corn. Not that I really need it, but simply since I am already here. You think I can make anything out of lumber? Eh, what? If there is a chance to buy something, a man has to buy it."

"Well, naturally."

"The five per cent—let it go as commission."

"But if I can't . . ." Reb Yechezkiel took a large wallet out of his rear pocket, opened it, took out a few notes, and offered them to Reb Mordecai.

"What can a man do when he can't?" Reb Mordecai groaned as he accepted the money.

And the deal was made.

Who knows whose grain from whose fields had changed hands!

And God was kind to Reb Yechezkiel. As though on order from Heaven, the ice avoided the rafts. Like matches, like slivers of wood, the logs floated in the turbulent water, tossing and trembling, but without moving from their anchorage.

Reb Yechezkiel stood by the shore and beheld the wonder that God had performed for him and saw that God had not ignored his prayer. For two days the peasants labored, dragging the logs to the shore. And Reb Yechezkiel, with his own eyes, beheld the effect of the Lord's intervention.

On Thursday Reb Yechezkiel said farewell to Reb Mordecai.

The unfortunate Reb Mordecai had to remain over Sabbath at Chaim's place since it was impossible to cross the river.

When Nutta was back on the driver's seat, waiting for his master, Chaim's wife came out on the steps. She gazed at Nutta and shook her large head. One idea was clear in her mind—what a fellow was this Nutta! He had had a feast for himself in her house. She had stuffed him with the best of everything, hoping that he might one day become a kinsman—through her niece. And there he sat on his wagon, with the horses waiting to carry him off. What a fellow! He had really taken her in, yet she could have no real complaint against him! For after all, what was he doing? He was driving off with his master. What else should he do? Stay in her place, forever? But she had reason to shake her head. And she stood on the steps, studying Nutta and shaking her head.

"What a fellow he is! What a fellow like that can do!"

Nutta turned his head away and stared out into the world, pretending not to see her; he whistled to his horses.

"Look how he sits, proud and fine on his wagon!" she spoke more through her head shaking than with her lips.

"What? Who?" Nutta asked, looking at her innocently.

"What? Who? And didn't you stuff yourself, and didn't you drink your fill, eh?" The old woman kept on shaking her head.

"Not a bad fellow, Nutta, a nice young fellow, one might say. Stuffed himself and made a fool of the old lady! I should live so! Does he want to get married! Is he looking for a suitable match?" said Reb Chaim, coming along and slapping Nutta on the back.

"Well, what else, Reb Chaim?" Nutta wrinkled his eyes and shrugged his shoulders. "If someone gives you something, you take it!"

"And didn't you promise to become a bridegroom while you were gobbling and swilling!" Chaim demanded.

"You should live so, you old fool!" Chaim's wife snapped at him as she turned and ran into the house.

THE LITTLE TOWN

Soon Reb Yechezkiel came out in his sheepskin and climbed up on the wagon. "The best of health to you!" Nutta cried into the window as the horses began to move.

"A healthy journey to you, and may you break your hands and feet!" cried the old lady. She sent her curses after him, feeling in her heart that he had somehow done her wrong.

Nutta answered her with a crack of the whip.

Keeping Accounts

There were four partners in Reb Yechezkiel's lumber business, but actually only three "heads" could be counted. Reb Yechezkiel, of course, was one of the heads. The second partner was Reb Chaim Rosenkranz, whose daughter was married to Reb Yechezkiel's son Motaleh. Motaleh, of course, was a third partner. And the fourth was Ozarel, the son of Reb Chaim Rosenkranz, who was married to the daughter of Reb Yechezkiel. The two older men counted as heads of the business, and the two younger men taken together were counted as the third head in the business.

Accounts were kept by the younger generation, Motaleh and Ozarel. They did their bookkeeping in the modern manner with paper and ink. They kept their accounts separately, but every few minutes one ran to the other for a consultation. One's accounts never balanced with the other's, and the only way to straighten them out was for the elders to take a piece of chalk and do the accounts over in the old style, by straight and crooked marks, until the business was finished.

But this was only the ordinary weekly reckoning that took place every Saturday evening. When the semiannual accounts had to be made at the end of each winter and summer, they sent for Reb Wolf the scribe, the well-known wonder-worker, and if there really was a difficult computation to be made there was nothing for it but to send for the lawyer, who was "a specialist" and wrote contracts for the big landowners.

To tell the truth, the elders could never understand what use there was in all this bookkeeping. No profit was ever made out of it, nor did they ever have to pay out money as a result of it. What use was it to know the sum total? Whether you knew or did not know the total, your blessings were neither greater nor smaller. And actually they were perfectly able to keep all the accounts in their heads; they knew in what transactions they had lost and in which they had earned money. They had lived their lives until now and done quite well without knowing anything about book-keeping, but now came the younger generation with its innovations, and one had to keep written accounts! So they kept their accounts although they knew beforehand what the result of every accounting session would be—a dispute. "And in the end," the elders complained, "what difference can it make? Is not Motaleh my son, the same as Ozarel? If there is a circumcision or a confirmation in one family or the other, don't we take equal pleasure out of it?"

The younger generation insisted that books had to be kept because this was a "necessity" in modern business. Well, so they went on adding and subtracting, and if disputes arose, with God's help, the arguments led to nothing serious.

In the younger generation there were nothing but disputes; the sons argued with each other, and the daughters quarreled with their mothers-in-law. There was a standing quarrel between Iteh, Motaleh's wife, and Golde, Ozarel's wife.

Golde, Ozarel's wife and Reb Yechezkiel's daughter, contended that much of her father's fortune had been sunk into the purchase of a house for his partner, Reb Chaim Rosenkranz and family. And contrariwise Iteh insisted that a great part of her own father's fortune had been utilized for the purchase of Reb Yechezkiel's properties. Again, the elders pointed out that it all would amount to the same thing in the end. "What does it matter," they said, "whether you inherit from your father's side or your mother's side since, after we are all dead, everyone will get an equal share?"

33

But how could one expect the younger generation to understand anything so simple?

Reb Yechezkiel's daughter Golde was a tall young woman who wore an elaborate marriage wig with three curls falling over her shining forehead. She had a snake's tongue and the whole town trembled before it. She was often to be seen in the streets with her little boys running before and behind her, tugging at her broad skirt, and crying, "Mama, a copper, a copper!"

She was the deadly enemy of her sister-in-law Iteh, and she complained constantly to her brother Motaleh, Iteh's husband, "Oh, Motaleh, you certainly fell into it, what a pity! How terrible you look—and when I remember you before you were married!" Her brother had only to step into her house for a word with Ozarel, and fail to find him at home, to hear this wail from Golde.

Motaleh was quite used to his sister's pity, though he had no idea why he was to be pitied. So he would only murmur, "All right, all right; be still, please," and leave the house. Sometimes, however, he was pained when she criticized his wife for, after all, Iteh was his wife; so he would turn on his sister. "What business is it of yours? She's married to me not you!"

"His wife! Just look how he defends her with his last breath! A fine daughter-in-law for Reb Yechezkiel Gumbiner! You know what she is? She is the daughter of Chaim, your father's stableman."

"Then my father's stableman's son is your husband. How do you like that?" her brother teased her.

"My husband—Chaim the stableman's son!" Her face grew red with anger. "So that is what Iteh has made of you! She'll bring you to an early grave! You'll run alive into your tomb just to get away from her." And she would begin to weep.

The house was filled with children, and as they saw their mother crying, they all began to bawl. After that Golde went to bed for the rest of the day, and when her husband came home, she fell upon him. "I suppose you stand by your wife, the way Motaleh does by his! If you heard your wife insulted, you wouldn't even say a word against it. You men!"

Afterward, when Ozarel and Motaleh were in the granary looking at the wheat and talking over affairs, Ozarel casually dropped a word about their wives into the conversation. "What was the trouble between you and Golde today?"

"Nothing, it was just nonsense."

"She went to bed for the whole day."

"How much did you put down for the Krosnitz?" the other asked, to change the subject. And more than once this sort of thing occurred the other way around, between Iteh and Ozarel.

It was the custom for each mother-in-law to raise a few turkeys for Passover, as a gift for her daughter-in-law. This had been a family tradition for years. One could see the young turkey cocks strutting around in Reb Yechezkiel's yard. They were destined for Iteh. And in Reb Chaim Rosenkranz's yard a few birds were being grown for Golde.

One day Golde came along, took the young turkeys out of her mother's yard, and carried them home. "They belong to me just as much as to her; they're my mother's turkeys," Golde defended herself.

Then Iteh ran off to her own mother, wailing, "Golde has carried away my turkeys!" Whereupon Iteh's mother seized the turkeys destined for Golde and gave them to Iteh. Soon enough the daughter-in-law came running demanding her customary gift, and naturally there was a healthy quarrel.

There was only one way out of it. The mothers-in-law quietly went off and bought another flock of turkeys, which they shared out between their daughters-in-law, and so the young women had twice their usual share.

35

The old folk were tired of the constant quarreling between the youngsters, for the endless quarrel embittered their households and their souls.

On the surface the daughters-in-law kept a sort of truce during the length of the year; they were neither angry with each other nor on good terms. If they passed in the street, they nodded distantly with their noses in the air. If, however, they met in the mother's house (it made no difference which mother) during fruit-canning days, they offered each other a polite "good morning" without actually looking at each other. The preserves were then shared out without exchanging a word. One would push the larger share toward the other, saying, "Let her take whatever she likes," and stare off at the wall.

"What difference does it make? Your children will eat the preserves in her house, and her children will eat them in your house —and the best of health to them all!" the mother or mother-in-law (as the case might be) would remark, while handing each her portion.

But when the time for the semiannual accounting came 'round, the two women, for no visible reason, would stop greeting each other in the street, and if they met in a parental house, they would sit facing each other in silence.

It was the night of the Sabbath before the annual accounting. There was a new atmosphere about the house. It bore a holiday air as though the house were decked in silken garments. The lamplight poured down on the long broad table, and the lamp seemed to be burning with special respect and altogether unusual intensity in honor of this day. Piles of documents and notepaper were spread on the table. At its head sat Reb Yechezkiel in his patriarchal chair. He held his glasses in one hand and a bit of chalk in the other while he carried out a bit of side addition for himself.

At the other end of the table, opposite Reb Yechezkiel, sat Reb Chaim Rosenkranz, a tall man with a long yellow double-pointed beard and a long hairy nose. Large beads of sweat dropped from the creases in his shiny broad forehead and hung on the hairs at the end of his nose. Reb Rosenkranz spoke little, and when he uttered a word, it was as though he were doing someone a favor. He watched everything. If anyone spoke he stared at him—and that was enough.

Ozarel and Motaleh sat on either side of the table. They were carrying on their computations out loud.

Motaleh muttered to himself, "Eighty-two on hand in Schenitz."

Ozarel, who seemed deep in his own accounts, suddenly started up as though boiling water had been poured over him. He shut one eye and regarded Motaleh. "What? When? What do you mean, eighty-two?"

"In Schenitz, didn't we give it to Lazar Rubin, eh?"

"Ah, Lazar Rubin . . . One hundred and twenty in Gumbin." The other went on with his own calculations as though nothing had been said.

"Dirty dog!" Motaleh cursed. "Snooper! Thought he would catch me. . . ."

They began to throw insults across the table at each other. The elders called, "Quiet! Quiet!" pounding on the table.

Ozarel was the "chief accountant." He was a Jew who lived in two worlds at one and the same time. He was a Chassid and a "Dutchman," a Jew filled with pious Hebrew lore and a worldly fellow who spoke German. He was at once an educated fellow and a man of the street. He was at home everywhere, and therefore he was the pearl of the family. A short round little Jew with a little round yellow beard, he sported a stiff white collar and a black tie, and like his father, he counted his words. When he finally spoke, he would shut one eye while he suspiciously studied his adversary with the other. He was suspicious of anyone on first sight, and yet he was on good terms with everyone. For himself, he counted himself a Chassid. He frequented their little house of prayer and liked to promenade in a long silken coat and a white collar. When he spoke he accented his *r*'s sharply, according to the fashion in Warsaw. He was a great friend of Mitkovsky, the only Litvak in the town, and when the Litvak held forth against the town's ordinary rabbi, he would nod his head and make a little gesture with his hands in such a way that if one liked one could believe he agreed with the Litvak, and if one wished one could believe he regretted the utterances of the Litvak heretic.

Today Ozarel was deeply engrossed in the accounts. He sat with Wolf the scribe over the main account book, which was known as "the correct account" or "the real book." Who, then, was this Wolf, and what sort of account book was this?

Wolf the scribe was a frail, skinny, tiny little nothing of a Jew but the master of master accountants. In this little nothing of a Jew a whole world of wisdom was concentrated, just as all the secrets of the ocean may be found in a drop of water. He was all dried up, with a face dominated by a broad furrowed forehead under which his eyes and his tiny nose were lost. The entire little man could be stuck in your pocket, and then if you needed a mathematician, you just opened your pocket and let him crawl out to walk. Who knew where he lived? He had neither wife nor children, and nobody knew whether he had ever had a family at all. The little man wandered around the town as though he were an afterthought, something that was found necessary when all the rest was already there. If anyone had a mathematical problem (not that he needed to have it solved but simply because it might be interesting to know the answer), he would come to Wolf with it. Wolf would wrinkle his brows until his forehead looked like a leaf out of an old book. The wrinkles in his brow were like faded numbers, and one might have imagined that the wrinkles put themselves together in such a way as to bring forth the answer to the problem.

And so Ozarel had brought in this same Wolf to do the annual accounting. Wolf the scribe never asked for anything easy; all his life he hoped only to find a problem difficult enough for him to prove his mettle.

Whatever the merchants expended and whatever they took in was noted down in a little book according to a system invented by Ozarel; on one page he would inscribe the expenditures and on the other he would inscribe the income.

For Ozarel himself this was well enough; he kept his accounts neatly, he claimed; but when it came to the old folks, the whole system fell into ruins. They were always losing their pencils, and when they had to write something down, they started to search in all their pockets while they cursed the "modern system" that Ozarel had introduced, and in the meantime they made temporary notes on the sideboard with a bit of chalk, or on the table or perhaps simply on a scrap of paper. When the annual accounting came, they had to hunt up the scrap of paper and examine the table and the benches on which they had scribbled their accounts, and then they would transfer these accounts into the big book.

The handwriting of the old people was not very clear, and the numbers scribbled down on scraps of paper and even in the notebooks often became rubbed out so that later there were innumerable arguments about the figures. One would declare that a certain number was an eight, the other that it was a five, but mostly they could make nothing at all out of the notations. They would ask the elders, who would say, "Go bother your own head." So then they would send to Berl the watchmaker for his magnifying glass. They would stare at the number through the magnifying glass, only to emerge with the same division of opinion. At this point Wolf the scribe would intervene. He would perform an algebraic multiplication on one side and an algebraic division on the other side and finally prove that according to mathematical logic the number in question was neither an eight nor a five but a three, and there was no way to stand against him.

The big book was like an instrument, a violin, for Wolf the scribe. Upon it he performed his melodies. The book was the apple of his eye, and he carried it with him wherever he went. Ozarel and Wolf the scribe sat together poring over the big book. There was a perfect stillness upon the household, which seemed to enshrine their task with an added importance. Two large silver candlesticks stood on the table among the scattered papers and notes, lending a solemn illumination to the occasion. The door creaked, the servant slipped in and out, bringing tea and carrying away empty glasses.

On a sofa in the corner sat Chezkel and Berel, of Reb Yechezkiel's family. They were motionless and utterly quiet, so as not to be seen and so as to not miss anything. And they were ready at a moment's bidding to fulfill the slightest task that might be demanded of them by one of the magicians at the table. More than once they started off toward the door, following their own idea of what was needed; they would bump into each other at the door and make a commotion. One of the men at the table would look up and the two lads would shamefacedly tiptoe out of the room; but a few seconds later they could be back again, sitting on the sofa. One of them would solemnly pinch the other's arm or leg, or give him a little bite. The other would reply by sticking a pin in his brother, and they would carry on their battle without uttering a word.

All at once, the sound of arrivals was heard from outdoors; the door opened wide and a group of leading townsfolk appeared, still dressed in their Sabbath clothes; some smoking cigars, some with pipes in their mouths, and a thick stream of smoke issuing from their beards. The pipe-smoking did not accord very well with their Sabbath garments, but managed to give them a half-holiday air. The room became filled with smoke and through the thick haze the two candle flames threw a warm homey glow over the group.

They offered a hearty "Good week to you," and then arranged themselves around the table, each according to his station. The door creaked more than ever, and somehow the room now lost its imposing atmosphere, so much so that Berel and Chezkel no longer were constrained by a sense of awe, but felt themselves at home. Now their tongues were freed, so that they left off pinching each other and began to quarrel aloud. The room recovered its old atmosphere. The accounts were soon set aside and Wolf the scribe rescued his big book and vanished.

A tall man with a long broad beard, who talked more with his hands than with his tongue, and who stopped everyone else's mouth with the stream of his own conversation, became the head of the meeting. Since the town needed the income a wonder rabbi would provide, and since a rabbi was urgently needed to provide a place where the Chassidim might gather at a holiday and on the Sabbath, and in general to bring life to the village, it was his opinion, he said, that they should invite the rabbi of Trisk, who had just come to a parting of ways with his brother. The rabbi of Trisk would agree to come, he knew for certain, on the simple conditions that he receive the town rabbi's little house of prayer for his use and that the town rabbi give him a certificate declaring that the supervision of circumcision was the province of the rabbi of Trisk.

"What! We still have our rabbi in town. He'll live to be a hundred and twenty! All that you'll get is a pain from your precious rabbi of Trisk!" cried Aaron Leib the cobbler, who was blind in one eye. He had his stick in his hand, ready for the tall Jew.

The cobbler belonged to the congregation of ordinary folk, the hewers of wood and the carriers of water, as they were called in the village. They were all on the side of the present rabbi; but the more learned Chassidim, who were followers of the wonder rabbi in Trisk, wanted to bring a rabbi of their own into town.

"Handel Leib, since when have you become one of our leaders?

41

Can it be that you haven't a crumb left in the world and are trying to get your nose into someone else's cake, eh?" The second attack upon the tall Jew came from a butcher who had gone to school with him as a boy.

"Peasants and fools are to be found everywhere. Nobody asked anything of you! When you are asked, then you can answer!" said the tall Jew, turning his face toward the head of the table.

Reb Yechezkiel, the most important citizen of the village, sat listening to the dispute without uttering a word, glancing occasionally at his partner to see what he would have to say.

"Speaking among ourselves—whoever comes to our rabbi here in town? What sort of a name has he got? Who is he anyway?" the tall Jew quietly pointed out to Reb Yechezkiel.

"A good week to you all!" a new voice rang out all at once in the room. It was a special kind of a greeting that could not be confused with the others. Several of the men turned around to see who this might be. It was Reb Yitzchak Yudels. He was a Jew of quite another sort. Actually he was a little man, but broadly built and with a large stomach. He did not speak in an ordinary voice, like other men, but with a kind of screaming singsong. He did not look at people as did other men but seemed to attack them with his eyes. He could be as gentle as a pigeon or as vicious as a snake. He always had a cigar in his mouth whether it was lighted or not, and one could tell when he was coming a quarter of an hour in advance by the way he scraped his feet. He was everyone's intimate friend. Reb Yitzchak Yudels played a vital role among the Chassidim. He was an expert on all religious rules and regulations, he could tell anybody what they should or should not do, and the whole town feared him. All the ordinary rabbis who were respected by the townsfolk were held in utter disdain by him; he simply dismissed them with a wave of his hand. He had a standing quarrel with the rabbi of the town. If a question of ritual came up, he made his own ruling, declaring that the rabbi was illiterate. The whole town was intimidated by him; they were amazed at his temerity and afraid to contradict him.

Ozarel, who had remained cool during the entire discussion, listening quietly as though without interest in the argument, became transformed when he saw Reb Yitzchak Yudels. For the important Chassid always patted him jovially on the back when they met in the prayerhouse. Now Ozarel was a new man, a Chassid.

"What are you all arguing for? No one wants your opinion," Ozarel shouted to the plain folk.

Reb Yechezkiel and Reb Chaim Rosenkranz were ordinarily considered among the family men, the unlettered plain folk. They prayed with them and had their friends among them. They were not educated men and could not carry on discussions of the Torah in Hebrew although they were able to read out the prayers by rote. They were of the folk who had great respect for learned men and would give way before them. If a learned man uttered a word, even though he said something that was not altogether right, something that an ordinary man would not permit himself to say, it nevertheless stood to reason that he must know what he was talking about. So even though he was on the side of the ordinary folk, Reb Yechezkiel kept quiet in the face of the learning of Reb Yudels.

It was Reb Yechezkiel's secret desire to have a sage for a son, a being from the other world, who would sit day and night over the scriptures. Therefore he had employed Reb Yitzchak Yudels to teach his offspring, but his eldest son had taken to business even as a boy and had gradually deserted the Torah. One hope, however, had remained to him, a son-in-law who considered himself a Chassid, who frequented the Chassidic house of prayer, and who kept the company of Reb Yitzchak Yudels. Now that he saw that Ozarel and Motaleh together were on the side of Reb Yitzchak Yudels, on the side of the Chassidim, the old man felt a certain pride, for after all the Chassidim were something special, something beyond their everyday world with their everyday rabbi. So Reb Yechezkiel did not raise his voice in protest.

Reb Yechezkiel was in hopes of securing a true student of the Torah, someone who would bring honor to the house, as a groom for his youngest daughter Leabeh, the child of his old age. This would be a son-in-law who would eat at his table all of his days and do nothing but study the Torah, so that in the years of his old age, when Reb Yechezkiel had given up his business and sat at ease in his house, he would hear the voice of the Torah rising in the room. And he had put the task of finding such a sage for a son-in-law in the hands of Reb Yitzchak Yudels, so now the hearty greeting of Reb Yitzchak Yudels, resounding loud and firm in the room, brought hope and pleasure to the old man. Chassidim—in his house! And the old man began to daydream about the learned son-in-law he would have.

He rose and winked to his partner, Reb Chaim, to follow him into another room, for it was a custom of the elders that neither one of them should put his hand into a new affair without the other's knowing of it.

After looking ironically around at the plain folk, Reb Yitzchak Yudels threw a remark to them, "Yes, you don't need anything. There is no hurry—and where have we got to in this town?" Scraping his feet, he went into the other room to join the two old men.

"I had a letter from Reb Mordecai Konskar. He mentioned that you met him in Trisk and that you met his son. Well, what more could you wish?"

The women were gathered together in the dining room around Reb Yechezkiel's wife Malkaleh. It was Malkaleh's habit to try out the last of the goose fat for Passover on the Sabbath evening of the annual accounting. From the other room, where the men were busy over their affairs, a low rumbling was heard, which

44

indicated the gravity of their discussion. The servant girl went back and forth carrrying in full glasses of tea and bringing out empty glasses. Each time the door opened there was a blast of cigar smoke and of noise that temporarily drowned out the women's talk, and the women were dutifully impressed by all that was going on in there. Here in their room the women sat indulging in the foolishness of a card game. It was a game called Sixty-six, played with a worn old pack of cards that the men of the house had given to the children. The youngest children clustered about their mothers, pestering them for the coins on the table. The mothers pushed them away and the children kept up their clamor from a little distance. In the midst of all this a bit of a lad rushed up to the table, seized the stake out of the plate, and vanished to the land where pepper grows. Go follow him!

The older generation of women wore bonnets trimmed with ribbons of all colors, and wide forehead bands edged with pointed lace. From each point, there glowed a different ornament. From one a red ruby, from the other a little diamond glittered, until each wrinkled old forehead was transformed as though by the tiara of the Queen of Sabbath. The younger generation already wore "modern" marriage wigs, with curls falling over their brows, and their clothes were mostly of Parisian textiles in many colors, according to the fashion at that time; their gowns were cut in wide pleats, as was fashionable then, with each pleat inserted into the next. Sometimes the pleats melted together and became one, or again they separated and went in different directions. Over their hearts they all wore little square silver plaques on which each had hung out her bridal gifts.

Iteh, the daughter-in-law, and Golde, the daughter, sat opposite each other in silence, for this being the day of accounting, they were in a state of war. If one of them got up from her place, the other made a derisive movement with her lips, lifted her eyes to the ceiling, and sighed a little, for this was their custom when they were at war.

They sat at their game, which was presided over by a little man who was known as the Daitschel because of his modern "German" manners. He was always bobbing in and out of people's houses, especially Reb Yechezkiel's, and was known as the ladies' man. Even in those days he affected the German way of dress, wearing a short jacket and a septagonal cap with a hard visor. He dressed in the German fashion, not that he wanted to appear as a German but simply because it seemed to be fitting for a ladies' man to dress in this way. He had a remedy for every illness and called his remarkable drug the Corpus Delicti. He could speak Polish and mingle easily with the Gentiles of the village, and so he was thought of as a man of affairs in the town. He was a little man who made himself at home everywhere and was everywhere accepted as one of the family. He was friendly mostly with women, and somehow no one thought anything of his running in and out freely among them, as though the strict regulations of orthodoxy did not apply to him. He knew all the women's secrets and did not mind being thought of as half a woman. He won everybody by his witty sayings; he had a gift for making people laugh although his talk was more foolish than amusing. His mimicry was equally silly; he would push up the collar of his overcoat, twist his little hat around, and pretend to be asleep, while his little beard waggled from side to side, and that alone was enough to send everyone into peals of laughter.

Naturally, he had to be in Reb Yechezkiel's house on the Sabbath evening of the big annual accounting. An aroma of melting goose fat rose from the kitchen, and he knew well enough that when the accounting was completed a big feast would be spread, for this was the custom, year after year, in Reb Yechezkiel's house.

At one corner of the table sat the young bride-to-be, Leabeh. Through her fresh cheeks her young blood shone, as lightly as the glow upon a rose when the sunlight floods its satin petals. Her quiet eyes rested dreamily in their wide beds, guarded by their delicate, quivering lids. Her black brows were also on guard, following every movement of her eyes, from the edge of her large white forehead that rested like a crown upon her face. Her hair fell in two girlish braids over her slender shoulders. She sat by herself, and a kind of bridal charm emanated from her sweet little face. Each time that the Daitschel raised his voice her heart missed a beat and her young breast stirred lightly. She was afraid he would make fun of her. And soon enough her turn came. "Do you know the matchmaker is sitting in there with your father and discussing a groom for you?" She dropped her head, and made a defensive gesture with her slim white hands.

"You'll have a groom just as soon as radishes grow on the new moon." The chamber was filled with laughter. Leabeh leapt up from the table and fled in embarrassment.

The copper utensils shone rosily from the walls of the spacious kitchen, seeming to wink across at each other. The deep baking dishes, the long narrow frying pans, the tall containers of various shapes hung from the walls in neat array, gave the room a home-like atmosphere and told a tale of great feasts of the past. . . . A fire flickered on the hearth, and the deep broad-bellied copper pots seethed and boiled. The full, rich odor of frying fat lay over the kitchen, with a promise of the feast to come. The long table that served only for the preparation of meat was covered with a sheet of copper; upon it stood a whole row of deep receptacles, large and small, ready to receive the melted goose fat.

In a corner of the kitchen sat Rachel Leah the old houseworker —a tall woman with little warts on her upper lip and with two or three hairs growing out of each wart. The old gray cat lay in her lap and licked her skinny hands. Surrounding her were Malka's grandchildren, boys and girls, some in little shirts, some in their trousers, some in dresses, some in their fringed vests, and

47

they were all listening to her tale about the fiery hand and the goose fat.

"Once upon a time long ago," she told them, "a woman was melting goose fat in her oven, and when she took the pot out of the oven, she saw a fiery hand reaching out of the flames, and she heard a voice saying, 'Good woman, good woman, give me a little of the leavings—and then no evil eye will fall on your goose fat!' And so that was what she did, and then she began to pour off the fat, and she filled up one pot, and she filled up a second pot, and a third, and she filled up six and eight and ten until she had no more pots in the house—and only then did the fat stop pouring."

The children listened to her tale and watched with large anxious eyes for her to take the pot out of the fire, to see whether there would be a burning hand in the flames.

But presently old Rachel Leah dozed off, and her old bonnet with the silken ribbons, which had been made over from a discarded bonnet of Malka's, dropped over her wrinkled old brow. Then one of the little boys reached out his hand and tweaked one of the wart hairs on the old grandmother's face. "Up hup-hup" went the old woman's shrunken lips, while her toothless gums snapped at the child's fingers.

"Grandmama, why do the hairs grow on your warts?" the little children asked.

"Because there is no man any more to recite the Sabbath blessing for me, and I do it for myself, and I drink the wine of the blessing," the old woman answered with her eyes half shut, a crooked little cackle on her twisted old lips.

While the old woman was amusing the children, one of the eldest boys, a lad of ten named Chatskaleh, was very busy casting a toy out of lead. He had found a bent spoon in the kitchen, and now he was putting a handful of sand in a little form he had made.

In another corner of the kitchen, away from the stove, sat Yente the servant girl, with a large pail of water before her. She had a lapful of potatoes, which she was preparing for the big feast. She peeled the potatoes and tossed them into the pail.

Nutta stood behind her and pinched her full round arm.

"Well, Yente, and what about us?" he asked.

"You think I believe you will marry me?" she replied. "You should live so!"

The Rabbi and the Wonder Rabbi

At last came Lag b'Omer, the day of rejoicing which commemorates the holy Rabbi Shimon-bar Jechua.

And the good Mother Earth, who bore the entire village, houses, barns, and all, upon her generous breast, now was rejuvenated according to the will of God; she was newly arrayed from head to toe in budding leaves and grass. Little green shoots poked their heads from under logs and stones; with a loving glance at the world, they shook themselves awake and sucked their bit of nourishment from Mother Earth, and Mother Earth uncovered her full breasts and fed and filled every open little mouth so long as it wished to suckle. Lord of the Universe, everything about us obeyed and fulfilled what Thou hast ordained since the first day of creation. The grass grew, striving upward, for this was the fulfillment of its duty: to grow. The little birds built their nests upon the old synagogue wall, just above the window of the women's balcony, and all day long they hopped about in the holy little street of the temple where the voice of the Torah echoed. They danced from roof to roof, they sprang to the window of the ancient house of prayer, and they leapt down, reaching the earth with a screech, which was their way of blessing their food, for they set themselves to picking up the crumbs of bagels, rolls, bread and butter—which had already been blessed by the little student of the Torah. They flew off with their blessed crumbs, and the blessings of the food served partly to redeem the human souls that had been transmuted in these birds.

In the heavens above, thin little clouds extended themselves and melted one into another and floated far and wide, losing their way over strange lands while they guarded their little world according to Thy behest from the beginning of time. And the flowing of the stream behind the village was like a tranquil prayer by which it hoped to render thanks to Thee, our only Father, for all that is; it flowed on, wave upon wave, from one strange land to another; and upon its journey it repeated a lengthy, peaceable story; and from the surface of the water invisible clouds of dew arose to refresh the fields that spread far and wide on either side of the stream. The clouds of dew lay over the fields all night long, slaking their thirst and bringing them new life. And from the fields rich scents arose, filling the atmosphere with life and awakening and refreshing every living being within reach.

The first festival of the spring ... Before every gate, before every door the housewives sit with their knitting in their hands, knitting stockings and gossiping. A few children have remained at home instead of going along with the others to spend the holiday in the fields; they linger around their mothers, tugging at their aprons, crying, "Mama, a copper!" The pious rabbi's wife, wearing her white holiday shawl, sits before her door, surrounded by the wives of the servants of the synagogue, and of the cantor and the ritual butcher. There are a few trees on the street; no one knows how they grew there since no one ever planted them, and no one knows how they survive when the boys clamber all over them, tearing off their scant leaves. Barefoot lads now come from the fields with heaps of yellow buttercups in their hands, and they cry out, "Flowers for buttons! Flowers for buttons!" The other boys slide down from the trees, and ring them round. They tear the buttons off their trousers and their coats, and buy flowers, running back to their mothers with arms full of blossoms and with their pants falling down.

A large white canvas is suddenly laid in the midst of the market place, and the music of a hand organ is heard. Children come running from all sides, then older folk appear. They make a circle around the musician. A barefoot fellow in a crushed visorless old cap, wearing some sort of knitted shirt and buckled up in a broad belt, turns round and round on the canvas; he has a long whip in his hand, and he snaps it over their heads, flicking off their hats, while the hand organ grinds on. Suddenly a tall lad appears; his face is covered with chalk, and he is dressed in tights from head to foot. There is a clock painted on his backside with the motto "Excuse me." He balances a huge pole on his stomach; an entire family climbs to the top of the pole to perform balancing acts and all sorts of tricks. The organ grinds on, and the fellow with the whip snaps it in front of people's faces and over their bare heads. A half-naked girl appears, wearing a little skirt which scarcely reaches her knees; her flowing blond hair is combed and braided, and she has all kinds of little emblems and decorations woven into the braids. She has a red-cheeked attractive little face, and she performs splits and contortions and jumps through a hoop.

There is still another entertainer who swallows one sword after another. When he has swallowed them all, his partner comes forth, but instead of pulling the swords out of his mouth, the partner pulls out a whole chain of kerchiefs and bonnets, the devil only knows why, and the organ grinds on, and the ringmaster snaps his whip around their faces and their heads. . . .

Once there was a tailor in the village; no one knew where the little man came from or whither the little Jew was going. He was one of the thousands whose life passes like a shadow under our eyes; no one notices when they are born, and no one pays attention when they die. The bread they eat must grow in invisible fields, and the meat they consume must come from cattle that graze on unknown pastures, for otherwise one would have to ask oneself, "Who ate the wheat of these fields? What has become of the cattle in the pastures?"

A little tailor, a Jew who had nothing to do with anyone except with God his Maker . . . Night still covered the sky when the tailor prepared to go to the house of prayer. Hidden behind the big stove, screened by the stand of holy books, he repeated his prayer of gratitude to his Creator for having brought him into being, for the bread with which he nourished himself, and for the mercy that would be his part when God should call him back unto Him. No one paid any attention to the little tailor on his way to and from the synagogue, and no one paid any attention to the little tailor sitting and sewing away on the greatcoats of the peasants, and if one noticed him, he seemed as natural a sight as the pole in the market place; no one ever thought to ask "What is that pole standing there for? What use is it?"

His wife, Chana, had taken upon herself the duty of lighting two candles in the abandoned old women's synagogue every Friday night. This was a duty she had taken over from her mother, may she rest in peace, and that her mother had taken over from her grandmother, and so on from generation to generation. No one bothered to inquire who lighted the two commemorative candles that twinkled from the windows of the ancient women's synagogue every Friday night; no one even thought to wonder whether the ancient housewives had awakened in their graves. There would have been more wondering had there come a fine Friday evening when the two candles were not to be seen; then somebody would have noticed that something was missing in the synagogue, although no one would have been able to say exactly what was missing. But God noticed, and God had sent a reward for the two candles that these simple women had been lighting for so long a time from generation to generation; God sent them a living light, Reb Daavidle, the rabbi of the town.

For many years, Chana, the tailor's wife, was childless; then God listened to her prayers and gave her a son. She named him

Daavidle. And this was the present rabbi of the village, Reb Daavidle. From earliest childhood, Daavidle showed himself unlike other children. He would not even sleep in his cradle without a covering on his head. When he was three years old, he babbled the blessing for food before he broke bread. He learned his alphabet from a little prayer book bought for him by his father, and when he was a grown man and a rabbi, he still carried this prayer book in his breast pocket. He studied in school with great industry; he was not a quick student, but what came into his head never left it. He was extremely pious and observant of the last syllable of the law. He never departed by a hair's breadth from the regulations laid down in the Shulhan Aruch. A hundred and one times he repeated the Scriptures, learning them from memory together with the commentaries, until he could find every letter of every word blindfolded by pointing to it with his finger.

When Reb Berl, may he rest in peace, the old rabbi of the town, was taken unto his fathers without leaving behind him anyone to fulfill his place—except a grown daughter of marriageable age—the townsfolk began to suggest that Daavidle should wed the orphan and fill the place of her father. The Chassidim were opposed to this: "What? You want to take the son of Lazar the tailor as our rabbi?" However, the shopkeepers and the little householders, who were hopeful of seeing one of their own sons rise to glory, stubbornly insisted on the combination. A terrible division arose in the town, but one day the ordinary family men assembled in the cemetery, set up the wedding canopy, and married off Daavidle to the rabbi's orphan daughter. Then they knocked on the rabbi's grave and called down to him: "Congratulations! *Mazel tov!* Your son-in-law will fulfill your place on earth!"

The Chassidim had a fearful respect for the anger of the dead; therefore they were silent, waiting for the first offensive step to be taken by the new rabbi. But Reb Daavidle had his Talmud and his books of the Law, and he sat at home studying day and

54

night. He conducted himself in a model way; a member of an ordinary prayer circle, he arose before dawn each day and recited psalms and prayers with the townsfolk until the rising of the morning star. He prayed with the first ten men who entered the synagogue and completed a congregation, and before each new moon he held the service of atonement in the chilly synagogue.

The Chassidim had never forgiven him for their defeat, however, and they were stubborn as was their wont. They referred to him only as Daavidle the tailor. One of them went so far as to insult him during a circumcision by remarking that a tailor's boy should know how to cut. The plain folk wanted to have it out with the Chassidim, but the rabbi insisted on keeping the peace and actually replied to the insult of the Chassidim by signing himself from then on, Daavidle, the humble tailor's son.

The Chassidim who sat with him in the house of prayer could not bring themselves to call him rabbi; they kept their distance from him. He, too, became estranged from them, preferring the company of the hewers of wood and drawers of water, and it was to them he gave all of his attention. He had no use for learning for himself alone but found it necessary to share with others what he knew.

Every Friday evening the plain folk would gather in the house of prayer with their Bibles in their hands, and Rabbi Daavidle would study the weekly chapter with them. He would explain the legends and the commentaries to them in such a way that the good men licked their fingers over his wisdom. Following the Sabbath afternoon nap, he would seat himself among the tradesmen and workers in the synagogue, take a prayer book in his hand, and repeat the Psalms with them, taking turns reciting the verses. He chanted each word, and his voice was heard beyond the synagogue; it reached down the little street, calling the townsfolk into the house of prayer. Youngsters and Sabbath loafers who were playing in the street put aside their games; teamsters and fishermen who were standing and gossiping with the women left off their talk and came into the synagogue. The little synagogue became more and more full, and the rabbi, lost in the midst of them all, stood repeating the verses while the congregation recited the responses, a verse from him and a verse from them.

They all knew that they had found a man on whom they could rely. If anyone were in trouble, he would come to the rabbi, and the rabbi had a cure for him—prayer. No matter what sort of Jew came, the rabbi would stand with him in a corner of the house of the Lord and begin to pray with him. The Jew, listening to the voice of the rabbi, which seemed to rise up out of a broken heart, would fall to weeping; he would talk out all his troubles with the rabbi and go away with a free conscience.

When Daavidle became rabbi, he took upon himself the fulfillment of a commandment that he was pledged to carry out; he was determined to perform this duty from generation to generation, God willing. This was the commandment first carried out by our father Abraham; the Lord's commandment of circumcision. It would be his task to preside at all circumcisions. Daavidle asked and readily won the consent of the householders of the town to perform this act. Circumcision became his special province, his duty, and his good deed before the Lord.

There came a day when Reb Daavidle paced back and forth in his room; his high forehead was wrinkled, and he groaned from time to time. His wife Hindeleh sat in the corner by the stove with her pale face in her hands, crying bitterly.

"Daavidle, I can't bear it! I won't let this pass without raising a hand! You must do something!"

"I tell you, this is an act of God! It is Heaven itself that prevents my doing anything! What can I do against God's will? I suppose it has to be this way. Shall a whole community be at war because of me? Shall the town, God forbid, be doomed? They wept before me—my heart was torn in two!"

"But the shame of it, God in Heaven, the pity! And yet, you

56

can't permit yourself to be the cause of bloodshed. Heaven forbid!"

The rabbi approached his bookcase, took out a book, and fell into meditation. "Ah, woman, woman, vengeance is a sin. Remember, be careful not to fall into this sin!"

"God in Heaven!" the woman groaned, covering her face with her hands, while the tinkling of her long golden earrings echoed her sighs.

Just then Yudel, the village teacher, appeared in the doorway. Yudel had a second function. He was a *mohl,* one who performed the act of circumcision, and often served when the rabbi officiated.

Yudel motioned to the rabbi's wife, "Excuse me, *rebbetzen—*"

The rabbi's wife was startled.

The rabbi noticed and signaled to Yudel with his fingers, "Well, are they coming already?"

Yudel nodded.

"As far as I am concerned, they have won. Surely all this is willed from on high. I was not meant to fulfill this sacred duty."

"Rabbi!"

"Shall people be deprived because of me? For my past, I have chosen another sacred duty—I shall fulfill the commandment to welcome the stranger. This, I believe, they cannot take from me. And what about you, Yudel? Have they taken the circumcisions away from you?"

"I don't know. I suppose . . . But what good can it be, without you, rabbi?"

"This is an inflexible law. According to the law, you are not permitted to resign, so long as . . ."

Suddenly a commotion was heard from outside the window. People came running, shouting, "The resignation! The resignation!" The voice of the blind old cobbler was heard, "Rabbi! Oh, rabbi of ours—you bring down the wrath of God on yourself!"

They pounded on the door; some pulled it open; others pushed it shut. Sticks swung in every direction. There was a crash, and something came flying through the smashed window. The rabbi's wife screamed and pulled on her husband's coattail. From outside a cry was heard, "The butchers are coming!"

The rabbi flung open the door and appeared in the street. A sea of faces confronted him—men, women, and children, workmen's caps, and silken skullcaps, and velvet Sabbath hats, and kerchiefs of every color. The street was black with people, as at a funeral. All were running and shouting, there were men pulling at each other's beards, swinging their sticks over each other's heads. A tall man stood out above all the others; with his long, lean arms, he swept aside all the heads before him.

"Sinners!" shouted the rabbi.

"The rabbi! The rabbi!" a cry came up from the crowd. Then there was silence. They dropped their heads, waiting. Each hid behind his neighbor, so as not to be recognized by Reb Daavidle.

"Jews, why are you fighting each other like goyim!" the rabbi cried bitterly, while his eyes filled with tears.

A sorrowful, penitent silence choked them all. Only the sound of a single voice came from the mass of heads. "The resignation! The certificates!"

Everyone turned to see who had spoken, but he was already lost in the crowd.

"What do you want? The authority? Here, you can have it, only let there be peace. Surely your rabbi, too, wants only peace."

No one offered a word in reply.

A short, stocky man emerged from the flock, approached the rabbi, and veiling his eyes with piety, as though he were about to repeat the blessing over the holy Torah, he announced, "The rabbi is waiting outside the town. We came for the certificate of authority."

The rabbi went into the house. The stocky man, Reb Yitzchak Yudels, followed the rabbi, and the Chassidim crowded behind the two, elbowing their way past the plain townsfolk.

Reb Daavidle paced up and down the room a few times. Then

he went to the shrine of the Torah that stood in the corner and began to sway before it in earnest prayer, saying, "Unto Him Who called the world into being, it is surely known that I do not resign out of my free will from the sacred duty that I took upon myself, the duty whose fulfillment I pledged with the price of my soul. I do this only for the sake of peace."

He went to the table, took a pen in hand, and began writing.

The Chassidim were silent. From the next room the sobbing of the rabbi's wife could be heard.

Soon enough, the rabbi rose. Reb Yitzchak Yudels reached out his hand for the note.

"No!" said the rabbi. "Have we forgotten our duty to welcome the stranger? Hindel, my coat!" he called into the next room.

Hindel came into the room with eyes red from weeping; she went to the wardrobe.

"Behold, woman, I am thankful and praise the Lord, who has relieved me of one duty and given me another—and you, you sit there mourning and weeping."

The rabbi's wife wiped her tears with her apron.

"Come, let us fulfill the Lord's commandment to welcome the stranger!" called the rabbi to the crowd as he stepped out to the street, dragging the teacher Yudel by his sleeves.

"Let us go and meet the rabbi!" shouted Reb Yitzchak Yudels.

And the whole crowd moved toward the edge of the town.

From every door people flowed; they snatched up their Sabbath coats, their velvet caps; shops were closed in the middle of the day; everywhere doors were shut, and everybody went off into the street. Townsfolk, seeing their own rabbi in the lead, forgot their animosity toward the Chassidim. For they told themselves, a wonder rabbi is coming to live in our town. Then his followers, the Chassidim, will come from far and near to pass the Sabbath with him, and the town will blossom. They put on their Sabbath coats and followed the procession. The parade grew longer and longer; craftsmen put aside their work; the shops were deserted by the clerks while the whole town proceeded along Konskar road to greet the rabbi. Even the Gentiles became curious and joined the procession.

From Reb Yechezkiel's yard Nutta came riding forth, with a second cart behind him. The horses wore new harnesses, decorated with brass. In one of the carts sat Reb Yechezkiel with his sons and grandchildren, in the other his partner Reb Chaim Rosenkranz with his sons, sons-in-law, and his grandchildren. When they reached the procession, they saw the entire flock was afoot, so they alighted and walked like everyone else.

The fields around, as though aware that they were all ruled over by one and the same God, seemed to have lost their boundaries and merged into one great field. An ocean of green grass spread as far as one could see. A breeze blew upon the grass, causing wave after wave to flow and vanish in the distant green sea. Little footpaths wandered through the green, leading far into the fields, where they disappeared in the sea of grass. A few isolated trees stood orphanlike and with an air of being abashed that God had permitted them to grow taller than anything in their surroundings. They swayed lonesomely as though praying by themselves in the fields.

Between the fields the deserted roads stretched far away, screened on either side by lanes of linden trees, whose long, freshly budding branches wove an archway over the road.

And the flock proceeded on God's way. In the fields they encountered some of the village teachers, who had led out the children for the first festival of the spring. The boys had made bows and arrows for themselves, and with their bows in their hands they joined the procession, marching to meet the new rabbi.

It wasn't long before the Chassidim found one another; linking themselves arm in arm, or their hands on each other's shoulders, they walked together, forming a little flock of their own within the flock. It made no difference to them whether a man was one of their sect or not; anyone who cared to took hold of a Chassid's belt or joined hands with him and went along together with the Chassidim. Children came running and blundered underfoot. They clung to their fathers' girdles, to their fathers' coats, and dragged after the crowd.

The procession grew and grew; from every side it gathered Jews unto itself. They embraced each other and began to raise their voices in song. *"In multitudes, the people glorifies the King!"*

Their voices mingled together and became as one voice, just as their souls seemed to be joined together until one voice arose out of a thousand hearts, resounding over the field and through the woods, while an echo chanted the response. *"In multitudes, the people glorifies the King!"*

In the heavens above, the shining reaches of the sky melted one into another; from all four corners of the world pale little silvery clouds came floating, gliding over each other. There was one corner where darkness glowered, but the black cloud was torn apart and the sun poured her light through the break in the cloud, and the stream of light fell upon a green meadow below on earth, making it shine like a mirror from among the other meadows.

And just as all the earth below became one, so the heavens above suddenly melted together; one shining cloud floated into another, and they mingled and became one and were like a second procession forming in the sky to accompany the villagers as they went to meet their rabbi. And below the heavens, the gentle wind moved the grass over the fields, and the grass swayed after the passing of the flock and bowed, and the lone trees in the fields shook their branches in greeting, and everywhere the voice of the multitude rang out, far and wide. *"In multitudes, the people glorifies the King!"*

The rabbi and the plain folk walked a little to one side. They saw how the Chassidim were linked together, how they had become one with heaven and earth, and they felt that they, the ordinary people, had somehow been left out of things, even discarded. And they could not help feeling a kind of awe before the

61

Chassidim who were enfolded in unity, who sang in ecstasy. And here and there from among the plain folk, one or another would slip over to the Chassidim.

Presently a huge cloud of dust rose heavenward from the road. The cloud of dust seemed to be galloping toward them, coming closer and closer, as though to announce, "The rabbi comes! The rabbi comes!"

Then the Jews rushed pell-mell into the cloud of dust, ripping it asunder; the cloud dissolved, revealing a large wagon. In the wagon sat the rabbi in a long white satin coat, buried in his velvet hat and beard and side curls. He was gray and aged, and he sat holding his hands crossed over his heart, his closed eyes fixed upon the sky. A passing frown appeared on his high, delicately aristocratic forehead.

"Peace unto you."

An ocean of hands, thin, long, pale, fat, thick, red-haired, and smooth hands, stretched out toward him. They reached one above the other, drowning each other, reaching upward again, and the rabbi took each one separately in a greeting of peace.

At last Rabbi Daavidle managed to reach the new rabbi. He put forth his hand and said, "Peace unto you."

"And unto you, peace!"

"Who might you be?" the new rabbi asked.

"I am the rabbi of the village."

"So. The rabbi of the village."

"I have brought you the certificate of my resignation," the first rabbi said, handing over the sheet of paper. The rabbi reached out his pale hand for the bit of paper.

"I greet you thrice in the name of the Lord, for it is my duty to welcome the stranger," the rabbi stammered, standing for a moment longer near the wagon. There was a murmur in the crowd.

"And who is your rabbi?" the new rabbi asked with a smile as he put the certificate into his breast pocket.

62

"No one."

"No one? Then you shall sit at my table." The new rabbi smiled. The rabbi simply stood there.

But in the meantime the Chassidim pressed forward, and the rabbi found himself pushed to one side. With their hands reaching upward to the new rabbi, the people surrounded the wagon.

"Let us say the evening prayer, Jews," the new rabbi called as he descended from the wagon.

Close to the road there was a thick little wood. The trees were woven together as though into a single garland. The congregation followed the rabbi into the copse. It was already late in the afternoon; the last rays of the sun peered through the branches of the trees. Here and there, between the trees, the sun reached a little circle of grass and turned it to gold. The little wood was utterly quiet as though a secret had been entrusted to it long, long ago. Then the skies let down a sacred red-blue curtain around the woods. Deep in the forest a lonely bird called and called again, as though it knew not for what. Far away in the woods someone was chopping down a tree, and the death song of the tree echoed high in the forest. And around the woods, the whole world lay, expectant.

The green growth had not yet come to fullness but had only begun to blossom. The earth had only uncovered her breast, and the vegetation had only begun to take nourishment and to draw life from its source. Everything about them had only begun to live and was awaiting a blessing, a sign, a release. The congregation was scattered in the woods; beneath each tree there stood a man, and the youngsters stood by the saplings and bushes, and everyone swayed in deep and earnest prayer. The rabbi's blessing resounded through the woods, while he waved his arm before them.

"Praised art Thou, O Lord our God, for having brought forth all that lives, and for having brought all manner of fruits in Thy Goodness. Make Thy Blessing to shine upon the face of the earth,

and bless us with all the goodness of the earth, as Thou hast done in the good years that have gone before. Blessed art Thou, O Lord our God, who provides us with all that is good."

Beneath each tree there was a soul, and within each tree there was a soul, and each soul prayed in unison with the other, and with each prayer that was uttered, one could see a change in all the living green world. The trees swayed together with the congregation as though they too were in prayer, but the trees could not speak, and so the human soul that was beneath each tree spoke the words of prayer, while the trees swayed in unison as if to say amen, amen.

Every living thing prayed and sang to God, and the heavens seemed to come closer to the earth and the earth to approach the heavens; the people and the trees seemed to form one congregation. The branches and twigs were linked together; the grass and the earth moved in prayer; the birds cried from one branch to another, singing the praises of the Lord; and the echo of the prayer came from among the trees deep in the woods. The woodsman's ax responded in the distance, and the sound of all the voices flowed together and melted into one single unity. All joined together and became a single prayer, a single heart, a single soul. And there, deep in the woods, the Shechina herself, the Sacred Spirit, hovered over the trees, joining in the prayer.

The entire universe is God, and through the universe, God was in prayer.

Soon all became quiet; the trees no longer swayed; there was no more movement in the grass; far away in the woods the singing bird became silent, and the echo of the woodsman's ax was no longer heard. The world seemed to have halted for a moment to listen. There, deep in the woods, was God, and He too listened to the ancient familiar melody, to the voice of the rabbi lamenting in the woods.

"Sound forth the great trumpet call of redemption, O Lord, let the miracle take place, gather us in from our exile!"

64

All about them became utterly quiet. A dim melancholy fog spread deep in the woods where the Shechina hovered. The fog spread further, deeper, and from the depths of the forest a lost and melancholy murmur was heard, echoing through woods and fields. Then the echo melted in the distance as though it were carrying away sacred secrets.

This was God's greeting to the congregation of Israel, out of the long, long past.

Soon the rabbi had ended his prayer. Under the trees a number of orphans were repeating the prayer in memory of the dead, and perhaps a few of the saplings also repeated the prayer for their fathers and mothers, or it might have been the children who prayed for them.

The rabbi returned to the wagon and mounted. The horses were unhitched, and numbers and multitudes of the congregation took hold of the wagon instead. They were packed closely together, head against head, and they stumbled against each other and against the wheels. The white satin robe of the rabbi floated over the ocean of heads and hands, and before and behind him there were waves and waves of heads and hands.

And behind the procession a dark, sad, and lovable little cloud of dew floated over the woods and fields, giving them drink and nourishment and filling every little mouth that was open to it. For this was the rabbi's prayer.

Thus they came into the town. A forgotten little cloud of dew that had risen from the river spread itself tenderly and with motherly care over the village, to watch over it and protect it. The little cloud rocked and hugged the village, and the village fell sweetly asleep. In a distant little street the crying of a child was heard.

In Reb Yechezkiel's house there was a chamber with two large windows that gave on the street of the synagogue, and from these windows two bright flames shone into the dark evening fog.

65

Out of that chamber, a tender dreamy tune floated into the lane. For it was there that the rabbi rested.

And there were also lights shining from the windows of the everyday prayer room of the synagogue, opposite Reb Yechezkiel's windows. Six little lights were shining into the night fog from the room where a simple everyday prayer from the heart of an old tailor was repeated, *"May the Lord forgive us our evil deeds, and spare us from destruction."*

Summer Evenings

As the Festival of Weeks begins to steal upon the town, the summer seems to be cut off in the middle of its life. All the world is like a princess sitting in her holiday garments, mourning the loved ones who have left her. A breeze sways the leaves. Every little blade of grass, every little leaf weeps quietly for the whole world's sake. What lovely summer evenings now! Clouds, in bright and dark masses, emerge from their secret worlds to cover the heavens. They melt together, far on the wide horizon, and then the beautiful open light and the dark clouds are hidden by the blue curtains of haze. Light lies over the broad river, mirroring itself in the glistening waves that flow one upon another, as though they are talking out their hearts to each other. Far away the sky bends down until it enters the water, and the water seems to rise up to heaven. The heavens and the seas join together in the first innocent kiss of love and go to rest together in the dense black woods at the end of the world.

Lovely summer evenings in the little synagogue street! Dark, melancholy fogs gently enwrap the quiet street as though they would mask it from human eyes. In the dense woods at the edge of the world the last reddish glow of sunlight shimmers, sinking like a lost, forgotten island into the blue sea of the sky. From a window of the old house of prayer a little light winks, and a mournful pious voice is heard along the lane, lamenting before Mother Night. And Mother Night carries off the lament into her own mysterious world and transforms it and mingles it with other voices until it becomes part of the choir of night. Frogs in the river croak to the same rhythm, and a lost little murmuring comes from the trees in the black woods, and the night gathers all the sounds together within herself and lets them fade away along the dark cemetery lane.

From the wonder rabbi's window two streams of light pour out, and he himself may be seen pacing back and forth. As his white gown passes the window, his shadow hurries across the white fence opposite. In front of their doors and their gates, the people sit half dressed, householders and housewives, craftsmen weary after their day of toil, getting a breath of fresh air. Young people stroll by the gates, arms linked, singing out a little melody.

> *When the count walked in the wood*
> *There a little maiden stood—*
> *"Maiden, Maiden, why are you here*
> *Alone in the wood? Have you no fear?"*
> *"I've come into the wood alone,*
> *And cannot find my own way home."*

The boys climb on the fence of Chana Sara's garden and reach for the branches of her pear trees that extend out into the market place. They seize the branches and tear off the green fruit. The gardener rushes out, and the children scatter, except for one little lad held prisoner by a branch. The gardener snatches the boy's cap, and the boy stands there whimpering and rubbing himself, afraid to go home to his mother. Cattle return from their pasture; the shepherd plays on his reed. The householders get up from their benches, take their cattle from the herd, and lead them to their stables. An accordion is heard from somewhere down the street where Stepan, the only Christian in the neighborhood, sits playing a love song for his sweetheart, and the tune of the accordion mingles and becomes one with the melancholy plaint of the shepherd's flute, a sad, heartbreaking little melody that fades away far down the street.

Lovely summer evening in the synagogue street! Far down in the dark little lane by the cemetery, the older lads, the students of the Talmud, saunter in their light summer coats, and young girls of respectable families stroll by in their cotton summer dresses. The youths walk on one side, the girls on the other. Now a lad glances timidly to the other side of the lane, hoping to catch a glimpse of his intended bride, whose golden engagement watch he carries in his vest. He feels embarrassed, and his heart beats fast. And if the maiden wishes to steal a glance at the lads in order to glimpse the intended groom, for whom she is sewing a prayer-book bag, she is abashed before her comrades, her heart pounds, and her light little jacket rises and falls over her bosom.

Lovely summer evenings in the synagogue lane! But these are the three weeks of mourning for the destruction of the temple, and in these weeks there may be no love play, and so everything has been put off until after the Sabbath of Consolation. The poplars that hold the village in their embrace know all her little secrets and silently guard the mystery of love. And the breezes from the other side of the fields carry the odor of the fields, refreshing the human heart. Then one's breast becomes filled and somehow very light, and there is a sweet and tender and terrible longing to be embraced, to be loved. Oh, Father in Heaven, the lovely summer evenings in the synagogue lane! . . . for those to whom they were known and those to whom they are lost.

And in the dark lane that led toward the cemetery, far down at the end of the synagogue lane, the world pressed her face against the heart of night, and night pressed herself against the heart of the world, and they embraced each other and wandered deep into the woods together and lay themselves down to sleep in the dense forest.

And on the dark path to the cemetery rise a number of old dead poplars, like terrible demons with their hands and feet cut off. They stand like the ghosts of prehistoric monsters, like witnesses from before the six days of creation, like silent witnesses from the beginning to the end of time. ... At midnight, the children are told, there appear the ghosts of "Germans tall with whips and all," and they take their places under the trees, and from the branches they draw sweet, heartrending melodies that pull and tug at people's hearts until they follow the music into the evil swamps.

In the fields, in the grass, outside the village, Chassidim lie with their heads to the stars and sing their song of despair.

> *You who live in huts of earth,*
> *Wherefore do you lift your eyes?*
> *Man and beast have equal worth.*

This they sing to the melody of the cantor who was buried alive in his grave, and their voices resound over the graves there on the hill. The tombs intermingle with God's earth, sunken under their seas of grass. And in their little graves the dead bones lie mute, with only a patch of sky above them. The breeze blows over them. They are mingled with the earth; the living verdure springs upward from them; and thus these ancient bones fulfill their true mission, the ultimate goal of life, that was before and will remain the everlasting. The whole world becomes one, the dead with the living, heaven with the earth, each blade of grass, each tree, all become one life, one world, one Godliness.

Alongside the lane, the night is mirrored in the river, and from a distance it appears to be another world entirely. The little lights of the boats that rest overnight in the water are reflected in its depths, and from a distance they look like dark gray animals whose paws blundered into the water in the dark night and who are unable to extricate themselves. From a distance, the little lights seem to be their eyes, pleading for help.

And on that dark path, deep in the night, God sits, covering his face with both hands. And as He weeps over the destruction of the temple two great tears fall upon the earth and cover everything with dew.

THE LITTLE TOWN

On the dark path to the cemetery, a young man and a maiden walked in the black night, Gabriel, the wonder rabbi's son and heir, and Leabeh, the youngest daughter of Reb Yechezkiel. She had seen him through a crack in the door that night when the rabbi stayed at their house. Before daybreak, while she still lay in bed, she had heard his voice in prayer coming in through her open window. As he repeated the holy words, his voice carried through the window and mingled with the odor of all the young green growing things that wakened from under the dew of night. His voice entered her chamber together with the scent of the blossoms and fluttered over her face and lingered over her, and all of itself her heart began to awaken. And from that moment she longed only for a glimpse of his sensitive face, which shone out like a bright moon from under his broad fur hat. But she did not understand the desire that was in her, nor did she want to know what it was. Yet every evening she went strolling in the synagogue lane. Something drew her there as to a meeting with the "Germans tall with whips and all," who fashioned wondrous melodies from the branches of the trees. And she was drawn still deeper into the dark lane, deeper and deeper . . . and he too must have been drawn by the unheard music, and he too must have allowed it to lead him on. They did not realize how far they were going. Night settled about their heads and took them to herself and wrapped them with darkness and screened them from the eyes of men.

The graves on the hill were witnesses that the young people never spoke a word to each other, nor took each other's hand. But he on one side of the land and she on the other let themselves be led by the heart-burning melodies that were drawn out of the old poplar trees by the long thin fingers of the "Germans tall. . . ." The same melodies resounded within them as though played upon the strings of their hearts. And the young people were drawn on and on, walking silently, listening to the inaudible music, to the secret melodies that were being played on their heartstrings. . . .

71

Silently, silently. . . . Night came down upon them and the dewy clouds floated before and behind them.

And everything around them was filled with love; the heaven, the earth, lay clasped together, lost in the woods; the night was in the world, and the world was in the night, and scented breezes came from the bare fields, slipping across their faces whispering secrets to them, secrets that were to be carried in their hearts and never, never to be revealed. And their bosoms breathed slowly, quietly, and in them there was a strange longing, and a longing lay over all the earth. . . . The whole world yearned for it knew not what. . . .

In the thick forest God lay wrapt in His black mantle, and He longed for His own sake and for the world, and at the edge of the world where the last red rays sank into the blue dark sea the day kissed the night, and they yearned for each other and for all the world.

Far on the horizon, a bright moon wandered day in and day out, filled with longing, and the little cemetery hid within itself and was filled with longing. . . .

And the young man and the maiden let themselves be drawn on, following the mysterious melodies. . . .

A little farther on was the river, and the lanterns of the night winked to each other in the depths of the water and told each other tales of other worlds.

The young man and the maiden followed the twinkling lights and let themselves be led astray by them.

They came to the edge of the water and sat down on the shore.

Suddenly a mighty ringing was heard.

The ringing came from the distance, as though a mother might be crying out in the dark night, "Help! Oh, what is happening! Help!"

The sky over the village suddenly became bright as though a

burning red cloud had come flying out of another world, had lost its way in the dark sea of night, and illuminated half the sky. Or perhaps a mighty hand had brushed a large part of the night aside and thrown it from on high, leaving the open heaven visible to the world. Or perhaps the sun had for once in creation been permitted to err and had returned to this place instead of going on to another land.

Down below on the earth there was a terrible glare as one cloud of fire rolled into another, and they came forth together, leaping into the heavens and setting fire to a part of the sky. Earth, air, and heaven embraced each other with a single flame. The veil of night was torn from the face of the earth, and it was day again. Cries were heard from the distance, and the village bell rang desperately as though it were a mother screaming for help.

The young man and the girl sit by the edge of the water. Bright rays of light fall into the river and seem to set it afire. And the burning waves flow by, whispering to each other, telling the terrible secret of what is happening behind them. Here the night still lies upon the river, and something stirs silently in the water—the dead come up from the cemetery, they creep over the fence, and they cleanse their souls in the river before ascending into heaven to stand and be judged.

The river flows quietly on, cleansing their spirits, cleansing them from sin, and the dead float upon the waves into the dark woods from which they will rise to heaven.

On the other side, the world is in flame; wall after wall of fire climbs skyward. The air is on fire, and the heavens too, and their fiery reflection is on the face of the water. . . .

The young people return to the village through forgotten paths.

Half-naked women, naked children snatch whatever they can of their possessions, bits of bedding, pillows, armfuls of kitchenware; they run with unearthly cries, their hair streaming, from one street to another, fleeing the fire. Little children clutch their mothers' skirts; the older ones help their mothers carry their

73

belongings. They flee shrieking into the black woods, and the fire pursues them, reaching out its tongue to seize them. Mothers carry their babies as they pulled them from their cradles, pillows and all. Brothers carry their little sisters; sisters carry their little brothers. They burst into the homes of strangers, lay down their little ones on strange beds, next to strange children. The conflagration drives people from their houses, drives them out of the village, like wild beings. And the wind carries the fire from roof to roof.

The fire had come out of nowhere, a beast springing upon the little village and destroying everything, everything. . . .

Jews and Christians alike hurried with pails of water, but the fire drank up the water with a laughing crackle and went on about its work. Dazed, scarcely knowing what they were doing, people tried to save what they could—some seized doors and windows and carried them off into the road. Wild-eyed mothers leaped into the flames with their hair streaming and their clothes flying, shrieking as they ran, "My child! My child!" and wildly frightened children ran naked in the streets, dragging bundles of household goods and screaming, "Mama! Mama!" And all the voices were drowned together in the crackling of the fire, and tongues of flame shot across the roofs, leaving behind one ruin after another.

Some of the householders, seizing axes and hoes, tear at the walls of their own homes. They hack away furiously as though a mad compulsion has come upon them to make an end of everything, to destroy whatever remains.

One of them smashes windows with his bare fists, then runs in the streets with blood streaming from his hands, but the fire does not diminish. The blazing paws of the raging beast march from roof to roof, and as though to silence the screaming of the children, of the mothers, of all the town, it furiously smashes one house after another. The lamentations rise to the heavens, and the village bells never stop ringing, ringing, as though pleading with the raging beast for pity, begging at its feet for mercy, and at

74

the same time crying out to the power above, in accusation of the wanton destroyer.

Now comes a cry of horror, "The synagogue is on fire! the synagogue!"

Then people rush from all sides. Fathers throw aside what remains of their household. Mothers put away the babies from their breast, the whole village gathers around the little synagogue. The tall windows are filled with flames, like two bright lanterns. Men groan and tear their hair, women press against the hot walls as though to shield them with their bodies. A few men pour pails of water on the flaming walls. But the fire only sucks up the water, sputters, and burns on.

Christians come running with axes and crowbars. They climb to the roof of the synagogue and hack at the tin covering. The Jews seize them by their ankles, pleading with them to hold back, but the axes tear the roof apart, and every bit of tin hurled from the roof rips its way through the heart of a Jew.

In the midst of this, the rabbi, weeping aloud, rushes to the synagogue doors, bolts them, and closes the shutters, stretching out his thin pale arms as if to hold back the destroyer. But the fire leaps down through the open roof, and now people cry, "The roof! The roof!" They break open the doors and the windows and burst into the synagogue. Already, the gables are afire, and through the roar of the conflagration one can hear the rafters falling one after the other. Now the flames are upside down, the tongues licking downward from above, shooting burning sparks and pieces of flame into the world below. Billows of black smoke burst from an open window; one cloud of smoke storms head on into another, ploughing through a broken pane. For a moment the smoke blackens the flames, forcing a way for itself, rising upward to heaven with the flames snapping after it. In the thick black column streaming from the broken window, mingled with burning sparks of fire and flying chunks of flame, are the shapes of men, leaping through the black smoke and the shooting sparks, some of them rescuing half-uncovered scrolls of the law, others with streaming prayer shawls holding pieces of the candelabra, boards from the holy ark. They disappear with them into the darkness.

The synagogue blazes; one wall gives up after another; from within one can hear the flames breaking down pillars, rafters, one after another, to be consumed by the tongues of fire. And from all around rises the bitter weeping of men, women, and children. They shriek, they groan, they wring their hands, and the village bell rings and rings, still pleading with the fire for pity, still crying out against the lust of a destroyer who would consume the entire world.

The day dawned gray and silent. Far on the horizon the morning star flickered bloodily in the pale gray mirror, and its reddish reflection was returned by the watery gray waves of the sky, as though waves of gray water had come from mysterious other-world oceans and made their way one after another into the heavens. The morning washed her newborn son, the new day, that came up out of the gray depths of the waters, washed him in wave after wave, so that he might shine and light up the heavens and the earth.

And the whole world wakened from sweet sleep; the leaves of grass, still drowned in the dew of night, began to stretch themselves toward the sun; the blossoms opened their little eyes and their little mouths and gave forth the flowery scents with which they had drugged themselves all night long. All wakened; the world threw off the garment of night which had enwrapped her while she slept with the dewy clouds; she wore the smile of the bride who wakens on the first day after the wedding. Everything glistened, smiled, and was drunk with love and life.

The fire was dying. Here and there it spent its last violence on a remaining wall, on a doorway or a pillar; it glowered over the wreckage. The village had become a ruin . . . smoking piles of

76

ashes and debris, burned roofs crashed over burned walls, glowing embers smoking and snapping.

Here and there one could see half a wall, with a mirror still hanging on a hook. Goose feathers from pillows and comforters fluttered in the streets, broken bits of earthenware rolled underfoot in the streets, and pieces of brass from Sabbath lights were scattered everywhere. And in the midst of all one might see the smoldering remnant of a Sabbath dress or a half-charred marriage wig.

Out of the glowing ashes tall black chimneys rose, sorrowing over the sacrifice that had taken place. Here and there stood Jews with long iron rods in their hands, trying to poke bits of houseware out of the glowing wreckage, pulling out half-burned garments or the legs of smashed tables. Each tried to assemble the pitiful remains of his household. Mothers ran from one house to another wringing their hands and gathering together the infants they had left in strange homes the night before. Little girls hurried to the strangers' houses where they had left their bundles of belongings, gathering together one little packet and another, and putting the packs on the backs of their little brothers and sisters. Schoolboys dragged half-burned books out of the fire, kissed the burned relics, and carried them all into the little prayer house, which had been spared by the fire.

The brilliant day and the brilliant sun, spreading their glory from out of the wide heavens, flooded the village with shining light. But the light fell only upon glowing ruins, stark chimneys, and homeless little children.

Here and there a simple householder stood by his smoking ruin pulling out a few boards or rafters that might not have been completely consumed, throwing water over the embers, and placing plank against plank, board along board, already planning in his mind how to put together his shattered house.

In the fields half-dressed women held their nursing babies in their laps; around them they had gathered up their bundles and their packs and their children, and the light of the sun poured down upon them all.

Among the plain folk in the village, it was secretly murmured that God in his heaven had taken the side of the town rabbi and had poured out His wrath upon the wood and the stones of the town.

The Halfway House

Slowly the town began to return to itself. Well-rooted villagers are not easily defeated, and a town is not easily destroyed. As soon as a man was able, he put together a cabin for his family. And the town became a town again.

At Reb Yechezkiel's, in the meantime, preparations began for the arrangement of the marriage contract. Leabeh, the bride, knew nothing of what was going on. Every morning she sat by her window and listened to the voice of the rabbi's young son, Gabriel, as he repeated his studies in the Scriptures, and his voice mingled with the scent of the blossoms in her garden, wafting into her fresh, clean little room, and slipping across her face, and breathing across her bare, young breast. The preparations for the feast of the marriage contract were to be seen mostly in the kitchen.

Grandmothers and aunts appeared as though risen out of the earth, and the cooking and baking got under way. A track of flour covered the stones from Reb Yechezkiel's house all the way to the bakery.

Reb Yechezkiel's dwelling bordered on a little alley overhung by a row of wooden houses or rather by a single structure with numerous layers of gables, one balanced on top of the other. There was no yard, and the Lord only knew how the top layers were linked with the bottom. The dwellings seemed scarcely to stand on the earth. The houses belonged to everyone and to no one. That is to say, the dwellings mostly stood vacant, with their windows broken, but the minute an "heir" wanted to move into one of the flats, a whole army of heritors appeared, each armed with papers and birth certificates to prove that the houses belonged to him.

The hand of destiny finally fell upon Leibish the milkman, who was selected by the town agent, for no reason in the world, to pay the taxes. A policeman came once a year and dragged four and a half rubles of taxes out of him. Leibish was neither a heritor nor a relative—but who could argue with the police when they brought in their documents and went off with the Sabbath candlesticks? And so the poor Leibish had to come every day and sweep the alley in front of a stranger's door. Now he was being tormented about building a fireproof wall. So he dragged through his days.

The whole town had prayed for nothing better than a fire that would once and for all burn down the shanties so that there would finally be an end to the argument about who owned them. Every day the schoolboys repeated their greatest wish, "May a fire break out in the middle of the day, so we can get out of school!" But just because the whole town wanted it, this time the fire had left these buildings miraculously standing.

Underneath the shanties that seemed to hang in the air was a cellar that seemed to lead into hidden nether worlds. Down there in the cellar was a baker's oven from the time before Terach, the father of Abraham, according to the village legend, and copper pots filled with golden coins were walled into the oven, but no one dared touch it for fear that the entire house would collapse and people might be killed. Day and night, a fire burned in the oven. It was said that the soul of the baker moaned in the fire because it could not rest.

In the cellar dwelt an old woman, Sarah, the baker's widow, with her six orphan daughters. God only knew how the poor woman ever came to live down there in the cellar, but since she was there people let her stay. On the other side of the basement lived a mattress maker, and the whole street was filled with cotton and feather flakes from his shop. The children nicknamed him "Bird Man," and kept shouting "Birds! Birds!" in his doorway. The old fellow would rush out, chasing them with a stick. Every

Sabbath eve, especially in the summer, the old Jew would collapse as though dead, thereby terrifying the entire town. "The plague!" they would cry and rush off to find Chyiall the apothecary, to come with his smelling salts.

On Wednesdays all the young lads of the town, the tailor's apprentices and the cobbler's apprentices, would gather to court the six orphan girls, who were scarcely a year apart in age. On a summer evening after work, when the night was dark and the shutters were closed, the boys would stroll by with their pagan little canes, walking back and forth past the cellar, and every few minutes one of the orphan girls would slip out, only long enough to show herself, glancing up and down the street; she might catch a kiss, a caress, from some lad and swiftly disappear into the cellar again.

It was hot there, in the evenings of the Festival of Weeks, when the good Jews of the town were in the house of study, which still stood, and the village wives went back and forth to the baker woman, bringing their butter cookies to bake, and the young men hung about the place, and the moon shone down with half an eye open and everything was muted in the half-drowned night.

All that was to be baked for the engagement feast was brought together in the cellar. Aunts and grandmothers clustered about Rachel Leah, the ancient crone, with the little hairs on her warts; she was the chief of all. She brought her huge mortar and pestle and spices from home, and for three consecutive days she stood there rubbing and pounding and grinding. Grandchildren swarmed from all over to try their hands at the mortar, only to be shoved away. A whole collection of baking molds was brought down from someone's attic; there were cookies in the shape of a star of David, in the shape of birds, of geese, and ordinary seven-pointed cookies. Out of her own head, Rachel Leah invented all sorts of shapes with points and corners. For every bride whose feast she prepared, she would devise a special emblem as a good-luck charm.

The cakes were wrapped up carefully, to be transported to the place where the marriage articles were to be signed. During this time Reb Yitzchak Yudels had become quite an authority in the house of Reb Yechezkiel; he had won the confidence of every woman and child. And the ladies' man, the Daitschel, was even passing his nights in the house. The women ran around in busy confusion, each one as though she had her hands full of things and knew not where to put them down.

The latest to arrive were Iteh and Golde, the daughter-in-law and the daughter. They had a habit of waiting until they were invited over and over again, and when they finally arrived, it was as though they had fallen from heaven. They would pretend they had no idea of what was going on, and in all innocence they would ask, "What could be happening here?" When the mother began to explain, they shrugged their shoulders and sat down each in her corner, wrinkling their noses to show they weren't mixing into the affair.

"What are you angry about?" the mother asked.

"I, angry?" Iteh lifted her nose a little and tossed her head.

"I, angry?" echoed Golde, with an affected little smile, as a curl from her marriage wig fell over her forehead.

And there they sat as though nailed to their chairs, and they looked with a distant eye upon the proceedings, watching everything that the mother and the other women were doing without saying a word.

Mother Malka ran to and fro, and at every moment glanced alternately into the eyes of her daughter and daughter-in-law as though she were not sure what she was doing was all right.

"How shall we dress the bride?" she finally asked.

"How should I know? Ask her," replied Iteh, with a glance toward Golde.

"Tell her to wrack her own brains," Golde advised her mother.

The mother straightened up from packing her daughter's clothes and set her arms akimbo. "Well! Now all is ready for the celebration!"

THE LITTLE TOWN

One fine morning the wagon was harnessed, and they rode off to the village that was halfway between the dwellings of the bride and the groom, for there the marriage contract was to be made.

Nutta brushed down the horses, tied red and blue ribbons in their braided manes, and tied up their tails; as soon as they got outside the town, he chopped off a tree's branches and bedecked the wagons with the leaves.

In the first wagon sat the menfolk: the rabbi and Reb Yechezkiel; Ozarel and Motaleh; Reb Yitzchak Yudels with Reb Schmaya, the old servant of the rabbi, who was dressed in his master's discarded clothes. Close and distant relatives sat in their velvet hats, smoking cigars. In the other wagons rode the women carrying the cakes and other provisions. On either side of the bride sat Golde and Iteh; perched perilously on top of their heads were tiny, circular black straw hats trimmed with black lace and feathers, in the fashion of bygone days. Golde had drawn out the locks of her marriage wig in the Warsaw style, so that they hung in three curls over her broad shining forehead. They wore their golden earrings and the modish chains and necklaces that were gifts of their own bridal days, when they too had made their journey to the halfway house. And now they remembered their own maidenhood, and shook their heads. Malka, the bride's mother, sat among the aunts. These last rode stiffly and silently, in their blue silken Sabbath caps, all beribboned, their thin lips drawn over their toothless gums. They were too excited to utter a single word, especially as the bride's mother kept stopping their mouths with honey cakes from her amply stocked apron.

And the bride, the bride herself, sat between Iteh and Golde. She wore a stylish hat, and her braids were already put up in a knot. She grew alternately pale and red, poor thing, scarcely knowing where to turn her eyes. Golde kept telling her over and over how she must behave and what she must say and what she must think when she was handed the bride money at the moment of signing the marriage contract, and how she should answer her future mother-in-law in case she should be asked anything. And from her side, Iteh kept darting stinging glances at her sister-in-law.

In order to appear in the best light before the bridegroom's family, they had brought along the wife of the old rabbi of Lowitsch. The *rebbetzen* was a far-off aunt, an ancient crone with a clean-shaved head like a sheep; she wore a black kerchief and a wide black gown with a little pillow in the bustle. She was a law unto herself. First she took hold of the ladies' man who had somehow managed to smuggle himself on the women's wagon, where he warmed his heart among the aunts and grandmothers. The *rebbetzen* took hold of him and threw him off the wagon, for to her he was still a man. Then she kept whispering advice and information into the ear of the bride, so that the poor girl became as red as fire with shame.

The ladies' man ran after the wagon for quite a way; when the *rebbetzen* had exercised her shaven upper lip until she talked herself to sleep, he caught hold of the wagon and climbed up in the rear, poking his dented old Sabbath top hat in among the cluster of ladies' hats. Hanging on the braces of the wagon, he too became drowsy, and his top hat nodded an amen to the nodding of the old *rebbetzen* of Lowitsch.

Thus the wagons arrived at the inn.

The Jewish inn stood at the juncture of two roads that led to two large towns in two different counties; each of these towns was the seat of a wonder rabbi. Followers of the rival rabbis, Chassidim with packs on their backs and sticks in their hands, separated here, going off along the different roads across the green fields and tossing stones at each other from one road to the other. Travelers in foreign lands, coming from various cities from either direction, stayed overnight at the inn. There was a special little prayer house for them because various little crawling things in the old prayer hut annoyed them, and they were important travelers, buyers and sellers out of strange lands. There in the inn the voyagers from far and wide would relate the tales of their wandering. The wagon drivers had long thick tangled beards that seemed to cover their faces entirely so that one could see only the little pipes that stuck out of their mouths. They were wrapped in thick layers of wool, and over everything they wore great sheepskin coats with large collars. Their high wagons were filled with lime and oil; at night their giant storm lamps showed from great distances. They all halted at the inn to feed their horses and rest their bones. This was the meeting place of Jews everywhere, and here they told each other what went on in their own lands, how it was with the Jews in the world, and how things went with our brethren, the sons of Israel.

It is evening; the sky is broken into a thousand pieces; the little white fleecy clouds and the little blue islands float in the bright shining sea, and the sea turns purple under the sunset blaze and then fades in the hour of the evening prayer. In front of the inn there are a number of wagons, tall wagons so heavily laden with wares that their axles seem to bend between the wheels. Jewish merchants are carrying goods from one country to another. The horses, unhitched, are feeding, digging deep into their nosebags as though purposefully gathering strength to draw the heavy loads on the rest of the journey.

The Jews are one people with one God, and they all await the same Messiah, but every little village has its own look, its own customs, one might say its own soul, with which it stamps its inhabitants. Here a number of Jews lie stretched out, all seemingly alike, sleeping and warming themselves under the sun's last rays, and the dust of the road covers them all. But on their horses and on their wagons there are the marks and signs of their various cities. On the threshold of the inn sits a Lithuanian Jew, an odd sort in a strange shirt with a short jacket that somehow looks like an overcoat and a hat with a high crown. Even in the summer heat he wears a pair of high boots. He must have come from very far, halting here to rest and to spend the night. He tells his fellow

Jews how things are far, far off in Lithuania with our brothers, the sons of Israel. He tells them how our brethren live there in fear and in need. This Lithuanian is quite a learned man; he speaks the holy tongue as freely as running water, only with a slight Lithuanian accent. The Jews respect him, and they groan, "What do we know? What can we do?" But somehow in their hearts they don't believe him. A Litvak—if they're not careful, he'll pull his tricks on them. Yet it's true that he speaks softly and seems to be pious. He stood for a long while at the evening prayer, over the eighteen silent behests; still he did not sway, and who can tell what a man hides in his heart?

Clouds of dust suddenly appear, rising from both ends of the road and settling thickly over the fields; the clouds come nearer and presently rip into bits as one hears the whistle of whips, and at length a number of wagons draw up in front of the inn. The wagons are full of wedding guests in velvet hats and women in wide skirts. The women are laden down with hampers, with brandy and honey cake. They all alight from their wagons. There on the groom's side are Jews from another district, with short beards and long beards, and they too have a tall, tall Jew, a sort of Reb Yitzchak Yudels, with a long yellow beard and long hands for pushing everyone around. And like Reb Yitzchak, he outyells everyone.

They all greet each other; the mothers-in-law, seeing each other for the first time, kiss and embrace. The old *rebbetzen* of Lowitsch gives orders to everyone, even members of the groom's party.

The drivers unharness the horses and feed them, then look each other over, with their hands on their hips. They call out jokes and make rough remarks to each other, simply by way of passing the time.

The wedding guests went into the house. The main room had a very low ceiling, with small windows high up in the wall. There the men sat. Reb Mordecai Konskar's young son Avrimel wandered back and forth in the room; during this time he had grown taller, and a little black beard was sprouting on his cheeks; he was wearing a satin coat with silken girdle. He was dark complexioned, and two long curly black ear locks framed the sides of his face. Everyone shook hands with him. Reb Yitzchak Yudels went over to him and talked to him as with a grown man.

In honor of the guests the innkeeper had put on his high shiny boots, which usually lay cast aside in the cellar all summer long. He placed two large candlesticks on the white-covered table and went out. The guests from both sides began to get acquainted. Among the men this went very quickly, they simply shook hands, said *"Sholem aleichem,"* and began to converse. And besides they were already related in a way, being Chassidim, followers of the same wonder rabbi. The learned folk among them soon began a sharp discussion of the Torah. Reb Yitzchak Yudels was already deep in an argument with the tall Jew who was the teacher of the groom. They had hold of each other's beards, and each was giving the other a true example of erudition. They got into a heated dispute, corrected and berated each other, and then made peace with an offering of cigars. The rabbi entered the argument but could not keep up with them. The Chassidim simply brushed him aside with a sweeping gesture. Meanwhile Ozarel came up and lent his ear to the dispute, wrinkling his forehead. At every point he nodded his head with his eyes closed, "Yes, yes, that is exactly how it is."

Then they began to give ear to the groom. He recited a minute argument out of the commentaries, leaping from one passage of the Torah to another and enlarging upon an opinion of the great Rambam. Here and there in the course of his argument he tacked on a reference to obscure authorities, and suddenly he tossed over the evidence brought forth on both sides of the dispute and posed a new question related to the kosher laws. He expounded it by mingling rival theories of slaughter with questions of the afterlife.

Reb Yitzchak Yudels tried to catch him up at point after point, but he kept slipping out of his grasp, dodging and dancing from one argument to another and managing always to land on his feet.

Suddenly the rabbi entered into the discussion, asking the groom to recite from memory a direct passage out of the Gemara with the commentaries of Rashi. Instantly, the young groom began to spout the passage, but in the midst of this, up rushed the tall Jew, Reb Osher Yischaras, his teacher, who pulled him aside crying to the non-Chassidic rabbi, "We have nothing to do with outsiders!" Reb Yitzchak Yudels, the Chassid, grinned with satisfaction, and Ozarel showed that he too was on their side. Reb Yechezkiel yearned to get into the argument, but he was intimidated in the face of learning. The rabbi stood stone still. Protests began; there was shouting; the argument grew more and more heated; and all of them were wrapped in the heavy smoke of pipes and cigars that filled the room and poured out of the open window as a fragrant offering to the Lord.

The two old graybeards, Reb Yechezkiel and his partner Reb Chaim Rosenkranz, sat in a corner of the room, their gray heads attentive, as the Chassidim carried on their dispute over the word of God. Each Chassid clung to his argument. Each Chassid supported his brother, one for the other, as though they belonged to a single household. Yes, there was a kind of partnership among Jews. And now they saw their own children mixing into the discussion. There was Ozarel, a veritable Chassid! And the groom —how pearls poured from the mouth of the young man, words of the Torah! He entered into argument with graybeards twice his age, and overcame them. Tears began to well up in the eyes of old Reb Yechezkiel, his dry old heart began to fill with new emotions, and he took hold of his old partner.

"Ah, my friend, God has allowed us to see this day. We were ignorant, but our children—our children—" and the two old graybeards embraced each other in the dark corner.

The room was drowned deeper and deeper in smoke that welled

88

out from the heavy beards and the thick whiskers and filled the house. Hats of velvet and fur bobbed hither and thither in the smoke, the two candle flames threw a sort of halo all around. The voices of Jews rose in argument, and the groom's young voice rang out like a bell as he poured forth his learning, sounding out over them all. Reb Yechezkiel was filled with pride. This would be his son-in-law, and the voice of the Torah would be heard under his roof! He went over to Reb Mordecai Konskar and half embraced him, holding back part way out of respect.

"Reb Mordecai, I want to take the boy from you, no matter how much it will cost!" And the old man wept tears of joy.

So the fathers went into the garden to discuss the dowry.

In the next room, the bedroom of the innkeeper and his wife, the women were gathered. On the walls were pictures of old soldiers and generals. Napoleon, too, was there, alongside a little Jew in an odd sort of hat, a relative in some strange land. The windows were overhung with foliage that still remained from the Festival of Weeks.

In the center sat the bride, freshly washed and combed; they had dressed her in her new gown with the fringes, and then they had seated her. "Sit quietly." All around her the women sat silently in their chairs, not one of them offering a word. Each waited for the other to start the conversation, and if one of them so much as coughed, she blushed. Only the old *rebbetzen* of Lowitsch moved around the room. Her arms were crossed, and her little bustle seemed to announce after her, "After all, I am the wife of the rabbi of Lowitsch." But the women remained quiet, their lips tightly shut. One might have thought they were waiting for some-one to smash a windowpane. Then, without anyone knowing exactly how it came about, they began to exchange a few words. From time to time one of them would show off by putting in a word of German.

From the other room they heard "his" voice, the voice of the young groom, interrupted occasionally by the voice of Reb Yitzchak Yudels. The bride's face grew red and her heart began to beat. Golde, with the locks rattling on her forehead, placed herself beside the girl; she took a deep breath, blew out her cheeks, and played with the golden chain round her neck.

And there on the bridegroom's side, believe it or not, there was a pair of sisters-in-law who were the duplicates of Golde and Iteh. Their Golde was tall, with a dark sunburnt face. Her hair was shaved; she wore a bonnet, wound around with a chain of pearls. She was more of a Cossack than a woman, and she was not to be taken in by anyone. She flattered her mother-in-law, and spoke a "city" dialect, saying *"yach"* instead of *"ich."* She talked only of how things were "with us in Warsaw." And their Iteh was a thin, delicate little woman with a narrow little nose, which kept twitching nervously. She wore a long lace bow around her throat and a light thin marriage wig with a part in the middle, a white shawl and a white shirtwaist. She spoke with an elaborate accent and a liberal sprinkling of German words, said *"icha"* instead of *"ich,"* and boasted of the "puttercake" served with coffee at her parental home. Whenever she took offense at the Warsaw Golde, she went over to her mother-in-law and said, "I want to go home," acting the part of a poor innocent little calf with her mother's milk not yet dry on her lips.

The first Golde looked proudly across toward the other Golde, as though from on high, like one young turkey challenging another. In her glance, she let it be known that she was the daughter of Reb Yechezkiel Gumbiner. She kept staring, waiting for the other to try to meet her eyes—and then there would have been a fine wedding, God forbid! But the second Golde was occupied with her conflict with her own sister-in-law. She settled herself close to her mother-in-law—the groom's mother—and began to praise the groom. The mother was filled with pride and melted like butter, whereupon the second Iteh moved over toward the bride and began to talk intimately and quietly with her as though they were beloved sisters. Soon they were kissing each other and telling each other what great friends they would be when they were sisters-in-law. The Warsaw Golde suddenly discovered that her archenemy was monopolizing the bride, so she too moved over toward the bride and with a loving little smile began to tell her how fond they would be of each other after the marriage, all the while darting dagger looks at her sister-in-law, in the hopes that her spleen would burst with jealousy.

And our Golde and our Iteh sat quietly on their chairs, twisting their thin mouths, licking their dry lips, showing that they did not want to mix into things.

Then Ozarel entered gaily, with his velvet hat halfway back on his head, and his hands in his pocket. "Why are you all sitting here as though you were strangers?" he demanded of his own family. And turning to the groom's mother, he asked, "Well, have you listened to the bride?"

Then the other Golde, the dark one, went up to the bride with a tangled ball of thread and gave it to her to undo. "Let's see what the bride knows," she said and put a series of questions to the girl. The bride answered them. The Warsaw Golde's bonnet bobbed in the air as she considered the bride's replies. And the poor bride grew redder and redder, while her heart beat loudly.

But this did not please our Golde and our Iteh at all. What sort of examination was this! Who were these nobodies from nowhere, who dared "examine" the bride! Their family pride was aroused, and they made an unwilling peace between themselves in order to attack the common enemy. Our Golde sharpened her tongue and attacked.

"As I live, imagine, people from God knows where trying to examine the bride as though she were being sold in the market place!" And with that she turned up her nose.

"In our circles in Warsaw," the other replied, as though biting the words off her tongue, "this is the way things are done."

But the other Iteh must have suddenly recalled her bridal days, for she began to weep—she had a gift of weeping at the slightest pretext—and she fell on the bride's neck and began to kiss and embrace her.

Then Reb Yechezkiel, the bride's father, came into the room.

"Come, women, don't take offense at each other! Let us bring together the bride and the groom, to see whether they please each other."

The Lowitsch *rebbetzen* objected strongly to this innovation, for it was forbidden that a couple should see each other before the marriage. But Ozarel insisted that the modern world required this, and turning to the Iteh of the other side, he said in a rich mixture of German and Yiddish, "Surely you agree. These old geese . . ." and he pointed to his own parents.

The women left the room, and the bride remained sitting in the corner with her face flaming red. She was unable to raise her eyes from the floor for shame and embarrassment. But the other Iteh, who had stayed with her, kissed her and wept over her as though she were about to be taken to the butcher's block. She alone knew and felt what the bride was feeling this moment in her heart. Perhaps she remembered her own maidenhood and wept for the time of her youth.

Then the groom was brought in by his mother. He was as pale as the wall; his ear locks wavered against his pale cheeks and he clutched his mother's arm tightly.

His mother brought him up to the bride.

"This will be your bride. Look and see whether she pleases you." With this she vanished from the room, as did the other Iteh, leaving the couple alone.

The children stood there as though they had just been beaten and as though they were afraid to move from the spot. The boy was completely confused; he did not know what to do with his hands. The girl stood by the window close to him; she heard the beating of his heart and somehow felt a great pity for him. She slowly raised her eyes and looked at him, and then she was not able to take her eyes away; she wanted to say something but could not think what.

They both wished only that they might remain standing like this without saying anything, without looking, and that no one should see them.

Then the mothers came in, and they asked the children, "Well, do you please each other?" And they clapped their hands and said, "They are pleased! They are pleased!"

The mothers became great friends and began to embrace each other heartily and to apologize to each other, and our Iteh praised the groom before the bride, and the Warsaw Golde clung to the bride, crying, "We shall be sisters for ever and ever. Amen."

Then the rabbi brought in an imposing document and it was given to the bride to sign. The bride signed her name, and everyone cried *"Mazel tov!* Good luck!" Then her future father-in-law Reb Mordecai Konskar gave her a long golden chain with a brooch as an engagement present, and the bride accepted it with a pretty "Thank you" and she kissed her future father-in-law's hand. After this the *rebbetzen* of Lowitsch picked up a whole stack of plates and smashed them on the ground, crying, *Mazel tov!* Good luck, good luck!"

Then both the Golde's and the Iteh's went up to each other and offered each other their lips, which usually gave forth only sulphur and pitch, and they embraced each other heartily and cried *"Mazel tov!* Good luck, good luck!"

Reb Yechezkiel wept like a little child, and if he had not been abashed before the Chassidim, he would have kissed his old wife. Instead he seized his partner Reb Chaim by his coat and hugged him.

The mothers could not be found, and from all sides people were shouting "Brandy! Honey cake!" and the old men continued to

93

embrace each other. Ozarel had slipped in among the women and was becoming extremely friendly with the other Iteh, speaking to her almost entirely in German. The little ladies' man with his dented top hat now came to life. He appeared as though out of the earth, and he made peace with the *rebbetzen* and immediately became friendly with all the women of the other side, telling all sorts of little jokes, except that he had a great fear of the other Golde with the feather in her bonnet. He feared her like burning fire and kept his distance.

And then from the kitchen, old Rachel Leah danced in toward the bride, carrying a platter of cakes and delicacies.

> *No one invited her*
> *She came by herself,*
> *A poor relation she may be*
> *But still she is my aunt to me.*

Night still lay over the village and the fields and over the whole world, and the moon came up among the clouds; the wagons still stood in front of the inn, and their storm lamps flickered in the night, casting their glow on the wagons of the wedding party. As the guests came out and mounted the wagons, they still chatted, and from the wagons the men still called out their last arguments, quoting a final passage of Maimonides at each other, and the women called out a greeting to the old grandmothers, to the old aunts, and to entire families. The snapping of whips resounded far and wide in the quiet night, and the echo came from afar. Then the wagons drove off to the right and to the left. In one of the wagons that went to the left there was an unoccupied seat; the bridegroom was missing, for he had driven off with his future in-laws on a Sabbath visit.

On the last wagon sitting among the women was the aged Rachel Leah. She had drunk a little too much, her eyelids drooped heavily, and half in sleep her thin old lips still mumbled the song:

> *No one invited her*
> *She came by herself,*
> *A poor relation she may be*
> *But still she is my aunt to me.*

Friday in the Little Town

It is a summery Friday afternoon.

The schoolboys finish off their afternoon recitation from the Book of Moses, skip the commentaries, and go home with their prayer books, their Bibles, and their Talmuds under their arms ready for tomorrow's "examination" by their fathers. Once they are home they get at the blueberries that their mothers are turning into jam; their mothers give them their berrying aprons, but they manage to smear up their faces; then they steal a few carrots out of the cellar. The mothers take their boots and coats and put them away in the chest until prayertime in the evening. Barefooted and half naked, off the boys go into the streets behind the synagogue square where all the rest of the lads are already waiting. With their hands full of stones they run into the market place and chase the baker's pigeons. The panic-stricken birds fly over the square, while the baker rushes out after the boys, who take to their heels and escape.

The burned town is half smoothed over; here and there one can still see a ruin patched together with half-charred boards. Everyone's property is separately fenced around. Here and there one finds piles of lumber and boards. Goyim are at work, while little boys clamber and leap around the lumber piles, and make seesaws out of the planks. A number of Jews, the idle and the unemployed, sit watching the goyim at work, giving them advice as to how to set in the doors and the windows. The Jews argue about their system of construction, and the goyim laugh at them.

In the market place there are green apples to be found and ripe little pears can be had for two coppers. A little boy runs by, blowing a whistle made from the throat of a freshly slaughtered duck, and the lads run out after him. A little girl hurries by on her way to the synagogue with a chicken in her hand, for some question has arisen as to whether the chicken is kosher, and the rabbi must be consulted. Then a woman passes, carrying a duck on a plate. The duck has proven impure, and she is about to dispose of it to the Christian baker. The fathers lead their young sons from the barbers where they have had their heads shaven like sheep, in honor of the Sabbath of Consolation. Jews with packs on their backs come walking from the road, to spend Sabbath in the village. Wagons arrive in the market place. They are loaded with Chassidim, with old Jews and youngsters and boys coming to spend the Sabbath with the wonder rabbi. The town is filled with new faces. Jews stroll freely about as though they were in Jerusalem, open and free, with their fur hats, their low shoes, and their white stockings, with their ear locks and their pipes. The town becomes lively with the Friday feeling; people run about, hurrying, and anyone can easily see that this is the eve of Sabbath, the eve of the great day. Even the sun seems to move over the town in a special Friday manner, letting her light pour down and her golden rays fall wherever they may, making no distinction as to whom they shall touch. Drunken peasants and their drunken wives in red kerchiefs and white coats leave the inns and ride off home; they kiss, weep, and laugh, hug each other, and dance. Their sleek, well-fed horses are decked out with ribbons as though they were on their way to a wedding; they leave the town in a great commotion, their wheels banging over the stones and pigs squealing in their wagons. Boys run after the wagons, shouting and yelling, their shirttails hanging out.

Laible the water carrier comes riding up from the river with his barrel filled; the children fall upon him, pulling hairs out of his horse's tail for use as fiddle strings. Laible curses them and flourishes his whip, but the children pay no attention; they keep on

97

pulling out the horse's hairs while they feed him blueberries and buttered buns, and the horse patiently bears everything.

The rabbi appears with a group of strangers. He goes from house to house, leaving a Sabbath guest in each house.

Along the street the wagon of the rich Reb Yechezkiel appears, driven by his man Nutta. He is hurrying home for Sabbath. Nutta unhitches the horses and mounts one of them, leading the other to the river, while Reb Yechezkiel sits down in his doorway and quietly slips a coin for the Sabbath to needy men who come to him in secret.

Everything in the street has a Friday air. The little clouds in the sky hurry away as though trying to reach their homes for Sabbath; more and more Jews appear in their long satin coats, in their white stockings and low shoes. Young men in satin and silk, carrying their change of clothing on their arms, go down to the river to bathe. These are young little Chassidim who have come to spend the Sabbath with the wonder rabbi. The town becomes cozy and friendly; the tailors and shoemakers deliver their last pieces of work; the apprentices receive their beer money and hurry into the shops to buy collars and ties, then run down to the river to bathe in honor of the Sabbath.

The river flows behind the house of the old ritual butcher. At night, the dead come from the little cemetery across the way, to take their ritual bath, but on Friday evenings it is the turn of the whole town. All the males of Kasner are gathered here, as naked as God created them. The field is strewn with white packages of clothing, while naked grandfathers, naked fathers, and naked boys sport in the water. The town has long been known as a town of swimmers; the citizens are proud of their prowess in the water. Fathers hold their boys on their bellies, teaching them to swim; the children cry out, and their yells split the sky, but their fathers drag them deeper and deeper in the water and duck their heads. The children open their eyes, screech, and are ducked again. Solemn-faced Jews who worry about business all week long now become playful and show off their tricks. One performs a fancy dive, another swims under water, and a third performs a somersault, crouching into a ball, clasping his hands about his feet, and rolling over in the water. A young man from Melawa astonishes the world with his feats of endurance; he lies under water for hours, like the fish, seizing people by their feet, then suddenly leaps up in the air, turns a somersault, and dives below again.

But they remember the saying, "The river devours a human life every year." In the midst of the sport, a scream is heard, "Help! He's drowning!" and there, indeed, someone is being whirled out where the current is strong. The poor fellow struggles to get out of the current, but he has been pulled in, and the waves hold him fast and keep dragging him under. The young man from Melawa dives expertly into the stream, gets hold of the drowning man by the hair, and pulls him out of the water. Meanwhile women and children have come running from the town, screaming, "Who is it?" "Chaim Mosheh, where are you?" They all seize the poor fellow and begin to roll him and to toss him about; they tie a belt around him, and thus they revive the dead.

The river is part of the town, but the field along the edge of the river belongs to the big landlord of the village; so he sends out a policeman with a dog to chase away the bathers. A shout rises, "The guard is coming! The guard!" They pick up their bundles of clothes and run naked to town; a whole army of naked Jews scramble along with their bundles on their heads while the goy and his dog chase them into the midst of the town. But there the Jewish butchers come out with clubs in their hands, and they free the town's Jewry from the arms of the goy. Already the sun is beginning to set far down on the road to Lintz; evening is coming. Things become quiet along the river; people are hurrying home. Only the last of the wagoners who arrived late in town now come down to the river to bathe, together with a few craftsmen who were late in finishing their work. The market women pack up their goods and go home. Freshly washed boys hurry down the street with empty bottles to fetch the wine for the Sabbath blessing from the spirit shop. One by one the shops close. And at the end of the street near the inn, on the way to the cemetery, a figure glows red in a cloud of golden dust. The sky over the town grows dark, one hears the custodian of the synagogue passing through the streets, rapping on the doors to warn that the Sabbath is at hand. Candles are already seen in many windows. But the half-destroyed cottages, the remains of the charred ruins, look like poverty-stricken relatives who have come to a wedding, ragged, yet in velvet Sabbath hats. Before several of the houses, the housewives and their little daughters sit, combed and washed and dressed for the Sabbath.

In the streets all is quiet and peaceful; the Sabbath arrives on silent feet, spreading restfulness everywhere. The Christians' church bell rings as though for itself alone, announcing the hour of prayer in the church. From the little study house the Sabbath candles glimmer, and one might imagine there is a rivalry between the church bells and the Sabbath candles. Each is calling its own to itself; pious Christians, both men and women, go through the quiet streets of the village to their church, and freshly washed Jews, their white shirt collars turned over their Sabbath coats, walk to their house of prayer. Chassidim in satin and silk, with white-stockinged feet, go to their rabbi's house, and the little town becomes ever quieter, ever more peaceful, ever more Sabbath-like, as though it had been divided between the little study house and the church, each having taken its own unto itself. Through the freshly polished windows one may see the glimmer of candlelight and the glitter of candlesticks. Maidens begin to appear, strolling in the little street. And the call of the cantor, "Come, O beloved!" sings out to the accompaniment of the church bell. The singing and the ringing mingle and become a single prayer to a single God.

Reb Yechezkiel and his son-in-law, the bridegroom, appear in the street, on their way to the study house. Young girls appear in the doorways and on the doorsteps along the street; well-bred respectable daughters peer out through the open windows and whisper to each other, "Leabeh's groom." "Leabeh's groom!"

Maidens and future brides stroll along the synagogue lane, wearing the golden necklaces they have received from their future in-laws. On the other side of the street, the young men walk, the grooms in their satin coats and their silken girdles, with their black side curls, and they too are wearing their golden gifts, the watches they have received as engagement presents.

Suddenly the cry of a mother breaks the quiet of the night-enchanted street. "My child! my Yitzchackel!" Women and girls come rushing from all sides, crying, "What has happened? What is it?"

"Yitzchackel went off in the afternoon, and he hasn't come back. Woe is me! He was seen by the river."

The woman weeps into the quiet street. A group gathers around her, and they whisper the old superstition, "The river takes a life every year. The river takes a life every year."

And the night grows quieter and darker; Sabbath arrives with silent steps and spreads restfulness in the summer world. Far off, there where the heaven lies on the water, the secret of the woman's little boy Yitzchackel, who has disappeared, may be known.

The mother runs down to the river's edge, there where the sky meets the water, where they both lie stretched out together, there to uncover the secret, to find out what has become of her child.

Friday evening had come. In honor of the bridegroom, the table at Reb Zechezkiel's had been set out in the large room. They had added the wings to the large table, as they did only once a year at the Purim feast when all the children and grandchildren gathered together. Malka, the housewife, had not spared any candles. She knew quite well that the greater the number of Friday candles, the greater would be the blessings of the Lord. The large table was bedecked with silver candlesticks of the ancient six-branched kind. Everything in the room shone bright under the candlelight. In honor of the groom Malka had brought out the silver table service that was used only for the Purim feast, and she had set out the silver beakers at the head of the table. The Sabbath bread lay ready for Reb Zechezkiel, covered with the Sabbath bread cloth. On the right hand, the groom's Sabbath bread lay ready, covered with ceremonial cloth, embroidered in silver thread by Leabeh for her groom. Malka wore her white silk dress with cloth-of-gold trimming; it was cut in the old-time style with wide folds that fell one into another, and over it she wore the silken shawl with the blue fringes that her husband had brought from the Leipzig Fair. She stood there in her tall Sabbath cap, covering her face with her delicate pale hands, as she said the blessing over the candles. Leabeh, freshly washed for the Sabbath, with her long silken braids falling over her blue velvet jacket, looked like an ideal daughter, who is obedient to all her father and mother's behests and behaves in a manner approved by all who are good and pious—may the blessing of peace and happiness rest upon her head! She seated herself next to her mother and together with her mother she recited the blessing.

Lord of the world, may this, my fulfillment of the duty of lighting Thy candles, be as pleasant to thee as the candlelighting of the High Priest when he fulfilled his duty in Thy holy temple! And may the eyes of my children shine with the light of Thy beloved holy Torah. . . . And may their fortunes shine in the heavens above.

The windows were open into the street, the croaking of frogs could be heard from the garden across the way, and far away in the black woods there was the reflection of a little light, hanging there in the deep night like a forgotten little Sabbath light, over which the frogs were saying the blessing. A dark fog hung over the water, covering everything; only one little light winked out from far away on the other side, and one might have imagined that the old river Vistula, the gray-haired grandmother of rivers, had also lighted her candles in honor of the Sabbath.

Wafted through the open window were the God-given summery scents of a thousand plants and flowers. They poured through the room in all their fragrance, caught up a word of the blessing, a bit of the Sabbath prayer, and drifted out again, carrying the blessing over the fields and over the woods, over heaven and earth, spreading the Sabbath blessing upon God's world.

The Jews were coming home from the house of prayer. The lucky ones brought along a Sabbath guest. The angels of Sabbath flew before them, carrying a Sabbath greeting of peace, and spreading peace over the town. And the Jews beheld the Christians who had come out in their weekday clothes and were sitting on the benches in front of their houses, with their wives and children, singing and making merry. The Jews had pity for them, thinking "Poor Gentiles, they have no Sabbath!"

And thus, Father in Heaven, Thy folk, Israel, were warmed under Thy hand. Everything seemed to be released and free; all was clothed in holiness, as though the Sacred Spirit herself had embraced the people of Israel, wiped the tears from Israel's countenance, caressed the people, smoothed Israel's ear curls along his cheeks as a mother caresses and comforts her child, and lovingly had said unto him, "Art thou my faithful son, Ephraim? Or art thou a playful child? As the favorite of my children, I shall always remember thee, and therefore my forgiveness shall always be ready toward thee."

And God's mercy was poured upon the world in the night. Reb Yechezkiel came home after the prayers were said in the study house and a goodly number of guests came with him.

"Good Sabbath."

"Peace unto you, *sholem aleichem,* from the hosts of angels of Sabbath, the angels on high."

And one might almost see the Sabbath angels spreading their two white wings, bringing peace over the room. Malka and the bride sat by the table, waiting for the blessing over wine and expecting from the husband and bridegroom the pleasant words that men speak to their wives on this occasion—"A good wife, who will find her?"

They sat down to the table. Reb Yechezkiel was at the head of the table, with the bridegroom next to him, and opposite them sat mother and daughter. All around was quiet; only the breeze that came through the open window kept up a continuous whispering. Every few moments, Leabeh shyly lifted her eyes and glanced across the table. He was so attractive in his satin coat with his dark face! And she saw the golden watch peeping from his silken vest, the watch that he had received from her. He was her groom. She would live with him in one house. Only they two, no one else . . . and her young heart beat so lightly, so quietly.

The young man sat silently, with his eyes lowered. What could he be thinking of now? About her, about his Leabeh? She blushed. Her father had brought a bridegroom home to her. . . . Ah, if only nobody were there to see, if her father and mother had gone to bed, then she would go to him quietly, for after all he was her bridegroom, and surely it was permitted to go to one's bridegroom, wasn't it? But Father and the bridegroom were singing the service in unison. His voice, how it rings, how it rises, pouring out through the open window.

"Peace and joy unto all Israel . . ."

And now she, the bride, rose and served the dishes at the table, setting a plate before her father, before her mother, and before him.

May he eat in the best of health! And her heart beat fast as she stood by his shoulder, and it seemed to him that something holy brushed past his face. . . .

Later in the meal the partner, Reb Chaim Rosenkranz, arrived with his wife and Ozarel and Motaleh, Iteh and Golde, with their children, and a host of other relatives and friends. They offered their greetings to the groom and asked whether the local cantor found favor in his eyes. This started a general discussion of cantors; someone sang a bit of a synagogue chant, and the bridegroom answered with a Chassidic melody. People in the street gathered beneath the window. The groom closed his eyes, rested his cheek on his hands, and his voice poured forth, flowing out in a song without words. Beneath the window more and more people assembled, and the daring ones put their heads in at the window. "Leabeh's groom!" the maidens repeated to each other while they pointed with their fingers. The door opened, and strangers began to come in, at first with an apologetic little laugh on their lips, saying, "It so happens . . ." but soon they walked right in, crowding the room.

Then wine was brought to the table, and the cups were filled again and again.

Soon Reb Yitzchak Yudels appeared, saying a hearty "good Sabbath." The people respectfully made room for him. Ozarel placed his hand on the Chassid's shoulder and loudly addressed him as a brother. Reb Yitzchak Yudels could not stay very long because "the rabbi will soon be saying his blessing." Presently the blessing after food was recited, and then the younger folk started off to visit the wonder rabbi, and the partners and in-laws, Reb Yechezkiel and Reb Chaim Rosenkranz, rose to go to the study house where their own rabbi went through the weekly portion, every Friday night, with the ordinary folk.

But Yitzchak Yudels pleaded with them; in honor of the groom, Reb Yechezkiel and Reb Chaim must come along tonight and visit the wonder rabbi!

At first the older men were hesitant about missing the weekly chapter, but their sons and the groom himself pleaded strongly, and Reb Yitzchak Yudels said, "You must get accustomed to the new way."

So at last the fathers gave in. Though still a little embarrassed, they allowed themselves to be led by their children to the wonder rabbi.

It was the first Friday night when they were not to be found at the rabbi's reading of the weekly portion.

In the house of prayer of the wonder rabbi, there is a mighty gathering. In God's congregation all are equal; though they be youths or elders, each has one soul, one body; all have the same love of God; all pray in one prayer house, and their prayer is one. A thousand voices rise out of a single heart; the whole congregation is fused into a single entity, a sea of black fur hats and black beards. All eyes are turned on the man in the white gown, who paces back and forth through the sea of black fur hats, making a path from one end of the prayer house to the other. This is the wonder rabbi. His hands are folded on his girdle, his eyes are turned toward the ceiling, and his spiritual high forehead is knotted into a single deep furrow. He has only a single thought, a single desire toward God.

And God is here, here in the midst of His congregation. He has mingled with His people; He has become part of the community; He is a flame in the lamp of the congregation. The Sacred Spirit and the congregation of Israel, the congregation of Israel and the Sacred Spirit—both have been wandering in exile, and here they meet, and they recall the ancient bridal time when they were first united. For is it not with them as between a bride and groom who have had a little quarrel and have separated; they have gone their various ways in strange lands, and now they meet again in a foreign stopping place.

And the rabbi gave voice to his hymn of love unto the Lord, the Song of Songs.

He did not sing, but chanted deeply and intensely, giving each word its full meaning and beauty.

Look not upon me, because I am black, because the sun hath looked upon me: my mother's children were angry with me; they made me keeper of the vineyard; but mine own vineyards have I not kept.

Tell me, O thou whom my soul loveth, where thou feedest, where thou makest thy flock to rest at noon: for why should I be as one that turneth aside by the flocks of thy companions?

If thou know not, O thou fairest among women, go thy way forth by the footsteps of the flock, and feed thy kids beside the shepherds' tents. . . .

I am the rose of Sharon, and the lily of the valleys.

As a lily among thorns, so is my love among the daughters.

As the apple tree among the trees of the wood, so is my beloved among the sons. I sat down under his shadow with great delight, and his fruit was sweet to my taste. . . .

My beloved is like a roe, or a young hart: behold, he standeth behind our wall, he looketh forth at the windows, shewing himself through the lattice.

My beloved spake, and said unto me, Rise up, my love, my fair one, and come away.

For lo, the winter is past, the rain is over and gone;

The flowers appear on the earth; the time of the singing birds is come, and the voice of the turtle is heard in our land: . . .

Rise up, my love, my fair one, and come away.

And the rabbi's voice did not seem to speak the words, so much as to taste them, and to offer them so that all who were present might know the sweetness, the loveliness, the devotion, that the children of Israel felt for the Sacred Spirit and the Sacred Spirit felt for the children of Israel.

And the rabbi's flock understood and yearned for the blessed words as a thirsty field yearns toward the blessed clouds. As the congregation absorbed each word, it sang in their hearts and caressed them, for each word was a greeting from the Sacred Spirit to the children of Israel in exile. *Were I a bird in the fields I would fly unto thee. . . .*

All the congregation joined themselves together, and they became as one heart and one soul.

The rabbi spoke the words with a love so intense that he might have been reading from a letter of love.

I sleep but my heart waketh.

Were I a bird in the woods, I would fly to you.

And those present felt close to each other, became one soul and one heart, for the rabbi said the words with such love, as if he read a letter, a dear good letter that came from a thousand miles away.

I sleep, but my heart waketh: it is the voice of my beloved that knocketh, saying, Open to me, my sister, my love, my dove, my undefiled: for my head is filled with dew, and my locks with the drops of the night.

I have put off my coat; how shall I put it on? I have washed my feet; how shall I defile them?

My beloved put his hand by the hole of the door, and my bowels were moved for him.

I rose up to open to my beloved; and my hands dropped with myrrh, and my fingers with sweet smelling myrrh, upon the handles of the lock.

I opened to my beloved; but my beloved had withdrawn himself, and was gone: my soul failed when he spake; I sought him, but I could not find him; I called him, but he gave me no answer.

The watchmen that went about the city found me; the keepers of the walls took away my veil from me.

Suddenly the rabbi was silent. He walked back and forth across the house of prayer without saying another word. His eyes grew larger and larger as he looked heavenward, and the furrow cut deeper and deeper into his brow. His spell of love seemed to have fallen upon the Chassidim, holding them all in a single embrace.

Then the rabbi started out of his enchantment, and with great joy, as though he had received revelation, he cried out, "Peace unto you! Peace unto you! The angels of Sabbath! The angels on high!"

And to the congregation it was as though a thousand angels had fallen in among them. It was as though the angels from on high came down to them and embraced them fondly and joined them in celebrating the Sabbath, in the house of their rabbi. They rejoiced together, old friends, fellow townsmen; everyone seized hold of the girdle of his neighbor, crying, "Peace unto you! *Shabbath sholem!* The peace of Sabbath! Oh, the eternal angels bless us! The angels on high!" And they went deeper and deeper into ecstasy, each man lived within the soul of his neighbor, and they were united in the joy of Sabbath, in a single love.

"Peace unto you! The blessing of the angels on high!" And the rabbi entered among them, mingled with the flock, clasped them by their hands, and with their arms all intertwined they cried out ecstatically, "Peace! Peace unto all! Peace be unto your coming!"

The rabbi became still again and stood in the center of the room with his eyes turned heavenward as though they were awaiting something there, begging something from heaven. He grasped his girdle more tightly and remained standing thus a long while, utterly motionless, and then he came to himself, and he went off into a little corner between the Torah shrine and the wall. He bent his head and stood there, deep in his own thoughts, and he murmured something quietly to himself. He slowly began to sway, and a silent, wordless prayer poured from him. From time to time he moved his hands as though he would call out or sing out through them. And then he would become still, once more sunk in himself.

All around him, row upon row of dark heads remained bowed in a sweet silence; a tender awe and affection embraced them all, and they groped for each other's hands and waited with trembling expectancy.

The rabbi awoke out of his spell, and with new energy he called to them, "Let us make the blessing."

His face shone as though it had been kissed by the Sacred Spirit and consecrated. A warmth emanated from him, embracing them all, drawing them all within himself.

The congregation made way for him. In the door there appeared a procession of women, with the rabbi's wife in their midst. Upon her high shining forehead was a band set off with diamonds, pearls, and gold. A Sabbath queenliness shone from her, and spread upon them all as she said, "Good Sabbath." From beneath her Sabbath headdress, the large diamonds in her long earrings blazed like great drops of the Sabbath itself, and the shining pearls that were spread over her heart, upon her silken dress, were like frozen innocent tears adding their glow to the holiness of Sabbath. And as she came to the table, surrounded by her daughters and daughters-in-law, the pride and grace shone upon her queenly Sabbath face. Her silken gown sang after her, her diamonds and pearls dazzled the eye, and all the gathering was filled with respect.

The rabbi filled the silver beaker with wine, lifted it high, and spoke the Sabbath blessing, *"And God blessed the seventh day, and made it holy."*

The blessing hovered over the heads of the multitude and then floated out through the open window into God's secret world of mysteries, and the weekday mantle was lifted from God's world, and all the world was wrapped in a gown of Sabbath.

The street was dark. The deep-set stars flickered in the blue sky like Sabbath candles flickering in a Jewish household, while the family sits around the table drowsing over the story books. Here and there the Sabbath light still burned brightly in a window, but soon it would go out. From the open window one might still have heard the sleepy end of a Sabbath song.

While the night lay over heaven and earth, the rabbi's blessing spread over the four corners of the world, and at last, all slumbered. Far off in the street one could hear the steps of the Jewish watchman, walking through the town all night long to guard it from another fire. From the open windows of the rabbi's house the psalm rose high over the street.

Two white beards, two gray-white heads showed themselves in the dark night.

Reb Yechezkiel and Reb Chaim were coming home from the rabbi's welcome to the Sabbath.

From the window of the little house of study a smoky little light still shone, and the tired voices of the sleepy men could still be heard.

They went into the study house.

At the table, which was faintly lit by a smoky dying lamp, sat the rabbi. Around him was his little flock of ordinary folk, tired after their week's work, and together with them he repeated the weekly chapter, *"And I pleaded with God in those days. . . ."*

A heavy weariness lay upon the sleepy congregation.

The gaunt figure of the blind cobbler could be seen, among those who were sitting there. He was snoring loudly and all the others in the little congregation were embarrassed.

The Sabbath

Sabbath morning—the sun rises in the heavens and the light of day spreads over the village. The day comes of itself; it needs no human help. The shops are closed and locked; no one is as yet awake. Not a soul is to be seen. A peasant comes driving into town with his wagon; he stops to feed his horses. From the deserted aspect of the street, he knows this is the Jewish Sabbath, then somewhere a little Jew appears in his doorway, in his newly washed underwear. He yawns openly and freely before the world. And presently a Chassid walks by, on his way back from his ritual bath, with water still dripping from his wet ear curls, falling on the newly laundered collar of his shirt, which is carefully folded over his coat collar. A tall thin Jew with a long white beard suddenly appears in the midst of the market place. He opens wide his mouth, and calls out like a trumpet, "Into the synagogue!"

And then women begin to appear in pressed white jackets; they run and beat on the windows, crying "Sarah, didn't you hear the call?" Iron latches are unfastened, shutters are opened, and white bed linen may be seen through the open windows. The sleepy ones gaze out toward the clock on the tower of the town hall. "What time is it?"

Now, one by one, the women come forth in their Sabbath finery. From one Sabbath to another, they labor lovingly over their garments, so that they may emerge in their best, to show themselves in the house of God. The fashion now is for wide silken gowns that are narrow at the top and grow wider and wider, until the women look as though they live with half a dozen children in their gowns. They love to strut in their embroidered jackets, and the most elaborate of these are left as legacies from mothers to daughters. Every coat is embroidered around the sleeves and the neck with broad designs in silk. On their heads they wear a sort of half cap made of two flowers wound together over upright wires, enveloped in a "Turkish" scarf, sometimes known as a synagogue scarf. Young wives of the modern world wear little two-pointed collars, tied with a silken shawl from Leipzig, and the two ends of the shawl are drawn into a wide bow over their hearts. This is very becoming, and heightens their feminine appeal. On their smooth marriage wigs they wear a cap of black embroidery, with a long black feather, tied with two silken ribbons around their throats. The maidens, dressed for Sabbath in their freshly pressed gowns with their white petticoats, stand in their doorways or in the windows along the entire street watching all who pass. Those who are all dressed up feel as though they are on parade, and walk slowly with a special manner, knowing that a hundred eyes are watching them and that everyone is discussing their every movement, and that all they wear is being weighed and measured by a hundred tongues.

Little boys walk before their mothers or their aunts carrying the women's prayer books wrapped in a handkerchief. And then the family men and householders come out in their long Sabbath coats and clean collars on their spotless shirts. Some already wear their prayer shawls, and some of them have their prayer shawl and their prayer books carried by their little sons who walk behind them. Chassidim appear in their long satin coats and fur hats, and white collars and silken ties, their neat attire attesting to the excellent housekeeping of their wives. Some are going to the ritual bath and some are coming from it. The street becomes ever livelier, more cheerful, filled with Sabbath atmosphere. The sun pours down from the heavens—a fresh new sun especially brilliant for the Sabbath. She pours her light upon the one side of the street, leaving the other in shadow. And on the leaves of the trees that blossom before the doorways the dew of night still glistens.

But the synagogue stood in waste and ruin, fenced around with boards, a coffin of a synagogue. All that remained standing after the fire was a sort of wailing wall, a pitiful remnant of the synagogue, and they went past it groaning and then went on to pray in the little house of study.

The prayer was already under way in the house of study; the cantor had prepared a few new songs for the faithful congregation of the town rabbi. There stood the cantor surrounded by his choir, by the boys, and by the obscure folk who wander about the streets all the year without anyone paying much attention to them, but who suddenly become important on the Sabbath day when they can make the congregation joyous or sad and when it is in their power to carry the villagers' prayers up to the heavens. At the door stood the "experts," the handkerchief maker with his little split beard and all of his companions. As usual, they were criticising the chorus, twitching their noses from time to time, or tapping with their feet, covering their eyes, or suddenly turning their heads and listening. "There . . . like that!"

Reb Yechezkiel and the groom arrived a little bit late as is fitting for a groom and a Chassid. Avrimel was welcomed with a psalm; the women looked down from their balcony, marveling at the cantor's rendering of the chant.

After the prayer, Reb Yechezkiel invited the congregation to come to his house for the blessing of the wine. Malka delayed the plain folk in another room, where the fish was being warmed, while Reb Yechezkiel waited for the Chassidim to arrive. Then Ozarel appeared with Reb Yitzchak Yudels and all his followers. They began to push and to shove, without sense or reason, pushing the plain folk aside. And in the great commotion that they made, the Chassidim stretched out their arms and seized whatever was on the table. Malka was filled with pride to find Chassidim in her house, learned men! And Reb Yechezkiel had virtually turned into a Chassid himself. The Chassidim pulled him into their circle and slapped him on the back while several of them began to sing.

Everything became quite merry. Malka handed out the fish, and everyone sat down to table; then people from all over town began to bring in delicacies as a gift for the groom. "Mother sends a pudding for the groom," the maidens would say, carrying in a platter that was covered over by another plate, with a napkin wrapped around the whole.

"Thank you, thank you!" Mother Malka would say. "Thank you in God's name. And when your own groom is sitting at your table, we will repay you with flasks of wine!" Her happy voice rang out over the room.

The table was covered with puddings, for each housewife in the village was recognized by the taste of her pudding. A well-made noodle pudding certainly came from an old housewife whose kitchen was managed in the ancient traditional style; a narrow pudding filled with raisins and other dainties was certainly from a modern "lady," scarcely a pudding any more but halfway a cake. A dry pudding well browned with goose fat, containing a sprinkling of raisins but plenty of pepper—that certainly came from a Chassidic table.

The street was still lively and gay. Through a number of windows one could still see people sitting at their tables, taking their day of ease. A number of family heads were drowsing over their prayer books in the midst of the blessing. The younger element and the schoolboys were stealing away from their tables. Before the blessing was finished, they ran out into the street, and up the hill at the edge of the town where the young men and maidens went strolling.

And the Sabbath lay over the hill. The town drowsed sweetly beneath its mother's apron, and this was the enjoyment of Sabbath. Schoolboys were gathered on the hill; they stood on the top, pretending to be generals spying out the town through telescopes, which they made out of their closed fists. Children slid down the hill one after another, tearing their Sabbath coats and their Sabbath boots. Women promenaded along the lane at the bottom of the hill and halted to shout up at the hillside, "Nahum, your Sabbath coat!" "Chaim, come down from there! Are you coming?" The lads pretended not to hear and kept on sliding one after another down the hill.

But suddenly a boy called out, "Here comes the rabbi! The rabbi!" and then the whole flock of them took to their heels, vanishing in the distance. Far behind the hill, the road continued, and there was the stream that cut through the town, and beyond was the watermill. The slapping of the water against the wheel could be heard from a distance. And beyond the watermill the older lads, the students of the Torah, went strolling far along the road.

After the meal, as is customary in a good man's house on Sabbath, Reb Yechezkiel crawled under the covers for a nap, and Malka did the same.

Leabeh, wearing a Sabbath dress with a white apron, went into the salon like a modern bride and sat herself by the window, reading a modern romance. Her groom walked back and forth in the salon, a bit more at home. They now felt a little as though they belonged to each other, although they had not yet spoken an intimate word to each other. She kept on reading, no longer disturbed or abashed by his presence, for after all they had been made bride and groom. She said nothing but tasted her joy within herself, feeling her happiness in her heart. For he was hers, a little groom all her own, and she counted his steps within her heart. Now they were no longer ashamed to keep their eyes on each other for after all this was certainly not forbidden. But they had nothing to say to each other, and so they remained silently together in the same room.

"Perhaps Avrimel would like to drink a glass of soda water?" she suddenly asked him, gaining a little boldness.

"Thank you very much," he replied.

So she brought him a glass of soda water, setting it down close to him. Then he picked up the glass and made a loud blessing, and she felt as though the blessing now included herself, and so she answered with a half-whispered amen. Then she felt deliriously happy, as though she had joined him and they had made a blessing together.

Then they were silent again. He went on walking back and forth in the room. He had an impulse to tell her the story of the lad from Lowitsch in the study house. But then he remembered that she was only a girl. How could she understand such matters? And she had an impulse to talk to him about her circle of girls—but after all he was a man. And so they were silent, yet they felt that it was good to be together, for now they were bride and groom, and after that—but they did not dare to think any further.

From outdoors the Sabbath sun shone through the windows and poured her light on the window sill and came into the room, brightening the silver candlesticks and the glassware. Outside the open window, where the blossoming tree shimmered, one could hear the laughter and the liveliness of the youngsters who were sitting on the benches in front of their houses. Maidens strolled by in the street, glancing into the window as they passed, to catch a glimpse of Leabeh and her groom.

In the afternoon the street was filled with the sound of prayer. From every window voices rose. Reb Yechezkiel, like a good family head, sat down, as was his habit, and first read through the entire weekly portion. After that the grandchildren began to pour into the room, and Reb Yechezkiel listened to each of them reciting his portion, while their grandmother dispensed their Sabbath delicacies, a pear, an apple, a handful of berries, swelling with pride over her flock.

The groom sat at his studies on the other side of the table. He recited in a loud full voice from the endless Gemara, recited to himself, held arguments with himself, disputed over the commentaries with himself, and finally apologized to himself. Presently he allowed himself to escape into the path of ecstasy and delved deeper and deeper into the mysteries.

Reb Yechezkiel was silenced in his simple Bible reading by the imposing flights of the holy Gemara that rose about his ears. To think that in his own house, under his own roof, the words of the exalted scholars of all the ages were flying about and contending with each other! Oh, father of all the rabbis! How beautiful this was, how wonderful this was!

On chairs in front of the door sat Malka and the partner's wife, and her daughter-in-law and her daughter. In their silks and their velvets, with their golden necklaces, they watched the strollers in the street.

With slow Sabbath steps, the sun went down below the village. Jews were on their way home to eat the third meal of the day. They walked leisurely, deep in conversation, the women in their Sabbath garments, and after them—let no evil eye befall them— swarmed their children and their children and their children. The little ones tugged at their mothers' aprons, demanding "Sabbath presents! Sabbath presents!" and the women pretended not to hear, walking on in quiet dignity. From the open window the groom's voice resounded, reaching out over the street, enveloping it in the holiness of Sabbath. The passers-by halted for a moment. "Listen to the groom! Listen to the groom!"

Leabeh sat quietly playing with her golden chain, listening to her groom.

Darkness had already come. Here and there little candle flames appeared in the dark of the windows, as they began to dispel the blackness that came into the rooms. From far away a little forgotten melody came wandering into the lane, a melody that was being sung at the evening meal at the wonder rabbi's table, and it passed through the little street and flew on to another world.

A few shops opened, and here and there a woman with a kerchief hastily wrapped around her head hurried through the streets with a worried complaint, "Heavens! My husband has fainted."

118

Some ran into the apothecary's for soda water, some ran to the doctor's for the hot-water bag, and the ladies' man dashed from house to house with his smelling salts.

A fright ran through the town, as though the angel of death had brushed it with his wing. They were afraid actually to speak of the matter, but it cut into their hearts.

The plague?

The moon made a path for itself between the dark clouds and appeared so pleasant, so friendly, that it could only be wishing a good week to all.

Here and there little groups of Jews stood and bade the moon welcome.

And far away the frogs croaked in the water . . . but who could tell what the future had in store?

The Holy Month

Now the early days of autumn came to town, and with them they brought the wool dealer who appeared every year just before the high holidays.

No one really knew whence he came or who he was, but he was the first visitor of winter. In the days of early autumn, before the high holidays, when the householders sat before their doors after breakfast, giving the children their coppers as they went off to school; in those days when the sun still reached into the streets but no longer warmed them, then the wool man suddenly appeared. He must have come from somewhere far away where winter had already arrived, for he wore high snow boots; he carried a great bundle of wool under his arm, for knitting woolen stockings. He was a thin little man, and he wore a wool scarf around his throat even on the hottest days, as a sort of reminder of winter. He was a mysterious little Jew who seemed to be sent into town as a harbinger of winter, and when he was seen in the town, everyone felt a shock and a feeling of apprehension.

The first bird of winter.

After him all sorts of newcomers appeared in the village, people who were not seen the entire year round, people with odd hats and strange coats cut in a foreign fashion, peddlers with packs of ritual vests, with strange charms and amulets and toys and horn rings for the children. From their presence one felt that far, far away somewhere there was a world, and in that world lived Jews, and that the poplar-lined road led to and from that world, away from and into our town. . . .

Strangers arrived in their little covered wagons, bringing blind orphans, or Jews with wooden legs, or lonely women. There were respectable-looking Jews with flowing beards, and there were families who came with written documents in their hands, stating that their homes had burned down.

Other visitors came, Jews who had the faces of Gentiles and even Gentiles with Jewish prayer books in their hands, relating how their fathers had been important landowners and generals and how they had been overcome by love for the Jewish faith and had given up everything in order to undergo circumcision at their ripe age. Somehow in their hearts the Jews cherished a fear of these newcomers, who were at once Jews and yet not Jews at all.

In the little street of the synagogue there was a pleasant feeling of excitement as the booksellers arrived in their covered carts with all sorts of literature—little prayer books and psalm books that carried the scent of Warsaw, of Berditchev, and also the scent of travel. The schoolboys pulled hairs out of the horses' tails, plagued them, and then led them out in the street where they could mount them. The booksellers lived in the little prayer house, setting up house behind the high cage where torn and discarded volumes of scripture were kept. There they brewed themselves tea while the Jews were at prayer; they spread out their volumes on long tables, and the lads of the town pestered their mothers for money for new little prayer books, for new study books—and what Jewish mother would not take the bread out of her mouth to save a few pennies for her boy to buy a little prayer book or a study book?

And then all sorts of sick people came riding into the town to visit the wonder rabbi. There was a Jew with an evil spirit in him that kept crying out like a rooster, there was a woman with an evil spirit that shrieked out of her belly, there were all sorts of Jews with all sorts of ailments, and each one had another pack of troubles. And suddenly there arrived a man who sought a trial before the court of the Torah against a dead man who gave him no peace but came every night demanding that he accompany him to the court on high. The whole town gathered at the wonder rabbi's to hear the dead man speak from behind a curtain.

And upon all this there lay a kind of Jewish charm, a spirit of familiarity with the other world of mystery, a veil, like the coat of dust that lies upon ancient holy books. One might have imagined that such a Jewish other world actually existed somewhere—a Jewish world consisting of one immense house of prayer, where the whole Jewish community lived as though in a case of discarded leaves out of the scriptures, enveloped in holy dust, and that upon all this there lay the spirit of Jewish family love and of longing.

It was a fine clear day. The women sat by their doorsteps knitting stockings and scarves. From a yard somewhere the voices of little children came out into the market place as they sat in school repeating the words of the holy Torah. And a woman repeated a phrase out of the women's prayer, *"In the name of the little innocent children who reached out their little necks toward God."* There was never such a sun in heaven or on earth; her sunbeams lingered over the market place like guests reluctant to depart, and suddenly one heard the blast of a ram's horn. The sound trembled in the air, startling young and old.

So the women sat on the doorsteps of their homes, knitting and embroidering. And wagons came driving up to their doors, and distant cousins and aunts from far away came visiting, wearing their mourning clothes, for this was the season for visiting the graves of their fathers in the old cemetery.

The old cemetery was spread out on the hill, with every tombstone hidden by a tree, and under every tree a sleeping soul, and they all looked down forever into the village. The rabbi of each generation lay surrounded by the good folk of his time in a separate little corner of this holy place, and here one could count the generations of the fathers of the village. Many of the names of the dead could still be found among the living; some of the names had been graven upon the stone and wood of the village, had become the names of streets or of courtyards. Reb Johanan's, Reb Mosheh's Yard. . . . It was quiet in the cemetery. From somewhere behind a tombstone an angry cat meowed, and elsewhere a mad dog's eyes glittered. The town billy goat with his harem of she-goats clambered over the graves, pasturing among them, and a quiet little breeze swayed the branches of the trees. Here and there living persons knelt among the graves, and a steady quiet sobbing rose from the tall wild grass, as was fitting in a cemetery, and one could scarcely tell whether the sobbing came from the dead or from the living. In one corner Chane Esther, the cemetery woman and the oldest crone in town, guided a young woman to where her father's bones lay resting. And the cantor's little children climbed into the apple trees, and between one requiem for the dead and another, they knocked down the little green apples.

At this time of year the man from the land of Israel appeared to gather up the money that had been dropped into the little collection boxes fastened on the door frames of all the Jewish houses, just below the amulet of holy words, the mezuzah. In every Jewish house this money was gathered for the land of Israel; whenever a housewife blessed the Sabbath candles, she dropped a little blessing money into the box.

He arrived like a shadow, a tall lean man with a pale, ascetic face; in his high furrowed forehead a deep secret seemed to rest, the secret of God's reason for the long, long exile, the secret of the time of the coming of Messiah. . . . He was one of those Jews in whose existence everyone believed; surely they lived somewhere, but no one knew where. The sight of such a Jew recalled something familiar to our hearts, though we could not say what it was. He aroused a forgotten loyalty, deep down in us, and made us feel as though we somehow belonged together. The man from the land of Israel wore a white satin coat, and he had long black ear curls, and he sat in an obscure corner in the house of prayer. A group of old Jews had gathered around him. There was Reb Mosheh David, who had taken upon himself the holy duty of burying the torn and worn leaves of the holy books in the cemetery, and there was Reb Yoshiahu Wolf, and Reb Nota, all those who spent the days of their old age sitting in the prayer house, long-standing members of the circle of psalm readers. They were the bodyguard of our teacher Moses and the faithful friends of David the King. They had long ago prepared their burial garments and made ready the little sacks of earth that they had procured from the land of Israel. And these old men listened well to what the man of Israel had to tell of the motherland.

They were never tired of gazing upon him, for in the folds of his garment there was the dust of holy land, the dust that blew upon the graves of the holy forefathers, and over the tomb of the holy mother Rachel, and within this dust there was a secret from afar.

Out of his pack he drew bits of stone that he himself had chipped away from the Wailing Wall, for he had stood there, reciting the evening prayer with a congregation of Jews. Each of the old men took the bit of stone in his hands, setting his iron-rimmed glasses upon his nose while he studied the true stone out of the Wailing Wall from the ancient temple in Jerusalem. This was the very stone from the temple, this bit of stone was from the days of old. The high priests had perhaps leaned against it, and this stone had seen the passing of every pilgrim who came with his sacrifices to Jerusalem. Then the man from Eretz Israel drew out a little sack of earth from his pack. This was the earth from the grave of Mother Rachel, there too he had been, on the road to Ephrat, as it is written in the Scriptures, there where our father Jacob buried our mother Rachel, on the road to Bethlehem—from there he had taken this bit of earth.

And the Jews studied the earth from the ancient tomb, from the grave of our mother Rachel, the grave that had been dug by our father Jacob with his own hands.

A voice seemed to speak within their hearts, *And thus have I not done. And in my coming up on the way from Padan, there your mother Rachel died upon me, and this was in the land of Canaan which is in the land of Israel and on the way to Ephrat.* Of this Rashi says in his commentary, *And therefore it was that I did not bring her into Ephrat, in order that I might bury her in the land of Israel. And since Thou art perhaps angry with me, I say unto Thee that all this was according to the word in the prophecy, for when the Jews should be driven into exile by Nebuzradan, then our mother Rachel would appear out of her tomb and plead for mercy, as it is written in the chapter. A voice of pleading shall be heard and then God would be kind unto her as it is written in another chapter: There is an answer unto thy deeds.*

And the old Jews were filled with longing, and here and there a tear dropped upon their spectacles.

Dusk had fallen upon the town and from a faraway land a wind blew upon the street; now and again an old man showed himself in his winter overcoat. Yes, he had already put on his winter clothes, and with his head bent into the wind, he went into the study house to recite the evening prayer. The young lads, the tailors' and the shoemakers' apprentices, put aside the canes they had carried when strolling in the fields and in the gardens, while they paid court to the pretty girls in the summertime, and now they went into the house of study like old men with their prayer books under their arms, and they recited a few psalms between the prayers of evening and of night, for the beginning of autumn, the month of Elul. Out of the little shops wide beams of light came from smoky lamps, giving the lane a synagogue atmosphere. On one side the sky burned with a hellish red glow; down there the evil ones were being roasted and burned and their blood streamed into the fire, flaming and flickering. Beneath the trees, the street was empty of life, not a lad was to be seen, nor a maiden. Dutiful little women rubbed their hands against the moist windowpanes of their shops as a substitute for the washing of hands, before they raised their eyes piously toward the heavens and uttered an amen to the blessing that could be heard from the house of prayer down the street. The prayer house was crowded with Jews, young and old. There was warmth in the house of God. With all their souls, the men had turned to their eternal creator. A preacher stood in the pulpit, exhorting them in his sonorous voice, reminding them of their glorious task, reminding them that they were God's children and that the Lord had only wanted to test their faith in Him, and that at every moment the Lord awaited their return. He told the parable of a prince who sinned against his father the king, under-lining the parable with a passage from the Prophets: *"If thou wilt return, saith the Lord, return unto Me."*

And then the congregation felt themselves to be like little children wandering in exile, lost from their Father in Heaven. After the preacher's admonitions they devoted themselves energetically to their prayers. It was the same weekday prayer for mercy that seemed to carry with it memories of the winter lamp burning in the little room, and it was led by the same Reb Osher Aaron with his same hoarse voice, but still it was not the same; something had come to life in the dark congregation, half hidden in the dim house of prayer. A forgotten longing stirred among the people, the long-ing of the exiled prince for his father the king. A shimmer fell upon them, a darkling, melancholy shimmer, as of a hidden spirit that entered into them and gave them a universal soul, and the simple weekday prayer became something altogether different, be-came a renewed word of God. A spirit glowed among the simple folk, the spirit of the Jewish congregation, the simple weekday members of the praying circle.

THE LITTLE TOWN

The congregation stood to the prayer of the eighteen verses. The prayer house was half dim; the little candles before the holy Ark were already dying; only somewhere in an obscure corner little drops of light fell into the ocean of darkness. A heavy silence lay over the heads of the worshipers. The single prayer shawl among the multitude of black coats was like a living being among dead shadows. A multitude of black shadows swayed this way and that, as though a wind of mysteries were blowing upon them and bending their heads one way and another. There was not a word uttered in the entire congregation, not even a cough was heard, but now and again, "O Father above!" was torn from an old ailing breast, and the silent multitude of shadows swayed with its secret swaying as though speaking an amen to his groan. A mute soul, wrapped in its black cloak, prayed in the darkness together with the multitude, and the prayer too was mute and dark.

And now it was night. The voices of the poplars that stood on the black cemetery had become muted as though the "Germans tall" had gone early to sleep. Cold winds blew from there, and the lane became dark; everything seemed to be wrapped in black; the shutters were closed over the windows, and from the cracks in the shutters little streams of lamplight escaped. The Jews were already at their labor, a cobbler's hammer could be heard tapping on his last, and the tapping resounded in the street, something familiar, like the chirping of the cricket behind the stove. It reminded people of the long dark winter evenings in the workshops lying ahead.

In and around the town the cottages were drowned in a sea of orchards. The sons of Israel stirred in the groves. Here and there a fire shone through the dark green gardens, and smoke arose. Somewhere a man's wife was cooking his supper, and the little flames among the dark green branches lent a loving pious atmosphere to the village and seemed to draw people to it. Here and there in the dark foliage little glowworms appeared like sparks of fire or like lost souls.

And God's world was like a chaste and loving bride who walked

127

all alone at the edge of the road, down the little street, toward the black lane.

The dark silent sky seemed to utter the prayer of night over the village: *"Cover mine eyes with sleep and mine eyelids with dreams."*

After the Holiday

The high holidays had gone by. The villagers had fasted for the Day of Atonement, and afterward, as every year, they had had their joyous recompense in the Festival of the Torah. Early in the morning Aaron Leib, the one-eyed cobbler, had wound a prayer shawl round his head, Turkish fashion, and danced through the village with the scroll of the Lord pressed to his bosom, and he had banged his fist on the table of the house of prayer, singing, "O Moses our teacher, O Moses our teacher!" But now the first night after the holidays crept upon them, the first night of winter.

It is a mute dead night! Not a light shows in the village; cold winds rip and blow without beginning or end. Here and there the shadow of a tree outlines itself, its naked branches swaying like the ghost of a dead tree in the night. The fantastic shadows of its bare branches make fearful shapes in the darkness. All about is silent, dead, and dark. Far down in the little street it seems that the form of dead Aunt Leah walks slowly along. In her white winding sheet she leans against the window of her kitchen to see whether her children are being mistreated by their stepmother. Here and there the wind plays with a torn sheet of tin roofing or with a swinging shop sign, banging it one way and another. Somewhere water is dripping, and the drops rattle down a trough. Far down the street one hears the grinding of a little mill; the kernels fall on the millstone, and it groans protestingly, pretentiously, as though it had knowledge of God and was complaining—the Lord only knows against what.

Lonely steps are heard in the dead of night. They echo upon the stones, and a Jew appears on his way to the study house carry-

129

ing his little prayer-shawl sack. He is on his way to say the morning prayers. And a frigid "good morning" reverberates in the street. A little light shines out of a high window as if hanging in the air, and the stuttering of a sewing machine rips through the dead night; a tailor is already beginning to work. From a back street there come the sounds of a wagon being hitched . . . and who is running there in the dark street in this dark night?

The deadly weight of the night still lies on the village and yet one already hears the life of the village struggling from beneath the burden of the night.

The night becomes grayer, and the morning begins to peer out as though through misty glasses. Out of the gray mist the forms of tall wooden houses begin to appear; they seem to be in the process of creation, slowly taking flesh and bone upon themselves. Morning lights show in the windows, a cold wind bends the trees in the street, and one might imagine that the wooden houses also bend a little in the wind. Peasants' wagons stand already hitched in the market place. Jews begin to busy themselves with parcels and crates, with boards and rods. They are going off to the market in a neighboring town.

Reb Mosheh the furrier comes riding down the street; he is hauling a wagonload of skins down to the river to be washed. The dew of night still clings about his wagon. The sky becomes grayer, as though it were wrapped in a prayer shawl, repeating the morning service, and had only got as far as *"How goodly are thy tents . . ."* The houses stand out more clearly against the gray background; here and there the lights in the windows are already extinguished, and the houses stand out now as though they had dropped their mystery, as though they had just come out of another world, crying, "Here we are as you see us."

Lads and good children wrapped in their warm fur coats, with their prayer sacks under their arms, enter the house of study for the day's lessons. It is full day now, but a few candles still shine out from the house of prayer. One hears voices in prayer and in study; it must be warm in there. Over the rooftops the white morning clouds lie cold and fresh; the first breath of winter blows from afar. Smoke rises from a number of chimneys; the women are already cooking breakfast—thick, fall cabbage borsch with potatoes—and a cold day of reckoning rises over the village.

Sometimes the sun suddenly appeared in the heavens, as though she had crept out to pay a debt, and for a moment people would feel optimism in their hearts, but almost immediately a wind would blow across the market place, stirring up the dust and the scraps of straw left over by the peasants, together with other rags and bits of refuse; the Lord only knew from whom or from where all this came to litter up the market place. The refuse danced in the wind, whipping into people's faces like the end of a witch's broom —a broom that swept away all hope. The little huts that had been built for the harvest festival of Succoth were still standing, but now the wind tore off their fir branches and carried the foliage away to the market place, and the bare little houses remained standing naked and ashamed, nothing but four empty walls knocked together from bits of wood, without a roof, without a bit of green; what use were they? What a sight!

And the three trees in the Jewish street stood drowned in their fallen leaves. The trees looked mute and dead, staring off into the market place. Now and again, seeming to come to agreement about something, they shook their bare branches, one of which still held a leaf at the end of a twig; they were mourning the summer. "So it is, so it is, my children."

Only yesterday the townsfolk had celebrated the Festival of the Torah as a veritable marriage feast. All their troubles had been forgotten. For this day, once in a year, people were bound to be happy. And so they had made merry. They had gone to bed half drunk, and when they woke in the morning, the stench was still upon their beds. As soon as they awoke they were restless, for during the holidays the Jewish grocer had consumed the bit of flour that remained in his sack, and a craftsman remembered that the pincers in his shirt pocket had somehow got lost together with his shirt. And so they came into the market place, stick in hand, ready and eager to earn a few pennies. The wind blew. A master-of-all-trades wandered around the market place, wrapped in his sheepskin coat. One after another appeared, some wearing their silken hats because their weekday hats had got lost somewhere in the merrymaking. The Jews wandered about, waiting for the peasant carts to appear, as for Messiah. They quarreled for no reason at all. On the threshold of Reb Zekiel Epstein's shop a number of grain dealers stood around, freezing in their little coats; there was nothing for them to do. The man-of-all-trades bought a radish for his lunch from a cart in the market place; the others watched him, sighing, and pointing at him with their fingers, for more than one of them was thinking to himself that no one else would eat lunch today.

Now there was a commotion in the street—the sheriff was carrying off two Sabbath candlesticks and a set of impounded Sabbath covers. A woman ran after him begging and screaming for mercy, but the sheriff paid no attention. The Jews stood there in their light coats, and their hearts began to tremble, "Oh, oh, the rent!"

The children were not in school; they had finished with their old classes and not yet gone into the new, and in the meantime they are wandering empty-handed and idle, getting in the way of their mothers. Their mothers scolded them, so they snatched a bit of bread for their pockets and ran about their business. In the Street of the Butcher, hides were spread out to dry in the sun, and fruit lay spread out on large sacks, apples and plums and winter berries. They snatched a handful of plums and ran out into the meadows, where the village herd grazed. A heavy fog lay over everything, but this did not matter to them. They gathered twigs and corn stalks and straw left in the fields and built a fire.

They sat around the fire roasting potatoes and weaving switches out of palm leaves stolen from the Succoth remains. The smoke rose from their fire and hovered darkly over the town. It looked as though the children had captured the town.

The teachers wandered around the market place trying to flatter the poor little storekeepers, the fathers of their pupils. The parents listened to the pleasant words, nodding their heads. Talmud students came riding into town with their little boxes of belongings. Still dressed in their new holiday clothes, they took their boxes on their shoulders and went from house to house, seeking the customary pledges of "table days" in different homes so that they might receive their meals in each of them one day of the week. And the lads of this village started out to studies in other towns. Their mothers accompanied them to the edge of town, helping them to carry their little boxes, sending them off to study among strangers, hoping that all would go well with them. The whole town seemed to be afraid of something. It trembled and worried for the future.

Beyond the town there walked a tailor with a long yellow beard and with swollen eyes, talking to a tall thin apprentice. The lad was dressed in a new sackcoat, which represented his summer's earnings. The tailor walked along with him and promised him all sorts of things. The young man listened silently. And there on the road, someone was already off with pack on his back, going into strange foreign places in the wide world, seeking his bit of bread somewhere, and his mother followed him for a distance, blessing him and weeping.

Toward evening the wagons returned from market, loaded with parcels, wooden cases, and boards. The lights shone out of the little shops and the sky was darkly clouded, the clouds lay thick over the little town and a cold rain fell; for so it had always to be; it always had to rain on market day. Perhaps it was on purpose; perhaps for no reason at all. The drainage ditches filled with water, and the water flowed over half the street. One could no longer pass from one side of the street to the other. People stood in their doorways looking across at each other. The ditch water ran into the shops whose thresholds lay even with the street. The Jews cleaned out the unbidden guest with shovels and rags, but the water that was shoved out of one door came back in through another. It took up a board, a plank, and carried it off into the street. The women ran after, crying, "Stop! stop!"

The sickly Gedalia Yudels walked along the house of prayer, looking as ill as death itself. He suffered from a lung disease inherited from his father and grandfather. Though as tall as a man, he was thin as a boy, so that one constantly feared that his tall body would snap in two. A heavy scarf was wound round his scrawny neck; he coughed and looked about with large wide-open eyes. Everyone in the village knew that he would probably die this month, for this was the worst month for tuberculosis, and they looked upon their fellow being who was still with them today, and who tomorrow would be a part of the great mystery hidden from us all, which we all so greatly fear. All became quiet in the street as Gedalia Yudels passed by; people began to say the prayer of repentance in their hearts, as though the angel of death with his long black wings had flown down the street. Little boys stood whispering together, pointing. And the street was filled with the fear of death.

In the evening the housewives sat with their neighbors around the ovens where apples were baking for the older lads who were studying the Gemara late into the night; the winter lamp stood lighted on the table, and the wives sat around it, mending winter clothes and telling tales. The young children, in the early grades, had been brought home by the teachers' helpers, and they sat by their little table playing their little games, waiting for their elder brothers and sisters to come home and amuse them. Meanwhile the house was still quiet; the dark night looked in through the dark windows; outside all was night, and here they clustered at home around their mothers.

Reb Yechezkiel's wife Malka had also returned from the market in Lowitsch; she was laden with packages and boxes. Like a good experienced housewife she had ridden to market to buy a trousseau for Leabeh, her youngest daughter. When she arrived with the boxes and packages the household gathered, the entire family and all their close and distant acquaintances, Iteh and Golde and Rachel Leah, and all the aunts, to examine the purchases, offer their opinions, and wish luck to the bride. Malka unpacked calico and cotton, the sheets and the linen, the tablecloths and all that went with them, and she related the history of each separate piece, how she had found it and how she had bargained for it, exactly where and how she had made the purchase, and told of the miracles that had taken place, which were as numerous as the hairs on her head. The women felt each separate item, weighed and measured it, and tried to guess how much it cost. And they never once hit it right. They were always a little too high or a little too low. As is natural and customary with women, their opinions were completely opposite one from the other; if one were to say "cellar," the other would have to say "garret," and so there began to be angry words and tightened lips. Then the women's tailor from Kalish appeared, a dark young man who had just been married and whose face still wore a youthful cheerfulness. He sported an eight-cornered hat, and was known as a reader of storybooks. Every Sabbath eve his house was filled with young people, and there was dancing. He was well known for his habit of tickling the women under their arms when he took their measurements, and indeed more than once he had received a slap from an outraged husband for this habit. He had brought along a large volume that he called his "journal." It was a book of women's fashions, and he showed them how the women of Paris were wearing dresses with narrow sleeves and layer over layer of frills around the throat. He informed them that in Paris women were wearing mannish coats with hoods hanging down the back. He was an expert in his work, he told them, and he knew all the latest fashions in the great world, but here there was no one for whom he could properly exercise his craft. Therefore he intended to leave for London right after Passover. He would cross the sea; in fact he already had his passage; he had his tickets at home. He told them all this in a fashionable new dialect filled with German words, right out of the storybooks. There was a modern tailor for you! A fellow like that—how could anyone ever make a good pious Jew out of him!

The children were gathered in the kitchen, boys and girls. The boys had just returned from the house of study, and the lights still burned in their little street lanterns. Among the children stood Rachel Leah, sharing out little honey cakes from her large apron. The cakes, shaped like little birds, she had baked especially for the children, for this was the custom from long ago—to hand out honey cakes to the children on the evening when the bride's wedding dress was given out to be sewn.

Three Weddings

Mazel tov! Mazel tov! For this was Leabeh's wedding day.

A quiet clear winter night. For a few days the snow came ceaselessly down over the little town, covering it from head to foot, and then one evening the moon came up. She found her way through the clouds and made the village so bright that the children on their way home from the house of study used their little lanterns more for amusement than to light their way. After the moon, the stars appeared, each from its secret resting place, and they swam from one cloud to another on their great journey, until they reached all the corners of the earth. The stars shimmered down upon the banks of snow that lay around and within the town like great flocks of white sheep huddled close to one another.

All was cheerful and homelike in the town; the shops were open; lamps shone from the windows; and youngsters jumped on the sleighs that glided through the streets. For there was great festivity in the town. Three weddings. The richest man in town, Reb Yechezkiel, was marrying off his youngest daughter Leabeh. Reb Yechezkiel's driver Nutta was leading Yente the cook under the wedding canopy, and the blind Akiba was presenting a scroll of the Torah to the synagogue.

The wonder rabbi himself would perform the ceremony at Reb Yechezkiel's. A whole army of Chassidim and of other important folk had arrived for the wedding; there was even a string orchestra, and Reb Noah, the clownish master of ceremonies, was also on hand. Oh, what a wedding this would be! Even Nutta's wedding would be quite a ceremony, for Nutta was going to stand before all Israel to put the veil upon his bride. Not for nothing was there a custom among the old families to marry off a servant on the same day as the youngest daughter of the house. And on the very same day there would be the festival for the presentation of a scroll of the law, the first ever given to the circle of early-morning psalm readers!

The entire village was filled with relatives of the bridal couple. They rushed about in sleighs whose bells jingled through the streets. The children jumped on behind to catch rides, and there was turmoil and commotion everywhere. One saw Chassidim in silken hats, velvet hats, fur hats, and special fur tricorne hats; they all did each other honor in the streets. Jews appeared with their boots polished in oil, in new-style holiday coats, with a split in the back. There were female relatives in towering headdresses, all beribboned, and in wide silken gowns. Aunts stood impatiently before their doors, bedecked with chains and brooches, waiting for the sleighs that had been sent out to fetch the wedding guests, a newfangled idea, since they had only a few steps to go to Reb Yechezkiel's. Young girls who only a few days before the wedding were running about in pigtails, which they had tightly braided so as to make their hair curly for the wedding, now appeared decked out in white gowns, with blue ribbons and white shoes. They carried little velvet bags in their hands, with money for the fiddlers. And for the groom there appeared young men in satin coats and silk hats; some wore fur hats of their family pattern—a sign that they were about to become betrothed. And then little boys appeared in new hats, and girls with their hair freshly washed came walking with their mothers to the wedding.

Music was already heard in the street; the whole town assembled, and there was dancing in the snow. Children made snowballs, in preparation for the moment when the bride and groom would be led through the courtyard of the synagogue toward the wedding canopy. And the moon joined in the sport, pouring her light upon the snow that lay like a warm blanket upon the town. All was bright and cozy; the stars winked down, the snow shimmered upward, jewel-like flakes whirled into the wind, and the white-capped cottages stood by, and the sleighs skimmed along, with their bells ringing, while little boys leaped up on the backboards.

Violins were heard in the street, playing long-drawn-out Chassidic tunes; Reb Schmuel Lintchester's violin sang into the street, rising in a crescendo. The stars in the sky were listening, and all the white world around gave ear. Chassidim sang sweet melodies; candlelight and lamplight shone through the windows; the streets became bright with light; women appeared in their doorways with lighted torches. The waiting horses beat their hoofs. The bride and groom were about to be led to the wedding canopy in the synagogue courtyard. Chassidim in black fur hats began to pour out into the street, a sea of black velvet hats and satin coats; women stood by in glittering kerchiefs with diamonds strung like stars across their foreheads. Their ample silk dresses rustled in the street; wax candles flickered in their hands; black velvet mingled with the bright silk gowns like black streams of water in white snow. In the midst of the procession was the rabbi in his long white gown, and all around him were his black-garbed followers. The *rebbetzen* of Lowitsch, with her wide kerchief bound around her temples, danced before the bride and groom, scattering raisins and almonds, while little boys and girls caught the raisins as they showered down. The rabbi's helpers drove away the children, clearing the path. And now the bride and groom appeared. They walked together, veiling their eyes with their handkerchiefs; their parents walked on either side. There was Reb Yechezkiel himself, wearing a tall fur hat and white shoes and stockings, just like the Chassidic father of the groom. The mothers were arm in arm with the bride, and the whole made a most aristocratic impression. The rich, and the Chassidim. The fiddles played, and the Chassidim sang, and the candles illuminated the procession.

The second procession followed immediately. Nutta led his bride to the wedding canopy. A little boy ran before them carrying his school lantern, with cut-outs of lions and bears glowing in different colors. Then came Yaeckel, the drummer; he had his swollen cheeks in a bandage, bim-bom! The whole street rang and reverberated. A lad had somehow got hold of the town alarm, which hung on a post in front of the town hall, and he began to sound it vigorously. Wagon drivers had taken the storm lamps off their wagons and were lighting the way of the bride and groom. Aunt Rachel Leah had joined hands with a wagoner who was a distant relative, and they danced before the bride and groom, while the drum banged away and the youngsters whistled and scooped up handfuls of snow, packed them tight, and let them fly at people's heads. The groom led the bride. In his Sabbath hat Nutta looked like quite a respectable fellow, but his eyes winked mischievously from under the wedding canopy. Yente the bride, dressed in Esther's Sabbath clothes, cried at the top of her lungs. The town rabbi appeared, amid the relatives and the wagoners, who wore their best coats and their black cloth Sabbath hats and had their boots greased. Here and there a woman in a wide beribboned dress, with a white bow on her head, sprang out of the crowd, seized an unhappy male guest, put her hands on her hips, and danced on one spot with him.

After the second couple, the third procession appeared out of a side street—the procession of the companions in prayer. Trumpets heralded their way through the village. What was this? Had Messiah come to town? Jews in masquerade were mounted on steeds. There rode a Turk with a prayer shawl wound around his head; a witch with rattling chains rode aloft on a broom; wild lads came running along, leading the town goat dressed in a long coat. Tar-dipped torches flamed skyward. Grapeshot rattled against the stones. The commotion reached to heaven. Did they want to bring down the walls of Jericho? Black masses of Jews with children clinging to their hands, seas of black velvet hats and coats, they came dancing with songs on their lips, dancing around the blind Akiba, who clutched the little scroll of the law and hopped about blindly with it. Our Torah! Our own Torah! The poor man had never swallowed a warm spoonful of food in his life, he had slept on stones, he had begged from house to house, put aside copper after copper, and in his old age he had ordered a Torah to be inscribed for him, a scroll of the law that would be as an offspring, to bless him after he was dead. And the Jews, the companions in prayer, leaped and danced in the street with him, and sang with him, "Our little Torah! Our own little Torah." Aaron Leib the cobbler threw off his coat, put on the barber's cap, and embellished it with chicken feathers. He seized the scroll of the law and danced and whirled with her. The blind Akiba clapped with his hands; his child, his heir, his good deed that would live after him! He kissed the Torah. Jews with their children in their arms danced around the book of the law, kissed it, hugged it. "Our little Torah! Our little Torah!" and the little silver bells that ornamented the scroll rang out with them in their joy, and the torches crackled in unison, and the trumpets sounded, and the Jews sang and cried out and danced and leaped about, and the little boys made snowballs and bombarded the procession as they danced along with it.

The three wedding processions reached the courtyard of the synagogue, which was surrounded by a low fence of half-burnt boards; under a white blanket of snow that reached as far as the fence lay the ruin. It seemed to peer upward to heaven from under its white cap. The moonlight poured down upon the destroyed house of worship. The three processions halted by the ruin, yet the music of the three did not mingle together; each melody from each instrument seemed to go its own way, sounding out separately, and one might have thought that the melodies were holding a contest in which each instrument vied with the others. The delicate Chassidic violins, the plain people's drum, and the common trumpet seemed to be struggling, each to drown out the other.

Outside the village, the whole world around was garbed in white. All was quiet and peaceful as though in a great cemetery. A strange white fog hung far over the sky, weaving together heaven and earth. The moon wandered all by herself in the silent wide infinity, and the cemetery lay upon the white hillside, with her graves scarcely visible above the white snow blanket. The wandering moon above picked out a tombstone here and there, upon which to pour its light. Beyond the fence of the cemetery, the dark river flowed. The townspeople declared that the river's source was beneath the rock of our teacher Moses and that its waters would heal diseased eyes. The water of the river, alone of all that was visible, was not yet covered by the white blanket of snow. Here and there in the black waters, lumps of snow had settled, and in the moonlight they made strange shapes—like weird animals sitting on their eggs. Far behind the cemetery, the black river lost itself like a black ribbon disappearing into white infinity, and no one could tell where its end might be.

All alone, with a pack on his shoulders and a stick in his hands, a wanderer passed along the road that went by the cemetery; he walked between the tall snow-laden poplars that stood shining in the moonlight like white-clad witnesses. Here all was silent and still; everything led its dead existence. From a distance old Kasner heard the tunes of the violins, snatches of song, and the distant echo of the trumpets and the drums. Only here there was no more struggle between the melodies; they no longer seemed to try to drown each other out; gently, as though they came from a hidden world, the melodies wandered here, and flowed together, mingling into one song. Each instrument contributed its tune, the violins of the Chassidim, the trumpet of the plain people, the drum of the wagoners. And it became the single melody of the village.

And the wanderer, together with the melody, and together with the dark ribbon of the river, became lost somewhere far in the distant white infinity.

Tricked

THE bridesmaids had made the bride ready. She had only to put on her wedding dress. The musicians waited with their instruments in their hands and their fiddles to their chins, and now and again one of them fingered the strings, tuning his violin. The deep-voiced cantor heaved an impatient sigh and Yankel, the clarinetist, blew impatiently on his instrument. The orchestra leader stood on a chair with two fingers stretched out ready to begin the beat; with his other hand he tugged violently at his beard, as though to take out all his anger on it. The groom and his father had not yet shown themselves. From the angered faces on the bride's side, it was easy to see that the trouble lay with the groom. But no one knew exactly what was the matter. The bridesmaids were filled with pity for the bride, who had to endure the dishonor of being kept waiting. They did everything in their power to dispel the painful atmosphere, laughing with forced gaiety, calling upon the musicians to begin. But the musicians were worried about their losses should the wedding be called off. They chased away the girls.

"Be off with you—go to your bride. There'll be enough dancing after the wedding."

The bride sat ashamed, with her face hidden in her hands, crying quietly. Her mother stood behind her, soothing her and patting her shoulder.

"God will pay them back for their sin against you, my child! God will pay them back."

In another room were the two fathers. Eliezer, father of the groom, a short little Jew, sat with his knobby bald head on his hand, biting his dry thin lips. With his other hand he stroked his short beard. And he was silent as stone. The bride's father was a tall powerful Jew with a great long yellow beard. He stood pleading before Eliezer.

"After all, don't shame me before the world. Eight days after the wedding—as soon as I sell the wheat—I'll give you the hundred rubles. Here is my promissory note! I beg you, accept my note."

With this, he tried to force a piece of paper into the other's hand. The little Jew did not budge. He made not the slightest movement except to stroke his beard. His body was immobile. He did not raise his eyes, nor move his head, but sat motionless and silent.

From time to time, one of the honored relatives would stick her head in the door and call, "Father—it's a long summer day, and the bride and groom are fasting."

"Fathers—the guests are beginning to go away. It's a crime against all those people."

"What can I do? He sits there like a murderer!" The father of the bride confronted his opponent. "Do you know what? Let us ask the groom whether he wants me to put on my coat and take my stick and go begging in the streets for the hundred-ruble dowry—right now, just before the wedding. Now, while my child sits waiting for the ceremony! I will do it! That's what I'll do. Yes, I will do it!" he cried, losing all patience.

"The groom will do as I tell him," the little Jew replied shortly.

"No, I want to hear it from his own lips. I want him to tell me that he will not cover the bride's head until he has the hundred rubles in his pocket." The bride's father stood on his point.

"If you insist on it, then you will hear it," the little Jew said. He got up, went to the door, and called, "David, David, come in here."

The groom sat surrounded by his young men, passing the time in little Torah disputes. But his mind was no longer on the Torah.

TRICKED

Something was wrong, that was clear. And it was possible that the wedding might be canceled. Actually, he would not have considered this a great misfortune. Clearly enough, if his father canceled the match before the wedding, it would be only because he knew what he was doing and meant it for his son's good. The groom did not yet know the bride. He had seen her once or twice during the preliminaries of drawing up the marriage contract and when he had signed the articles with her and exchanged a *mazel tov*. It was a pity, undoubtedly, that a good Jewish daughter should have to be humiliated, but his father knew what he was doing, and surely there was a reason for all this. He felt uncomfortable that the affair was dragged out for so long a time, and he tried again to exchange bits of Torah wisdom with his friends while he threw hidden glances toward the other room where the bride waited. He saw nothing but the edge of a white skirt. The glimpse of her wedding dress gave him a sudden glow of pleasure. For this was his destined one. But as yet he had no true emotion toward the being in the white gown. And now that his father called to him, he knew that the match was in question and that he would have to make the decision. His heart beat a little faster.

"David, do you want to get married with a three-hundred-ruble dowry?" his father asked.

"Who said three hundred? Four hundred!"

"Here is my note." His future father-in-law tried to push the paper into his hand.

"A note—what is a note? Nothing. It's a three-hundred-ruble dowry, and if that's all you want, it's all the same to me."

David's blood rose to his face. He saw the three hundred rubles as an insult to himself. For a first-class young man there were four and five hundred rubles to be had these days. He had a good head on him and was an industrious student. How could he accept only three hundred rubles? How many excellent matches with excellent connections he had refused, only because no more than three hundred rubles was offered! And now, to be married for only three hundred rubles. How could he show his face before his friends? Before all the young men in the house of study! A three-hundred-ruble groom! He was ready to throw off his wedding coat that very minute and to depart with his father. But he controlled himself since his friends and the guests were in the next room.

He twisted his ear curls angrily and said, "My father knows best what is good for me. I rely on my father's judgment."

There was no help for it. The bride's father had to put on his coat and take his stick in his hand and go out to borrow the hundred rubles for the dowry. And the bride had to sit there waiting, with her hair unbound and the marriage scarf in readiness, until one hundred rubles were gathered together in silver and in coppers from the members of her family. The coins were tied up in a handkerchief and placed in the hand of that silent little robber, the groom's father.

"David, go and cover the bride's hair," the little Jew said, approaching the groom with the handkerchief full of silver and copper in his hand.

That night, when David was alone with his bride, she suddenly became ill and fainted. After he had sprinkled water in her face and brought her to her senses, she opened her eyes, looking at him in a strange and frightened way as though begging something of him with her eyes.

David, not understanding what could be troubling her, asked, "What's wrong, Dvorele?"

Instead of answering, she took David's hand and placed it over her heart. David felt her heart beating under his hand like a little hammer, and he was frightened.

He asked her anxiously, "Are you sick, Dvorele? What's the matter with you?"

Dvorele remained silent. She only looked at him mutely with

her large eyes. Her black pupils shone out of the bed in the darkness, pleading with him for he knew not what. Again she took his hand, placing it over her heart. She sighed in the quietness.

"I am sick, David."

"But what is it?" he asked fearfully.

Her eyes now shone even more brightly and pleadingly.

"I have a weak heart."

"A weak heart?" The husband began to tremble. His hands shook as he drew away from her.

"Why didn't anyone tell me anything about it?" he demanded angrily.

"My father was afraid you would refuse the match."

"A bride with a weak heart," David mumbled to himself.

He was quiet for a moment, not knowing what to do with himself. As it was still night, he could not dress and leave her. So he sat down on the edge of the bed.

"Tricked," he murmured to himself.

"It's not my fault. My father told me to say nothing. But you are now my husband and so you must know. That's why I'm telling you."

David was silent. He looked out the window in the vague hope of seeing a morning star. Surely he would go home with his father in the morning. A bride with a weak heart! It was not he who was in the wrong! He had been tricked. The rabbi would agree to granting an immediate divorce. It was only painful to him that the night moved so slowly while he had to remain here in the same room with a stranger. With a woman he would never see after tomorrow. Then he felt something warm moving closer to him, snuggling behind him and touching him. He wanted to move away, but the touch was pleasant to him. And so he remained sitting there.

"David, are you angry?" she asked.

He did not answer. But he thought to himself, how can it be her fault if God has cursed her so?

And so he felt pity for her.

"Does your heart still give you pain?" he asked without looking into her face.

"A little," she answered quietly.

"And what is there to do when your heart pains you?"

"You put a cold towel over it."

"Do you want a towel?" he asked, still without looking at her.

"Yes, there is a bowl of water with a towel—just there."

David felt his way in the dark and found the bowl and wet the towel and brought it to her.

"Place it over me, David," she asked. "Right here over my heart."

David placed the towel over her heart, and his hand unwillingly touched her bare warm breast.

"And is there nothing to do for a weak heart? We could go to a specialist," he said aloud but as though to himself.

"We've already been to doctors and to specialists, but nobody knows what to do."

David sat and was silent. Before his eyes he saw the life before him—with an invalid wife. To be tied all of his days to a wife who would be ill, always ill, ill on the Sabbath and on the holidays, always unhappy. And perhaps it would affect the children too. The children would be weak. Or perhaps she wouldn't even be able to have children. Then they would have to live like this—he alone with a sick wife. And there would be summery days when Jews go singing and strolling with their young wives past the synagogue, and his wife would lie abed an invalid.

David no longer thought about divorce. He saw himself tied to his invalid wife and was filled with self-pity. Only yesterday he had been a carefree youth. He had seen his future so bright; now everything was dark before him. Why had this come to him? What wrong had he done? He blamed no one. Only his fate. And again he felt nothing but pity for his little bride. Poor thing, how could she be blamed? Yet he wanted somehow to find a ray of hope.

"And what do the doctors know?" he said bravely. "If God in his heaven wills it, you can become perfectly well!"

"All the doctors said that if I should find a good husband, who would be good to me, then my heart would become well again."

He remained silent, and his heart was pierced with love at her words. There was such softness in her voice, such gentleness, that his heart swelled within him. And he murmured to himself, "After all, this is my fate."

He heard a low sobbing behind him.

"Dvorele, why are you crying?" he said, bending over her. "Don't cry, Dvorele."

"Why shouldn't I cry since I have such a fate, since God has punished me so?"

David could bear it no longer. He buried his face between her breasts, and he wept into them.

"But your fate is my fate too, Dvorele."

And he did not know whether he was weeping tears of bitterness or of joy.

A Divorce

I SEE something in your face that is not good," the woman said anxiously, as her husband Yudel came through the door, still in his sheepskin, with a shawl wrapped around his head.

Yudel did not answer. He sat down without removing his sheepskin or his fur hat, without even taking off his overshoes. He simply sank to the nearest chair—one of their good chairs—and he was silent. He looked anywhere and nowhere, as though this were not his home but a public place where people waited for the coaches.

"Why do you have to frighten me? Why don't you say something!" his wife cried out in one breath.

Her cheeks flushed, and the little blond hairs on the two warts at the corner of her upper lip stood rigid. The man still remained silent.

"But I am terrified," his wife said with a beating heart. "God forbid—what can their answer be? It's not really *that?*" she faltered, in an inhuman voice.

The man nodded his head sadly and stared into a distant corner.

"Oi, mama!" the woman cried out. Then she too sank on the nearest of the good chairs.

And so they both remained seated for a few minutes without a word and without looking at each other.

After a while the woman moaned, "Woe is me! To think that I should have lived to this."

And sobbing and sniffling, her face wet with tears, she dabbed at her nose and said, "You certainly didn't tell them, Yudel. You certainly couldn't have told them!"

157

"I told them, I talked, I pleaded." The good Jew waved his arms as he spoke. "But it's a law that's written. The rabbi said, 'If a man lives ten years with a woman without having children, then they must be divorced. Maybe it will be better for her too. It can be that it was not a true match.' "

"Better for her!" the woman sobbed. "Woe unto my years! How can it be better for me! Who can make it better for me, a miserable creature. Who can help me? I lived ten years of my life with a man. Oi, Yudel, take off your coat. God forbid you should catch cold," she said, still sobbing.

Without a word, Yudel took off his sheepskin. There he stood, a Chassidic young man with a round little beard—scarcely more than a youth in appearance. And he sat down again in the same chair, as quiet as a stranger.

The good woman's wailing was heard by their neighbor, who came into their house from her kitchen, still holding a pot in her hand. She threw an eager glance at Yudel while she asked of the weeping woman, "What did he say, the rabbi?"

"Divorce! Oi, Nacha, my dear, divorce! Woe unto me! Divorce!" the good wife sobbed.

"Oi, my poor dear!" The neighbor sucked in her cheeks. "What a misfortune."

But in another moment she thought of something.

"Look, may you live forever, but how can you let him sit there? He has just come from the road. He surely hasn't had a bite in his mouth all day."

"Do you think I know what I'm doing? Oh, my soup is burning," and the woman ran to her pots.

With tears still streaming from her eyes, she made the table ready and told Yudel to wash his hands. Yudel obeyed quietly, like a stranger, and then he sat down at the table. Their neighbor, after a few sad attempts at conversation, groaned and left the room.

A DIVORCE

When the young man was seated at the table, his wife sat down opposite and spoke to him heartbrokenly.

"What will become of the business? Who will take care of it? And what about our place in the market? Woe unto me! Who will look after it all? And the household things." The good wife let her eyes rest on the rows of shining pots and the dishes neatly arranged in her cupboard.

"There will have to be a judgment according to the Torah, and whatever the rabbi will decide, that's how it will be," the young man answered in the same quiet voice.

"And with you, Yudel, and with you?" She shook her head, and a new stream of tears poured from her eyes.

Another thought occurred to the woman: he was a handsome man about to be divorced—but she left the words unspoken.

The young man repeated the blessing, out loud. After the blessing, he took the Gemara and tried to study. It was painful for him to watch the suffering of his little wife. There was nothing for him to say. During their marriage he had found little to talk about with her, for what is there to discuss with a woman? He had lived as a Chassidic young man should live with a woman, in righteousness and in cleanliness. Then surely it was the will of God that they had had no children. Actually, he had not been so eager to have children. Children—naturally, why not? After all, if one is a Jew, one must have children. But he did not miss them. His wife was a proper little Jewish wife. She observed all the laws and she had loved her husband as the Jewish law requires. And so, as a man should, he had journeyed to the rabbi once, and then he had gone again, to ask that they might have children. And the rabbi had told him to be patient. But when the ten years had been fulfilled, then the rabbi had said they must be divorced according to the Jewish law. And since the rabbi had spoken, and if this was the law, then there was not much to think about. After all, they were Jews. And—well! And she, the little woman,

159

must understand too that there was nothing else to be done. For behold, she was after all the well beloved, a Jewish wife.

But he felt a great pity for her and for himself. And so he read the passages of his study in a loud voice. He sang out the Gemara just to forget a little, and then for no reason at all, since he was with a woman in the house.

She listened to his Gemara melody and her heart pounded even more. She had heard the same melody since the time he had been a guest in her father's house. Now that he would be a stranger to her, this was no longer her husband's Gemara melody. And she began to cry afresh.

"Oh, why have I lived to see this day, Father in Heaven? Have I not been humiliated enough, that I am barren? Have I not been punished enough, since you have given me no children? Must you now take my husband from me? How have I sinned before you?"

The young man's heart was pierced by her words. He had felt great pity for her childlessness. Ten years he had lived with this woman, and she had been a true Jewish wife, a pure one. She had watched over him with her protecting eye. So he covered his Gemara with the cloth and began to pace the room as he spoke to her.

"Don't cry, Sarele, don't cry. It must be the will of God. After all, we are in his hands. What can we do? And perhaps it is all for the best. Perhaps I am not the partner that was destined for you. And God will help you. You will find your partner. And you will yet be blessed with children, Jewish children, such as you have well deserved."

He did not notice that he had come closer to her and had reached out his hand and that he was stroking her hair and her cheeks and her shoulders.

"You are a good Jewish wife," he continued, without looking at her. "I know it. I know that you are deserving and that God will help you. Yes, He certainly will help you." And tears dropped from his eyes upon her hair.

She stood close to him, happy to receive his caresses, and listened quietly. For it was the first time since their wedding that he had spoken to her so lovingly and tenderly and that he had fondled her. And her heart was warmed.

She cried out softly, "Oh, Yudel, Yudel, my Yudel. My only, only Yudel."

He stroked her face and her hair and her back. Wordlessly, silently . . . but suddenly he recalled that this was a woman, and moreover a woman about to be divorced. So he left her abruptly and sat down to his Gemara.

Aloud he read in a high singing melody: *"And thus spoke the Lord our Father . . ."*

And she sat quietly in a corner listening to his Gemara melody and silently weeping.

In a few days the wagon of Shlomo the driver was ready to carry them to the nearest town along the Sochotna River (for such a town was the proper place for a divorce). There they would go to the rabbi to be separated. The woman sat on the wagon, weeping, while a number of others stood around the wagon and wrung their hands. And they looked from one to the other, pointing at Sarele, repeating the misfortune that had befallen her.

Shlomo the driver called out to the women, "Be careful, beware that you don't ever have to go to town on my wagon to the rabbi for a divorce!"

And so they arrived in the town and came to the rabbi, and on this day the rabbi made no effort to perform the good deed of making peace between a man and his wife. At the divorce there was more weeping than at a funeral; all the women of the town assembled behind the synagogue and joined in the weeping.

After the divorce, it was time to drive home. But now they

could no longer ride in one wagon. So he rode home with Shlomo the driver, while she remained waiting for another wagon.

When Yudel seated himself beside Shlomo, she cried out after him, "Tie your shawl around your neck! God forbid, you might catch cold."

"Heaven forbid—to speak like that to a strange man! A stranger!" cried the women who were standing nearby.

For, after all, it was after the divorce.

"Do you think I know what I am doing?" the divorced woman cried out, distractedly. "A stranger!"

The Dowry

THE day after the wedding the groom sat at the head of the table in the new shirt that he had worn to the wedding, in his new linen suit from Lodz, and in his shining new boots. He was dipping large pieces of honey cake in the sauce of marinated herring. For the first time in his life he had the chance to eat honey cake instead of bread. And as though realizing that not every day would be the day after the wedding, he was doing well for himself. Facing him at the other end of the table sat the bride, and although this was a hot summer morning she was still showing off the heavy linen dress from Lodz, the finest garment in her trousseau.

The festivities had endured far into the night, and the bride was tired. The heavy marriage wig that she wore for the first time made her face seem older and paler than it really was. The groom, deeply absorbed in the joy of consuming cake dipped in herring sauce, nevertheless found time and opportunity to throw a hidden glance of love toward his bride. And when the glances of bride and groom met, the groom smiled and the bride put on an expression of annoyance and turned her head away. The husband, it seemed, understood the bride's annoyed look and was content to loosen his new belt, letting out his new trousers with one hand while his other hand was occupied with dipping cake in the sauce. The master of ceremonies, who had been brought along by the groom's parents from their town, stood up and offered another toast in honor of the groom and in honor of the bride and in honor of both their families.

But no one listened to his oratory. To the groom, nothing

mattered any more. As for the bride, the words didn't enter her head. And the relatives around the table had aching heads from yesterday's drinking and from the late hours of the festival. They wavered sleepily in their places, clutching one another's elbows. On the beds, on the benches, and even in the corners, various uncles and aunts lay entangled. Children and grandchildren slept, snoring loudly. From the crowded beds there protruded the checkered trousers of the uncles and the flowery gowns of the aunts, and boots and shoes over varicolored hose.

There was one man, however, who was happy. The brother-in-law of the bride was expansive, lively, and full of cheer. A short little Jew with a round beard and a pair of yellow ear curls, coatless in a homemade wide-sleeved blouse, with his silken skullcap cocked to one side, Moshe Kazack paraded in the center of the room. In one hand he held a mug and a flask of cherry brandy that he had discovered somewhere. With his other elbow, he awakened the tired and sleepy guests around the table, forcing them to drink.

"Boruch Clopot, is this how you celebrate the wedding of an orphan? Why, you swore you would dance in a barrel of water! Hey, women, bring in a barrel of water! Boruch Clopot is going to dance for us. Schmya, what are you sleeping for?" And he awakened a poor Jew who had fallen to the floor.

But the one person whom he gave no peace was the father of the groom. He attached himself to this long, thin, tall Jew, who kept playing with the long points of his mustache and with his smooth little beard. The merry one forced him to drink, cajoling him with a wide variety of friendly imprecations.

"May you never live to feast with me at the birth of their child! May you never live to dance with me at the wedding of the youngest of their grandchildren if you won't drink another *l'chayim* with me."

And then he went off to plague the groom and the bride and the sleeping aunts.

166

"Aunties, how can you sleep? Are we not celebrating the wedding of an orphan?"

So he went from one guest to another, from one aunt to another, pouring the cherry brandy over their hands, over their new gowns, over their silken clothes. And he had something to be cheerful about. For actually he was the real protector of the bride, the one who should give her away—if one did not count her uncle from Lodz, who had also helped in her upkeep. The bride was an orphan without mother or father; she had been raised in his house, and he had married her out of his house.

But just as the protector on the bride's side had good reason to be joyful and full of pranks, the father and protector of the groom—the thin tall Jew—had little reason for celebrating. It was not for nothing that he refused the cherry brandy. He sat on at the table, smoothing his mustache and his beard, and when he was not smoothing his mustache or his beard, he simply drummed on the table with his fingers while he counted over the dowry in his mind. There was the Singer sewing machine that had been named in the dowry—he saw that machine as he had seen it on the first day of their bargaining, when they had brought it before him.

"You see that machine?" the bride's protector had demanded. "The bride herself sews everything on that machine, with her own hands! She can earn a living from that machine alone!"

Last night, in announcing the wedding presents, they had called out the machine at least ten times. First they had called it out in the name of the brother-in-law.

"The wealthy and honorable brother-in-law of the bride bequeaths a new Singer sewing machine as a wedding present!"

Then they had called it out on behalf of the uncle.

"The wealthy and honorable uncle and aunt of the bride, long may they live, bequeath a new Singer sewing machine as a wedding gift!"

Then they had announced it for a cousin, and after that they had simply announced it for anyone whom they wanted to honor.

But where were ten million Polish marks that were mentioned in the contract? It was true, of course, that the ten million marks were now worthless, for between the time of the making of the contract and the wedding itself their value had dissolved like salt in water. Still, where were they? Yesterday at the time of the wedding there had been an effort to bring up the subject of the ten million marks that remained unpaid. Immediately there had arisen such an uproar from all the bride's uncles and aunts that he had retreated in silence.

"Do you realize," they cried, "that you are shedding the innocent blood of an orphan! Her poor dead mother and father will never leave you in peace!"

Why had he ever got himself entangled with an orphan? If anything at all came up they stifled him with their "innocent blood of an orphan."

He was afraid to speak of the money. And yet, really, what would be the end of the matter? The bride's protector had promised that on the morning after the wedding he would turn over to the groom a share of his legacy from the father-in-law—who should rest in peace—and that the legacy would more than fulfill all that had been promised by way of dowry.

Yet here they were—the morning after the wedding. The music had already stopped playing, honey cake and brandy had already been consumed, and there had been enough dancing. So what was he waiting for? What more confusion was he trying to add with his cherry brandy? The groom would certainly not be able to set himself up in business with cherry brandy.

Finally, the groom's father could endure matters no longer. All at once he arose, gave a final smoothing touch to his beard, and then pounded on the table.

"Well?"

"What do you mean, well?" The guests were all startled.

"I mean, what will be the end? It is time to pack and be on our way."

THE DOWRY

Everyone became attentive. The master of ceremonies stopped making toasts. The brother-in-law stood still in the middle of the room with the flask of cherry brandy in his hand. From one of the beds a sleeping aunt awoke, poking her feather-covered marriage wig into the room. The groom even stopped eating. The bride rested her tired head on her hands, and the beating of her heart could be heard through the entire room.

"Ah, you mean—you mean the dowry? Good."

"The dowry or not the dowry. You promised something. A legacy from the father-in-law, may he rest in peace. He must have left something?"

"Yes, yes, of course. We'll see about it right away," the bride's protector promised.

The master of ceremonies disappeared among the beds where the aunts were sleeping and began joking with them. In a corner the bride's two protectors got together—her brother-in-law and her uncle, whispering.

Soon enough the bride's protectors concluded their whispered discussion. The bride's brother-in-law disappeared. In a moment he returned; by each hand he led a little girl. The girls were nine or ten years old, or perhaps a bit older; the pair were curly headed, with bows in their braids, and they wore new little pleated skirts, but their feet were bare. It seemed that the shoes they had worn to the wedding yesterday had been borrowed and had had to be returned already. Their thin faces and hands were smeared with jam and crumbs of honey cake.

The bride's protector, the merry brother-in-law, brought the little girls directly to the groom, and without so much as a glance at the groom's astonished father, he announced in a loud voice that betrayed his inner excitement, "Groom, here is your dowry!"

With this, he pushed the two girls toward the groom's knees, leaving them to the young man while he retreated to the middle of the room. From the bride's corner came a sound of low sobbing. The groom, his simple eyes wide open, stared first at the bride's

169

protector and then at his own father. The frightened children, either in terror or because they had been told what to do, clung to the groom with their little hands clasped around his legs. Without thinking, the groom put his hands on their heads.

From the beds more and more of the aunts, startled out of their sleep, their marriage wigs askew, stuck their heads forth from under the feather comforters.

"What does this mean?" The groom's father remained standing with his mouth agape.

"My dear friends," earnestly began the bride's brother-in-law and protector, who now stood in the center of the room, swaying as though in prayer, "my dear friends, you all know that when my father-in-law died, may he rest in peace, he left five orphans on my hands. I was then only a young man, two years married. I had received no dowry. My father-in-law had promised me half his house, but this was taken away by his debtors. We were left naked and in want. Nevertheless, I took it upon myself to raise the orphans. This, I said to myself, is my dowry—left to me by my father-in-law. And I say to you, my friends, that five orphans make a fine large dowry, and in their name God in His heaven helped me, not only to raise these children, but to arrive at the happy day when I could give one of the orphans away in marriage. And today, what right have I to the entire legacy left by my father-in-law? Yesterday I was still uncertain whether I might entrust the new groom with a share of this legacy. But today, since the wedding is over and he is already a brother-in-law like myself, I am turning over to him half of what was left to me by our father-in-law—for what right have I to the entire legacy?"

The guests remained seated. The little room was still and quiet. The uncles exchanged glances with the aunts who had awakened in their beds. They winked a little to each other, and here and there a cheek was pinched. But finally the groom's father beat upon the table.

"And with what is he going to go into business?"

"What do you mean with what will he go into business? With the same stock that I had to begin my business—with orphans!" the brother-in-law declared.

Then all of the bride's relatives together, the uncles and the aunts, the protectors and the protectresses, joined in their indignation, some waving their arms, some with eyes flashing, but all wagging their tongues. They descended upon the groom's protesting father, "You call that a small thing, orphans!"

"I should only have their blessing upon me always, God in heaven!" a belated auntie called out from her bed.

In the face of such a reply, the groom's father could only choke down his anger and remain silent. He lowered his raised hand, sat down again at the table, and said, agreeably enough, "Do you think that it's for me I'm concerned? It's for him."

He pointed to the groom. "Let him say whether he wants to take such a burden upon himself."

"What do you mean, if he wants? Whether he wants or he doesn't want, isn't he a Jew, no different from myself?" the brother-in-law demanded.

From the bride's corner the sobbing became more distinct. The groom's large eyes stared out. He lifted his head and listened for a long time, pityingly, to his bride's sobbing. And then, as though having listened to a judgment within himself, he tightened his belt with one hand and said, "I am just as good a Jew as he, and if he could do it, I can do it."

More industriously than ever, he began to dip ever larger chunks of honey cake into the herring sauce. And he handed the morsels to the orphans who stood beside his knees for them to taste.

Yiskadal V'Yiskadash

WHEN the SS men walked Yitche-Meir into the assembly yard for Jews in Warsaw's Praga section, a veritable sensation was created. There was a furor, one might even say of joy, among the other SS men who were standing around in the big yard. The Group Leader himself—a twenty-year-old with a little black mustache and small eyes that might have been made of petrified stone—came out of his office to behold Yitche-Meir.

At this time the SS men had moved one of its Jewish assembly centers for the Praga section into a brick building, formerly a school. It was surrounded by a large yard, and every sort of Jew had been on view in this yard: Jews who had been dragged in for labor, Jews who had been picked up off the streets or hauled out of their homes. Amongst them were clean-shaven Jews in European dress scarcely distinguishable from Aryans. And there were real Jews in long coats, with full-grown beards. But so complete and full-blooded a specimen as Yitche-Meir had never before been captured. Yitche-Meir's Jewishness was trumpeted forth by his entire being. His beard was full, thick, black, and shining with a kind of electric current of Jewishness. His black ear curls were twisted into long braids, and they rattled against his thick side whiskers. His large black restless eyes sparkled. As for his clothes, he wore a torn coat, shiny with wear, tied together with a cord. But most authentic were his white-stockinged legs protruding from the two splits in his long coat.

The SS men clustered around him, absorbing the details. They couldn't think what to do with their prize. They stared at their

175

acquisition and trembled for joy. The Group Leader stood there with his hands stuck in his trouser pockets, and even his hard-bitten face was relaxed by a thin little smile of pride. All their eyes feasted joyously upon the offering that stood before them.

"What's your name, Jew?" one of them asked.

"Yitche-Meir Rosenkrantz."

"Yitche-Meir, a beautiful name. And Rosenkrantz, too!" the SS men laughed. "And what is your profession, Jew?"

"Rabbi."

"Rabbi! a fine profession."

"And what are you?"

Yitche-Meir had made up his mind to any possibility and prepared himself for anything that might happen, from the moment the SS had taken him. He was at peace within himself. He showed no sign of nervousness. Even his lively shining eyes were veiled in their yellow-white depth.

"A Jew naturally," Yitche-Meir answered, for the question was not very clear to him.

"A Jew naturally. That's wonderful!" The SS men laughed again.

But the Group Leader swallowed his smile. Once more his face became stony. He wanted to put an end to this comedy, but the Jew was so outstanding, such a treasure, that he could not but let his glance bathe a little longer in the spectacle. His face was like the face of a cat when she holds the mouse imprisoned in her paws and studies him with her piercing eyes. Only here, one element was missing—the fear of death, staring out of the eyes of the mouse. The Jew showed no sign of anxiety or fear. His eyes did not blink. His tall figure was not bowed. His lips did not tremble. He stood like a statue of stone. The lack of fear in the Jew marred the Group Leader's pleasure in the inspection of the sacrifice. He felt irritated. Suddenly he shot out his arm, and instantly his fingers were entwined in the hair on the Jew's face, catching his ear curls, a bit of his mustache, and locks of his side beard—a thick and solid fistful.

"Repeat after me—I am a Jewish pig."

Yitche-Meir repeated, "I am a Jewish pig."

"Louder," the Group Leader said.

Yitche-Meir said it again.

"Still louder."

"I am a Jewish pig!" Yitche-Meir cried at the top of his voice.

At this point, the Group Leader tugged experimentally, but Yitche-Meir's hair was so strongly imbedded in his flesh that nothing gave way.

"Damn," the Group Leader shouted. He pulled harder. But still the hair did not come out.

"This is a genuine Jew! Here is a genuine Jewish beard!" the officer jestingly announced to his spectators.

Somewhat embarrassed that the Jewish beard had not given way so easily, he braced his foot in the Jew's belly and pulled with all his might. This time the beard gave way, and in the Group Leader's fist there remained a torn bit of ear curl, some mustache hair, and several thick locks from the Jew's heavy side beard.

"Here, you try it," the Group Leader said, motioning to one of his men and pointing to the Jew's beard.

The same scene was repeated. Now there began a trial of strength against the Jew's beard. A real contest. Some showed that they could pull fistfuls of hair from the beard in two or three tries. One of them—a stocky, youthful SS—won a bet over the Jew's beard. One mighty pull and a great section of Yitche-Meir's beard lay in the youth's palm.

Yitche-Meir remained standing in the same spot in his white-stockinged feet. His skin shone through the holes in his torn rags. And his full shining beard of a moment ago, his richly sprouting beard, was now filled with large holes. There were entire pieces missing. The beard consisted now of scattered strands of hair stuck together by the blood that ran from the open wounds left on his face when the skin had been torn off. Yitche-Meir's beard was no longer a beard. It was now a wet pulpy mass stuck to a man's face. But Yitche-Meir's eyes had not changed nor had his whole mien.

The SS men now realized that the Jew had entirely failed to scream during the beard-pulling process. The Group Leader could not make up his mind whether he should accept the Jew's reticence as a sign of courage and character or of Jewish arrogance and conceit. For the first, he was even ready to give the Jew a bit of credit. But for the second, he decided to give the Jew such a lesson as would make him forget his Jewish pride.

And so he asked Yitche-Meir, "Are you in pain?"

"A little, sir," answered Yitche-Meir.

The Jew's reply slightly mollified the Group Leader. However, he wanted to make sure that the lesson had been learned.

"And what are you?"

"I am a Jewish pig!" Yitche-Meir replied in a loud voice.

"An intelligent Jew. A fine Jew!" the Leader announced, pleased.

"Well, now, we shall see what you can do—hitch him up to the wagon," the Group Leader commanded.

So they took Yitche-Meir and dragged him over to a cart that was standing in the yard. There was a new sort of harness on this wagon. There were ropes ending in a wide leather strap, much like those used by the porters of Warsaw. They hitched up Yitche-Meir, and a number of SS men climbed on the wagon. One of them sat on the driver's seat with a whip in his hand, and he began to drive Yitche-Meir.

"Git-up, Jew. Git-up!" He lashed out with his whip.

Yitche-Meir's long neck stretched out from his ragged shirt and from his coat. His stretched-out neck was like that of an ostrich, with a large lump in it. Because of his plucked-out beard his large head looked disproportionately wide and clumsy. And like an ostrich, he put forth his spindly legs, spreading apart the white-stockinged feet. Yitche-Meir's broken shoes became stuck in the mud; his feet sank under him. A river of sweat ran from his brow. And the sweat ran even thicker from his long neck and down his long bony body. He gathered all his strength to pull the wagon, which was heavily loaded with SS men. But the wheels sank into the mud.

The harder Yitche-Meir pulled, the more stubborn was the wagon. Yitche-Meir tried to alter his stance; first he tried to start off on the left foot, and then on the right. He tried to pull with one shoulder and then with the other. The whip lashed down on him, and he strained with all of his might to pull the wagon. But the only result of his efforts was to bring forth laughter. The wagon did not budge from its place.

"Get him another pig to help him!" cried the Group Leader, who stood watching the scene with his hands in his pockets.

The pleased little smile that had glistened on his face was gone now. His face was a mask of bitter black violence. A second Jew was dragged out from somewhere, a much older Jew than Yitche-Meir, with red sleepless eyes and with a trembling beard. They hitched the Jew to the other side of the wagon shaft. The whip lashes now fell on the heads of both. The old Jew took hold of the shaft from his side and Yitche-Meir from the other side. Yitche-Meir dug in his feet, and with all his force dragged at the wagon. The old Jew also tried to do what he could. The wagon did not budge.

"Let him feel the whip!" the Group Leader shouted.

The driver stretched out his arm, and the whip fell again on Yitche-Meir and again on the head of the old Jew. Yitche-Meir caught his lashes of the whip but remained quiet, only trying to pull. But every blow of the whip that fell on the old man produced a scream.

"Oi, oi, Father in Heaven. Oi! Voe, Mama!"

This only encouraged the playfulness of the SS men.

"Oi, oi, Papa! Oi, oi, Mama," they mimicked after the Jew.

But, all at once, Yitche-Meir was able to do it. As soon as he heard their mocking "Papa . . . Mama," he stretched forth his neck and shoulders in the harness. He seized the shaft in his knotted fingers. He pulled forward with his breast and with all the strength that was still left to him. His feet dug into the earth and pushed his body forward. And the wagon was jarred from the earth. Yitche-Meir ran, dragging the old Jew with him.

"The Jew did it! The Jew did it," the SS men shouted, stamping their feet on the bottom of the wagon as they rolled along.

"A reasonable Jew!" the Group Leader cried out. "Unhitch him."

They unhitched Yitche-Meir from the wagon. The sweat of his body had soaked through his torn old coat, and there was a band of sweat across his chest where the leather strap of the wagon had been.

"A reasonable Jew. A respectable Jew. Group A. Beard to be shorn. But that's enough for him for today," the Group Leader called out to his men as he left the yard to return to his office, his hands in his pockets, without another glance at Yitche-Meir.

They took Yitche-Meir and stood him near a wall. After a while a Jew was brought out of the prison. This Jew was still a young man, luckily chosen for this work. He carried a large dull scissors with which he cut off the remains of Yitche-Meir's beard, his ear curls, whiskers, and most of the hair from his head, leaving a "ladder" of clipped and unclipped hair on his scalp. Without his beard Yitche-Meir felt like a man without a soul—he felt as though he were no longer a human being, as though he had been turned into a beast. And thus he was led down into a prison in the cellar.

There between the cellar walls, lying on the bare ground or thin sacks of straw, he found those of his brethren who had been taken off the streets that day and dragged to this assembly center for slave laborers.

It was an evening early in autumn. A commando of Jews returning from their day of labor was brought down into the cellar. There were old and young among them, cleanshaven Jews in European dress and Jews in long coats and the little black hats of Warsaw. Some of them, like Yitche-Meir, had had their beards torn and plucked; their heads were also shaved in "ladders." Others had escaped with their beards intact—perhaps by oversight. There were a few there whose beards were already growing anew, and still others who had no beards at all.

The Jews dropped to the earth in sheer weariness. Their faces and their clothes were filthy and black, covered with a mixture of the earth in which they labored and the congealed sweat of their bodies. They lay there quietly. A few breathed raucously, and their gasping seemed to emphasize the weary silence around them.

Not all were lying down. Some sat. All of these had thrown off their shoes, their boots, and the rag windings from their feet. They were holding their feet in their hands. Their feet, swollen, beaten, and torn, looked as though they had pounded over hundreds of miles, crawled over mountains, bruised themselves against stones. They were inflamed and red, and an odor came from them. It seemed as though the people who sat and lay in this room had been absorbed into another world, the universe of their feet. They had lost all interest in life, forgotten their existence as humans. All other needs were driven aside, and there remained only one burning point of interest, the one great pain that grew out of their feet. It seemed as though the entire being of these men had gone out of their bodies and of their souls. It had sunk down and concentrated itself, twisted itself into their swollen feet; they had thought or feeling for nothing else.

Suddenly a voice was heard. *"Yiskadal v'Yiskadash"*—the opening phrase of the daily prayer.

Heads were raised, faces turned. In one moment they had all forgotten their feet, as though they had been torn from their trance by the prayer that was so well known to them and that seemed so remote in this place. They saw a Jew in a dirty, old, ragged coat, with a little Jewish skullcap, and a large colored handkerchief tied around his head, as though he had a toothache. He stood by the wall swaying in prayer.

It was as though Yitche-Meir's *"Yiskadal v'Yiskadash"* had called them back to their old world, the world they had thought to have left forever, the world that remained on the other side of the wall when they had been driven to this place. A few Jews stood up from their places, ceasing to minister to their feet. They came to the corner where Yitche-Meir was standing and began to sway together with him. Others remained sitting, watching the door with fearful restless eyes. A voice was heard, and then another— "Make it quick."

"Hurry, hurry, before they come in."

The prayer was speeded. The prisoners finished rapidly. They recited the blessing in unison, and the silent prayer of the eighteen exhortations was finished before there was an alarm. Immediately afterward a long whistle cut through the crowded cellar. They hurriedly left off rubbing their feet, wound their rags around their wounds, and pulled on their shoes. They stood up and marched out in regular formation, in pairs, each man carrying his tin dish.

They marched out like soldiers to the pump that stood in the middle of the big yard. They pumped water, washed, wiped themselves with their coattails, and then marched in military formation to the long shed where they took their places on the rows of benches. In a lean-to were huge cauldrons in which Jewish women prepared their thin potato soup. With the soup and a piece of bread they sat down to their meal.

Yitche-Meir, with his torn cheeks bound in a rag, marched in line like a well-disciplined soldier—just as though he had already been here a long time. The SS men who kept an eye on the prisoners could find no fault with him. Before Yitche-Meir took a bit of food into his mouth, he repeated the mealtime blessing. The first half of the blessing he swallowed under his breath. Only the last

words were heard—*"Who bringeth forth bread from the earth."*
And the Jews, who had hurled themselves like wolves on their
crusts of bread and the soup for which they had waited all day,
now waited with their spoons at their lips. Yitche-Meir's prayer
had reminded them. Many murmured the prayer after him, while
others were satisfied with a simple amen, which they muttered
self-consciously.

The two SS men who stood by the door of the kitchen noticed
that something was happening here, but the thing took place so
quickly that they could not comprehend it. The prisoners were
eating again, just as always. Each washed his tin plate, and
Yitche-Meir did the same.

On the second day, even before the dawn looked down into the
cellar, the exhausted Jews were awakened not by the whistle of
their taskmaster, but by Yitche-Meir's *"Yiskadal v'Yiskadash."*
Some of them arose early and prayed together with Yitche-Meir.
Others waited for the whistle.

Yitche-Meir stood in line in the yard. The ends of his torn coat
were pulled up and stuck in his belt. He went out to labor with
Group A. The group marched some distance outside of the city.
They reached a field where a road was being built. There Yitche-
Meir saw other Jews working in groups under the eyes of the SS.
The road was half finished. One group of Jews dug in the earth
while others carried off the dirt on wheelbarrows, dumping it on
the roadbed. Another long row of Jews, bared to the waist, lifted
stones from a huge pile and carried them to the roadbed. A number of younger men were hitched to a huge steel roller which they
pulled over the earth and stones. Yitche-Meir was placed among
the rock carriers.

The SS men ordered him to take off his coat, like the others.
This he did. They told him to take off his vest, and then his
fringed sacramental undervest, and his shirt. He did as he was
told, hesitating only when he came to the sacramental vest—as
though waiting for a clarification from the Torah. But a glance

from the SS men brought him back to the world. He undressed, remaining only in his trousers, which were held up by the suspenders over his bare shoulders. His face was still bound in the colored handkerchief. The SS men tore the bandage off his head, together with his skullcap. Yitche-Meir's face was revealed in all its nakedness. A bearded face when deprived of its hair seems truly naked; it has a hunted, inhuman look as though it were forever being pursued by the beard's ghost. Yitche-Meir, who had only yesterday caused such a sensation among the SS with his shining dark beard, today looked like an ordinary convict covered with dust and grime.

The SS guard could find no fault in the obedient Yitche-Meir. There was not even a beard to take hold of. So the guard only gave Yitche-Meir a kick in the belly with his boot and sent him on to labor. And when it came to work, the SS men saw that the new slave was a model of industry. Yitche-Meir labored without a halt, even with a kind of good will as though to please himself with his own competence. He loaded up his arms with rocks, balancing them against his chest to the limit of his strength, and he carried the load with rapid steps, putting the rocks down in their place in the roadbed. He gave himself not a moment of rest or respite.

The early autumn day was hot. The sun burned down upon Yitche-Meir's bare head and sweat ran from his brow, softening the thin layer of skin that had started to grow over the torn flesh of his face. Little streams of blood began to force their way out, mingling with the streams of sweat that flowed down from his hair. The mingled streams dripped upon his breast and down his back until his entire body was soaked in sweat. Nevertheless, Yitche-Meir kept at his task, making one trip after another without a rest. From time to time as he walked back for more stones, he wiped his body with his bare hands. But when his arms were loaded, the mingled stream of blood and sweat dripped freely on his half-naked body.

184

So industrious was Yitche-Meir in the performance of his task, that he even called forth the approbation of the SS. "A good Jew. A fine Jew. There is a respectable Jew! Come now, what are you?"

"I am a Jewish pig!" Yitche-Meir called out in full voice.

"Good little Jew! A fine little Jew! An intelligent Jew!"

At noon Yitche-Meir made the same use of the half-hour rest period as the others. He sat holding his feet in his hands.

In the evening when the Jews were led back to their point of assembly, Yitche-Meir and the others saw a huge gathering of people in front of the little fence that surrounded the brick building. Coming to the gate, Yitche-Meir noticed that a high gallows stood out in the yard with three bodies swinging from it. Their legs dangled, unnaturally long and bare. Their boots had been removed.

The returning slaves stared at the hanged men, whose bodies had been left there for them to see. A few Christian women knelt on the stones with their eyes closed in prayer. Others stood by in silence.

"Oi, Motte Moishe is gone—" someone in Yitche-Meir's row murmured under his breath.

"Blessed be the Lord," Yitche-Meir repeated to himself.

"He tried to stand against them. I told him not to resist. A breach of discipline, they call it," the other Jew kept murmuring.

"We are all in God's hands," Yitche-Meir said, as though to himself.

This time the workers were more silent than ever as they returned to their prison. They did not even discuss the happening when they were in the cellar. They threw themselves down on their sacks or sat holding their feet.

Thus they remained under the shadow of the black wings of death. They were even afraid to groan. They only sat there holding their feet. *"Yiskadal v'Yiskadash . . ."* they heard Yitche-Meir's voice, louder and firmer than on the day before.

185

This time there were voices raised in protest. "What does he want! Does he want to bring down disaster on your heads!"

"Hasn't he seen what happens here?"

And this time Yitche-Meir had fewer followers in his congregation. More and more voices were heard crying, "Quicker, quicker, quicker."

Yitche-Meir rattled off the words, *"And thou shall love the Lord thy God with all thy heart and with all thy soul and with all thy strength."*

"Enough, enough already," anxious voices arose from all the corners.

Yitche-Meir swallowed the rest of the words.

Thus several days passed. Yitche-Meir was outstanding in his self-discipline, his industry, his strength of will, and his thoughtfulness. He became the favorite of the SS men. They set him up as an example for the other Jews.

"There is a respectable Jew!" They even told him jokingly that they would set him up as Group Leader, over all the Jews. He labored with a will; not a single muscle was spared. All this until Friday. But when Friday afternoon came, the SS men observed a restlessness in Yitche-Meir. Each time he approached the rock pile for his load of stones, he paused for an instant, glancing at the heavens, to see where the sun stood. Once or twice the SS men roused him out of his distraction with a stroke of the knout over his head. But Yitche-Meir grew more and more uneasy. His large disturbed eyes continued to scan the sky restlessly.

However, the men were at last led home from their work. Yitche-Meir kept hurrying as though he would run ahead of the group, and the Jew beside him could scarcely hold him back. Fortunately, they were back in the assembly place before a star could be seen, for Yitche-Meir had kept his eyes glued to the sky the whole way. They had scarcely got down into their cellar, before Yitche-Meir turned to the wall and began his recitation. *"Yiskadal v'Yiskadash . . ."*

"Faster! Faster, faster!" But this time Yitche-Meir would not let them hurry him. After he had recited the entire prayer, he brought forth a piece of bread that had been wrapped in a bit of paper and hidden in his pocket. He raised the piece of bread before him and began to speak the blessing. "And on the sixth day—"

With the help of the Lord, the whole thing passed smoothly. There was not a single interruption.

But the next morning, after awakening them all with his *"Yiskadal,"* Yitche-Meir remained standing by the wall. The drawn-out whistle had already sounded, and the men were already hurrying to take their place in the ranks. Yitche-Meir remained standing by the wall swaying in prayer.

"Yitche-Meir," someone pushed him, "come!" Yitche-Meir did not respond. He merely continued swaying.

"Yitche-Meir!"

"Pull him away."

But Yitche-Meir would not let himself be dragged. He stood there swaying and swaying.

"He is risking his head."

"Come!"

For the last time, a voice was heard crying, "Yitche-Meir!" They all marched out. Yitche-Meir remained standing by the wall.

Soon there descended on his head a rain of blows from the knout. He heard the SS men screeching and shouting, like an army of devils dancing around him.

"You cursed Jew!"

Yitche-Meir let the blows rain upon his head; he continued to sway. He received a kick in his side. He did not budge. He stood facing them, with their fierce eyes and their sharp-jutting white teeth.

A fist smashed into his face.

"Get out! To work!"

"Sir," he said, "today I cannot. Today is the day of rest."

Yitche-Meir tried to bring a friendly smile upon his bloody and swollen face.

"What!"

"Today is our Sabbath. Today is our day of rest. Today I cannot go out and work."

The SS man did not beat him any more. He seized Yitche-Meir by the back of his neck, led him out of the cellar, and brought him into the office of the Group Leader.

The SS man clicked his heels and stretched out his arm. *"Heil Hitler."*

"Heil Hitler. What's the matter?"

"Breach of discipline."

The Group Leader's little eyes became even narrower. His face grew solemn. He seemed to be reflecting for a moment. He recognized this one. This was the Jew with the great beard. He had a report on him—a good worker. Despite the Group Leader's excellent training in the special school for taskmasters, despite the complete lack of human feeling in his heart, there was something about this Jew—perhaps the way Yitche-Meir held himself during the entire time, perhaps the memory of the sport that had been afforded by his phenomenal beard—there was something about Yitche-Meir that awakened the last shred of feeling in the officer. He wanted to save this wild full-blooded Jew. He got up and went over to the Jew, who stood unperturbed before him with an idiotic smile on his bloody face.

The officer took the whip from the SS man and brought it down once upon the Jew's head while he asked, "What are you?"

"I am a Jewish pig!" Yitche-Meir responded with his full voice.

"Well, now, go to your work, Jew," the Group Leader cried out.

"Please, sir, today I cannot. Today is Sabbath."

"Take him away!" the Group Leader shouted.

"Heil Hitler."

"Heil Hitler."

The Group Leader picked up his telephone. Something must have worked on him. For he put back the telephone, and called to the SS men who had already led Yitche-Meir away.

"Halt. Show him the gallows."

They led Yitche-Meir over to the hanging place and showed him the gallows. "You know what that is, Jew?"

"Yes, I have already seen it. It is where they hang people," Yitche-Meir answered.

"You will hang if you don't go to work."

"What can I do? Today is Sabbath, the day of rest."

The Group Leader was informed of this response. He telephoned to his superior and received his orders. "Hang the Jew Yitche-Meir Rosenkrantz for breach of discipline."

At six o'clock in the evening, Yitche-Meir was led to the gallows, together with two Catholics who had also been sentenced on that day. Yitche-Meir kept murmuring the Sabbath evening prayer to himself.

He was not at all uneasy at the sight of the gallows. The only thing that made him uneasy and caused him continually to look at the sky was his concern that the Sabbath should be over. As he saw that it was still day, he approached the leader of the guards who were marching them to the gallows.

"Please, sir, you have been so good to me, I have a request to make."

"What is it, Jew?"

"Please wait until the first star is seen in the heavens. Today is the day of rest."

The guard was for a moment stunned by the Jew's strange request. Then a thin smile came over his face.

"All right, Jew. We'll hang the others first."

The two Catholics were placed on the gallows. But Yitche-Meir's turn came before he had quite finished the prayer marking the end of Sabbath. *"Thou art One and Thy Name is One,"*

189

Yitche-Meir murmured to himself as they threw the rope around his neck.

That evening when the work party marched back from their labor, they once more found a crowd standing in front of the gate. From a distance they had already seen Yitche-Meir's bare feet, from which the shoes had been removed, seeming to stretch out unnaturally long.

Most of the Jews kept their eyes on the ground, and they choked back their groans. "Yitche-Meir is gone, too."

They were silent. But when they went back into their cell, they did not throw themselves on their wooden beds. They did not sit holding their feet. Directly, there was one of them standing by the wall of the cellar, and he began to sway and to recite in a full voice, *"Yiskadal v'Yiskadash . . ."* And this time there was no one to cry "faster, faster." One Jew after another planted himself alongside the leader, and they all began to sway. *"Yiskadal v'Yiskadash . . ."*

Yitche-Meir had left a congregation behind him.

A Child Leads the Way

O NCE again—what sort of establishment did you say this is?" the Gestapo lieutenant asked, turning the full stare of his cynical, steel-cold eyes upon the tall figure of the elderly directress.

Gray and motherly, she stood before the desk in her own office, while the young lieutenant had seated himself, cross-legged. His revolver lay near his right hand, his swagger stick at his left.

"Sir, I have already explained to you. This is a Jewish religious institution for young maidens of Jewish faith," the directress replied in a quiet voice, in her best German—acquired at the Frankfurt High School for Girls.

"And how many maidens are to be found in this institution?" The Lieutenant smacked his thin lips over the word "maidens," and his Hitler mustache seemed to accent his emphasis.

"Ninety-three."

"Ninety-three! That's a good number. And how old are these maidens?"

"From twelve to eighteen."

"All maidens?" The Lieutenant kept his piercing needle-sharp gaze upon the woman's face. And the steely reflection of his blue eyes was like icy fire.

The directress did not respond.

"Answer, Jewess," the Lieutenant said quietly but with the fateful tone of one whose words are underlined by the power of life and death.

"I have stated the number. Ninety-three maidens, Herr Lieutenant."

193

"All maidens?" the Lieutenant asked again. This time his voice was higher pitched.

"Except for four supervisors and the directress, who are married," she replied.

The Lieutenant thought over the reply and pursed his narrow lips. Was this a satisfactory answer to the question he had put? He decided not to press it further. Yet he was irritated by his failure to secure a more explicit reply from this woman.

Fingering his leather swagger stick, he shouted impatiently, "And what do they do in this institution, these ninety-three maidens?"

"They receive religious Jewish education. They are brought up in the true Jewish tradition."

"In true Jewish tradition! I like that. That suits us very well." The Lieutenant recovered his light cynical tone. "And what is the name of this maidenly institution?"

"The Daughters of Jacob."

"Jacob's daughters! That's good, too! And who is this Jacob who possesses ninety-three daughters, all maidens?"

"He is our patriarch. Our institution is named after him."

"The Jacob in the Bible? The one who cheated his brother and afterward his father-in-law? You see, we are well acquainted with the biographies of your great men."

"Yes, it is the Jacob of the Bible."

"So your institution is named after him. That's good too. That also suits us very well. . . . Now listen, Jewess Madame Directress, as daughters of Jacob, the Biblical patriarch, we are prepared to confer an unusual and exceptional honor upon these maidens. They shall receive the high and undeserved distinction of being visited by ninety-three—is that the correct number—ninety-three? —pure German young Nazis. Tomorrow at eight o'clock in the evening. Our orderlies will provide soap, clean sheets, and fresh linen so that the maidens may make proper preparations for the great honor which we are about to bestow upon them. And for this occasion—in order to help them to receive our pure Aryans suitably—we will provide a liberal supply of alcoholic drinks for your establishment. And you, Jewess Madame Directress, it is your personal responsibility to see that the maidens are properly prepared for the high honor they are about to receive. Have you understood, Jewess?"

The directress swayed to the right and to the left. Just as she was about to fall, she recovered her self-control; she remained upright and raised her head. Her face was now strained and white. Her lips were pale and tightly closed. But her dark brown eyes seemed to grow larger in their deep sockets, and her eyeballs bulged from under her eyelids, staring mutely into the Lieutenant's face. Her eyes sought his, and at last she caught his gaze. She stared fixedly into his eyes while she remained silent.

"Understood, Jewess?"

Still the woman remained silent.

"Answer me!"

The woman remained silent.

The Lieutenant picked up his revolver and placed it against the woman's breast. "Answer me."

"I will prepare my maidens for the high honor that is about to be bestowed upon them." The woman repeated the Lieutenant's words, and looked away with her prominent eyes, into the far, deep, silent heaven.

"That is all for today," the Lieutenant said.

He put the revolver back in its holster, picked up his swagger stick, and left the office of the Daughters of Jacob.

The daughters were assembled in their great hall—all the ninety-three maidens, from twelve to eighteen. All of the supervisors, teachers, and monitors were there too. The older girls stood in the rear and the younger in the front row, just as they did before a holiday or for an important ceremony. The directress, tall, slender, and distraught, stood on the platform. During these few hours her hair had become even whiter. The last strands of black that had glistened among the white had disappeared, and so she had tied a black scarf around her head. Two candles burned in the Sabbath candlesticks that stood before her.

There was no need for her to explain things. All of them, from the oldest to the youngest, knew that the thing they had awaited and feared, each day, had come. Now it was real. Now it stared them in the eyes. Now they had to examine this thing and decide what to do. And they all knew what they must do. Each one of them thought this to herself in silence. They had thought it out during the months and years of the German occupation. Sometimes they had whispered to each other about it at night in their beds, but mostly they knew it in silence.

Now they had gathered together at the call of the directress to hear from her what they had to do. To hear the words spoken openly—the same words that each had spoken in the privacy of her own thoughts. The thick silence endured for a long time. The directress and the teachers looked at each other for long silent moments. Neither the directress nor the maidens opened their lips to break the holy silence that filled the hall. No one broke the silence even with a sigh or a groan; they only stood facing each other—the students and the teachers looking one upon the other.

Then the directress went to the blackboard on the platform; she picked up a bit of chalk, and writing slowly, she inscribed two Hebrew words on the blackboard, "*Kiddush Hashem*," the sanctification of the Holy Name.

Only then did she find her tongue. And in the ordinary tone that she used for announcing their lessons she said, "Today's lecture will be on the subject of *Kiddush Hashem*.

"*Kiddush Hashem* is one of the holiest commands laid down for us in the Torah. We must not seek *Kiddush Hashem*. But when *Kiddush Hashem* comes to us, we must not avoid it. We must think of it as the highest duty imposed upon us by God, in order that we may fulfill the holiest of his commandments. This we have learned from the earliest of our martyrs, from all of those who were murdered for their faith throughout the entire length of Jewish history. God has enjoined us to love him with all our hearts and all our souls. *Kiddush Hashem* gives us the opportunity to serve God with our souls. As the rabbis have ordered, we have the right to make use of self-destruction in order that we may not be utilized for evil. This was the belief of our fathers. When they, too, were in danger of being forced into sin or of being forced, God forbid, to accept another faith, they slaughtered their wives and children with their own hands before killing themselves. From this we learn that in times when we are in danger of sin, when we are in danger of weakening, God forbid, then we have a right to destroy ourselves. Death by our own hand is considered by the God of the Universe as a sanctification of His Name. Therefore, we shall take this solution in our situation, and we shall prepare ourselves to come before the seat of glory in purity and holiness. Daughters of Jacob, are you prepared to fulfill the high commandment of *Kiddush Hashem,* with love and with joy and without regret, in order that there shall be no blemish upon your souls when you come before the seat of the Holy?"

"We have heard the Lord's command," a low murmur was repeated.

But a bitter childish whimper was heard from one of the youngest girls in the first row. The directress spoke no more of *Kiddush Hashem.* She addressed herself to the crying child.

"Rifka, come up here to me."

From the first row of benches a black-braided little head was raised. It was a girl of about twelve. Her head was tilted to one side, as though it was too heavy for her slender throat. And her thin little legs seemed scarcely capable of carrying her little body. She was barely able to mount the platform. The directress helped her up and seated her on a chair close to herself.

"Rifka, why are you crying?" the directress asked.

"I am afraid to die," the child sobbed into her little hands.

"And aren't you afraid to live, Rifkale?"

The child was silent.

"Answer, Rifkale, aren't you afraid to live when you see what stands before you?"

"Yes, I am afraid," the child sobbed again.

"Stop crying, Rifka, and answer me clearly. You must take the trouble to answer, because it is very important for all of us. Will you try, Rifkale?"

"Yes."

"Here, drink a little water. Now, answer me."

"Yes, teacher."

"Why are you afraid to die?"

"Because I don't know what it is," the child said, tearlessly, yet in a voice filled with fear.

"And do you know what life is?"

"Yes, I know."

"What is it?"

"They kill all the Jews."

"No, Rifkale, it is even worse."

"Yes, I know. They burn Jewish children in ovens," the child replied.

"No, Rifkale, still worse."

"Still worse?" the child asked in wonder. "What can be worse?" she demanded, in her childish singsong voice.

"It is because you don't know what is worse, Rifkale, my child, that you are fit to be our leader to the seat of the Holy. Do you want to do that, Rifkale?"

"You mean I shall be the leader?" Rifkale smiled through her tears.

"Yes, Rifkale, you will have the glory of seeing and hearing things that none of us will witness. You are one of the infants whose purity awakens the pity of heaven. You will be the first to go, and we shall follow. And you shall tell us what you see and what you hear on the way. Will you be our guide, Rifkale?"

"Yes, teacher." The child smiled through her tears with a glad heart.

"And now you are no longer afraid to die as your sisters do in *Kiddush Hashem?*"

"No, teacher."

"Then repeat the words that your sisters have spoken: 'We have heard the Lord's command.' "

"We have heard the Lord's command," the child repeated.

"Now go back, Rifkale, and take your seat amongst your sisters."

Rifkale returned to her place on the bench.

"Daughters of Jacob," the directress called to the rows of maidens, "prepare yourselves and be ready. Wash your bodies. Dress yourselves in clean linen, and then come here all of you together. Tonight at twelve o'clock we shall present ourselves to God. Together we shall all observe the greatest commandment in the Torah—the commandment of *Kiddush Hashem.* . . . Rifkale, go with them. Your sisters will tell you what to do." And the directress put the little girl into the hands of the older maidens.

At twelve o'clock at night the Daughters of Jacob, ninety-three Jewish maidens, gathered together again in the meeting hall, with all of their teachers and all of their supervisors. Each was dressed in her clean white nightgown. Their hair was unbound, and their feet were bare. Each sat down in her place. The directress was dressed in mourning clothes, a black scarf covering her hair. She took the youngest of them, Rifkale, and sat the child close to herself on the platform. On the platform in front of the directress there burned the two candles in the Sabbath candlesticks. On the table next to her prayer book, a white slip of paper lay unfolded, disclosing a little pile of white powder. Each of the maidens found on her desk an open prayer book and the white paper upon which lay the white powder.

The large hall was dimmed. The corners were in complete darkness. All that could be seen were the white nightgowns, the mourning garments of the maidens. Their white faces were visible, and their eyes were fixed on the two little flames that burned in the candlesticks before the directress.

"Daughters of Jacob, let us rise and we shall repeat three times, *Hear O Israel!*"

The maidens stood up in their places and repeated three times, "*Hear O Israel, the Lord our God, the Lord is One.*"

"And now, Daughters of Jacob, the holy moment of *Kiddush Hashem* has arrived. Let us bless the command, which it has been granted us to fulfill. And let us repeat the last prayer. Repeat after me word for word, "*Beloved art Thou, O God, King of our universe, for Thou hast made us holy with Thy blessing and Thou hast permitted us to die for the sake of Thy Name.*"

The maidens repeated after her, "*Blessed art Thou, O God, King of our universe that we have lived and awaited this moment.*"

The directress picked up the white powder that lay before her on the prayer book. She lifted the paper so that all might see. She put it to her lips and with her eyes closed she swallowed. The daughters did as she had done. For a moment all was quiet.

"Have all of us fulfilled the commandment of *Kiddush Hashem?*" the directress asked.

There was a chorus of weak voices. "All."

"Our little sister Rifkale will lead us to the seat of the Holy. Let us be quiet. Let us listen to the child Rifkale. She, before any of us, will see, and she will hear and she will know where we are going. Give me your hand, little sister Rifkale. Tell me, what do you see?"

"I see nothing. I see only light and light. Wait, now I smell something. What a wonderful fragrance! Just as though hay were being cut in the fields."

"Tell us more, Rifkale, tell us."

"Now I hear music as though flutes were playing at a wedding. They are playing so softly and gently and there are children singing too. Oh, such a holy song! Just as in the synagogue when they sing *Kol Nidre*.

"Now I see a woman all dressed in white. And a long white scarf flows in her steps. She is so tall and beautiful. Oh, Mother dear! I have never seen such a beautiful woman. She looks like a Jewish queen. There is a Sabbath crown on her head, and she walks so proudly and quietly. Oh, how she places each step. But why is it, oh, Mother dear, the woman is weeping so? She is so beautiful and yet she weeps. The tears rain from her eyes as she goes. The tears fall from her eyes like two little stars and they fall on her naked feet. Why is the Jewish queen weeping?"

"See, Daughters of Jacob, who comes to greet you! Rachel weeping for her sons. Let us bow down before her."

"And now all is so quiet, Mama dear. I am so afraid. It is so quiet, as in a synagogue before the evening prayer. It is as though the sun were tied in a black scarf. And there is such goodness over the entire world. I am shivering. I am so afraid. Teacher, hold my hand. The woman is coming wrapped in a thick black scarf. Oh, Mother dear! I have never in my life seen such a woman. She is so tall. She is so tall, taller than anyone. And she is so deeply wrapped in black. Her face shines through her black scarf with such a light, as though it were made out of the light of heaven. Oh, I cannot look into her face. My eyes are blinded. I must close my eyes. I cannot see anything any more. I feel only the rays of light that stream from her face and fall upon me. And they warm me and embrace me. Oh, she is taking me. It is as though streams of water were pouring over me and I feel so free. I have wings now. I fly from one place to another. It was the woman who made me fly. The rays that came from her! I am bathing in rivers of light. I am flying through clouds of light. God bless and keep all of you. I am flying away now. There on the cloud over there my mother is standing, and her arms are outstretched to me, and I am flying to her."

"I, too, I, too!"

"And I, too."

From all sides of the great dark hall there came weak torn voices calling with their last strength, "Mama! Mama! Mama!"

The Duty to Live

O N the way from Shochlin to Gombyn in the old Poland, between the thick woods and the dark pools that are to be found on both sides of the road, there marched two high-booted Germans driving a long line of children with their whips as though they were driving a flock of geese. The children cried, and some of them were bleating "Mama," like lambs bleating out a long *Maaaa*. Others were no longer calling "Mama"; they trudged along, sobbing. The Germans paid no attention to their weeping, but when a child unintentionally—or perhaps intentionally—got separated from the flock, or when a child tried to sit down on a stone by the edge of the road, or instinctively looked for protection toward the tall dark pine trees whose shimmering arms reached out from the woods as though inviting the children to hide among them, then a burning stroke of the long leather whip would flash over the child's head and cut his skin, while a brutal white-haired hunting dog would sink its teeth into the child's leg. Sometimes the child ceased to feel the sharp teeth of the hound. It simply remained lying on the road. And then the German guard would whip the dog away from the dead body. But when the children still had some life left in them, they would limp back screaming into the ranks.

After a time the crying of the children diminished. The calls of "Mama" became softer and at last were lost. The children were weary after their long march in the heat of the day. They were hungry and thirsty, and their little eyes were sticky with sleepiness. Their little feet became raw under their cotton stockings and blistered from the stony road. They wanted only to lie down, even here on the road, even if the whip screamed over their heads. But an unknown fear—the fear of death in which the instinct to live is rooted—gave the children strength to bear the hardships of the endless day. The instinct to live, which is ingrown in every living being, in every germ of matter, was stronger than their desire to drop and rest. Therefore, the older children carried the younger. They helped those who crawled and those who fell behind. And they struggled on under the lash of the two whips that the high-booted German guards cracked over their heads.

The flock of children was gathered together from the Jewish population of the town of Shochlin. There the Germans had dragged them out of Jewish homes, sought them out in their hiding places, torn them from the arms of mothers, and even snatched them out of cradles. In order to get the parents to send along the children's clothing, the Germans had declared they were taking the children for a summer vacation in the country, "where they would get better nourishment." The mothers knew that their children were being dragged away to be slaughtered or to be burned, to the same fate that had befallen the children of other towns—of Lovitz and of Kutno. Still, out of the need to cling to a last straw of hope, they forced themselves not to disbelieve the Germans completely, and they dressed their children in their holiday clothes, put their best coats on them, and packed up their last bit of food for them. They gave their children their toys to carry along—for what use would the toys be without the children? The mothers fainted, falling like flies in the doorways. Then they would recover and run after the children, with their eyes bulging and their hair wild, looking half insane. They would run after them until they were out of the city. They were not allowed to go farther.

The fathers had long since gone, carried off by the Germans, to slave labor or to death. And now the mothers stood, held back by the bayonets against their breasts, as they watched the Germans driving away their children. And they screamed after them, "Channeleh, take care of Shlomoleh!" "Mosheleh, guard Rocheleh, as the eyes in your head!" until the children were lost to sight, covered in a cloud of dust that rose after them. Thus they were marched away into the woods. Some of the mothers went mad. Others cursed God for having permitted this to come to pass. And after that, some went and tied stones around their necks and threw themselves into the river.

Among the grief-mad mothers who watched the Germans driving off their children on the road to Gombyn, from which they would be led to the river Vistula and never more be seen, was Zelda, the pushcart woman. Her menfolk—her husband and her grown son—had been taken off in the first wave, just after the Germans had come into the town. And now all she had left had been taken. Her twelve-year-old girl Iteleh and two-year-old Shlomoleh, the son of her old age, were in the flock being driven away by the Germans. Zelda did not tear her hair, nor did she curse. She did not scream like the others when she saw the Germans driving away the children. She only shouted into the group of children, "Iteleh, Iteleh, do you hear me?"

"Yes, Mother." She recognized her daughter's voice amongst the children's cries.

"Do you remember what I told you?"

"Yes, Mama."

"Then do it."

"I'll do it," she heard her daughter's voice.

Then Zelda drew her head scarf over her marriage wig down to her eyes. And so she went back into the town.

Iteleh trudged along in the group, carrying her two-year-old brother Shlomoleh. This was not too difficult for her. She had been used to carrying children in her arms from the time she was five years old. When her mother would get up in the morning and go to the market to buy goods, she would leave the household in Iteleh's hands. At first Iteleh had raised her brother Moshe Aaron. She had raised him with a bottle and a nipple. But Moshe

Aaron had died young. He had caught the whooping cough; the poor thing had suffered in her arms for two nights and then died. At the same time her mother had been pregnant with this little brother, Shlomo. And so Iteleh soon had Shlomo on her hands. When her mother had weaned him, she gave the baby over to Iteleh, and Iteleh raised him with a bottle and a nipple until the Germans came.

Now she carried him on one arm, while on the other arm she carried the little pack that her mother had given her. In the pack there was a bit of bread and a little honey. There was Shlomoleh's bottle of water mixed with a little milk that the mother had obtained—God only knows how—and there was a rubber nipple.

For though little Shlomoleh was already two years old and could speak a few words—even though he had already reached the stage of asking "why?" "why?" "why?"—he nevertheless had the infantile habit of not being able to go to sleep without his bottle or at least a nipple in his mouth. It is true that the mothers of the poor nurse their children longer at their breasts than do mothers of the rich. As though to give their children a memory of childhood pleasure to carry along into the wearisome struggles that lie before them in life, the mothers protract the nursing of their children. This becomes a kind of instinctive compensation for all the lacks and hardship that the child of poverty has to endure in his infancy.

And now as Iteleh marched along, with the weight of the child on her frail arms, she kept in mind the bottle that was in her little sack. She walked carefully so that it would not spill.

Her mother had given her one instruction, just before she had been taken away from the house, one thing she must always remember, must keep in mind every moment. And as she walked among the children and looked into the dark shadowy woods that stood on both sides of the road and kept growing darker as the evening approached, even now she thought of her mother's injunction.

THE DUTY TO LIVE

For when the Germans had surrounded the town and began to break into the Jewish homes and to take away the children, Zelda had not lost her senses. She had neither screamed nor shouted; she had not torn her hair like the others. She had simply called her daughter Iteleh out of her hiding place in the cold cellar.

"Iteleh," she had said to her daughter, "they will find you there. They will take you away, you and your little brother, just as they take the other Jewish children. Now listen to me. Listen to me with all your mind. You're grown up already. You understand things. You know what the Germans do with Jewish children."

"Yes, Mother, I know." Iteleh nodded her head, scarcely moving her lips.

"Iteleh, do you know what duty means?"

"Yes, Mother, Father taught it to me. It is our duty to repeat *Modeh Ani*, the holy prayer."

"Yes, to repeat *Modeh Ani*, and to go to the synagogue on the Day of Atonement and on New Year's Day, to listen to the blowing of the ram's horn, to light the Sabbath candles, to honor your father and mother, all this God told us to do. And all that God tells us to do is good and becomes a duty. Now, do you know what God tells us to do today? Today, God tells the Jews that they must live. To do everything, to overturn worlds, but only to remain alive. Do you understand me, Iteleh? You and your brother are being led to your death. They are slaughtering Jewish children. They are killing all the Jews."

"Yes, Mama." Iteleh nodded her head.

"Do whatever you can. Everything and anything is permitted— only to save your life. There are no other duties. There is no more Sabbath; there are no more holidays; there is no more blessing of the candles. Only one duty remains—to stay alive. God wants the Jews to survive. Iteleh, I am putting your brother into your hands. He is the only male left to us. Preserve his life; be a mother to him."

And the words "preserve his life; be a mother to him" now rang in Iteleh's ears. Ceaselessly, they demanded that she do something. That she do something now, even here, to save her brother's life. She kept looking about, seeking a hole, a shadow, a little house in the woods, a stream, any place where one might hide. But she was sensible enough not to risk a false step. She knew very well that a single false step might cost her and her brother their lives, and therefore she was careful that all might not be lost.

The Germans had two dogs, one on each side. If a child strayed from the road, the hound immediately rushed after it, barking. And yet Iteleh knew she had to manage something here in the woods before they came to the station by the river Vistula. The woods were still in the neighborhood of her town. They belonged to the owner of the manor of Korovitz. Behind the woods there were scattered cottages. She knew a few of the peasants who lived in these cottages, for she had helped her mother carry her bolts of cloth to sell among the peasants. There was one named Kaminsky in whose place her father used to spend the night when he had to stop over in the village. In another little cottage there lived the woman Yadwiga, who used to leave her children in her mother's house when she came to town for the fair. And she knew one or two other peasants from whom her father used to buy animal skins. And at the edge of the wood on the other side there were the large ponds of Korovitz, where fish were caught. The Jews of the town had always bought their catch from the fishermen, carrying it into the town to be sold for the Sabbath. Perhaps there she would be able to find a corner where she could hide overnight. And then tomorrow she would see what to do. She would go and knock on the doors of the peasants.

A little farther beyond the woods on the way to Shochlin, there stood the big church of the "Black Sisters." That was the Jewish name for the nuns of the Sacred Heart, who were always dressed in black. The nuns often came riding into town with their own horse and wagon, and they bought supplies in the Jewish stores.

Sometimes they would buy cloth at her mother's stall—linen and woolens and cloth from Lodz. People said that the nuns were good to Jewish children. They took them into the church and hid them. It was also safer among the nuns, because the Germans were hesitant about forcing their way into a church. But it was said that they converted Jewish children. She would not let them convert her little brother. No, not in any circumstances. No, she would not permit it. She would not even go into the cloister. It would be better to hide in the woods or to try to crawl under a haystack. Then she could try to approach a peasant. Somehow she would know what to do. If she could only get into the woods! She must get away in the woods before they reached the open road to Gombyn.

And thus Iteleh marched on, carrying her little brother and carefully holding the sack as well as the few bits of clothing that her mother had put under her arm. She kept on making plans, scarcely noticing that the woods were thinning out and that the fading reddish rays of the evening sun could now be seen between the sparse trees.

"Oh, Mother! We're coming to the end of the woods!" Iteleh cried out to herself in fright as she suddenly noticed that there were fewer trees. She glanced at her little brother. He had fallen asleep in her arms with his finger in his mouth and the murmur "Mama, Mama" trembling on his lips. For he had not ceased calling out the word, together with all the other children, the entire length of the way. "It's a good thing Shlomoleh has fallen asleep," Iteleh thought, "now it must happen before we come to the last trees. Now—now—but how can I do it, while the two hounds are on the watch?"

She could feel their sniffling wet nostrils behind her; she could hear their breathing. "But it must be done, it must be done! God, God, make it happen!"

And as she was saying this to herself, a convoy of wagons filled with German soldiers approached from the opposite direction. The wagons raised so much dust on the dry country road that everything was covered in a cloud of sand and filth. The two Germans hurriedly drove the children to a side of the road, using their whips freely. They drove them into the ditches so as to make room for the convoy. The dogs ran furiously along the entire length of the convoy, barking violently and keeping the children in line. And in this Iteleh saw a sign from God. It was God's will that the Jews should survive.

"Children! Follow me into the woods!" she shouted, running pell-mell, with all her remaining strength, into the forest. The children ran after her. She heard the dogs barking behind her; she heard the Germans shouting; she heard revolver shots; she did not turn around. She ran back the way they had come, so as to reach the thicker woods. And to avoid leaving a trace behind herself, she was careful not to drop anything. With one arm she pressed the awakened terrified infant to her breast. With the other hand she clutched her little sack. She zigzagged, ran from tree to tree, hid in the heavy shadows of the trees, until she came into a thick cluster of brambles. The brambles stuck into her bare feet, but she felt no pain. She hid among the bushes, sitting down for a moment to catch her breath. She kept one hand over the baby's mouth so that he might not give her away with his crying, which had now begun in full force. With the other hand she got out the little bottle of water and milk that her mother had given her. And she forced the bottle into the baby's mouth to quiet him. The child sought and found aid and comfort in the nourishment. He nuzzled his face into his sister's breast while he clutched the bottle with both his hands, sighing from time to time. He found peace as he suckled.

As soon as the child became quiet, Iteleh crawled out on all fours from under the bush. It seemed to her that she was too close to the road. She could hear the dogs howling as they rooted around the trees, rounding up the fleeing children. Once when it seemed to her that she heard the shouting of the Germans directly behind her, she crawled out on all fours and looked around to make sure that no one was on her trail. Then she took the child in her arms and the sack along with him and started running with all her strength toward the pond. The night was coming down into the woods, weaving its darkness from tree to tree, and shielding her beneath its curtain. But when she emerged from among the trees, at the edge of the pond, she saw the full moon shining in the sky. It was a night late in September when the reddish moon glitters like a great open eye that sees everything. Nothing is hidden from it. Iteleh became terrified of the naked emptiness in which she found herself. The pond lay open and broad, guarded by the surrounding trees, and the moon hung above, its full shining light uncovering everything. She was afraid to remain by the pond. It seemed to her that the moonlight pointed her out and gave away her hiding place. And it still seemed to her that she heard barking and the cries of the children.

Iteleh turned back into the forest and sought a dry bit of ground where she might rest. But scarcely had she sat down when her fright brought her to her feet again. She still seemed to hear the Germans coming with their hounds. She started deeper into the woods. Her knees now began to buckle beneath her. Her bare feet stumbled over roots. The child became heavier and heavier on her arms. Frightened and weary, she began to shiver with anxiety. Her arms fell asleep. Her feet seemed to be broken. She wanted to sit down and rest, but, if she rested a moment, it seemed to her that the Germans were coming and so she would start up and walk and walk and walk.

At last she saw a light shining between the trees. She was at first frightened by it, and yet it gave her hope. She slipped between the trees, coming closer to the light, until she saw that it came from a peasant's hut. With a beating heart she crept to the fence, but as she felt for the lock she was frightened by the barking of a dog in the yard. She hid behind the fence and waited. The dog would not be quiet. He barked and barked. Finally the door of the hut was opened. She saw someone coming out of the house. The light inside was extinguished. A shadow approached the fence.

"You'd better go away from here. The Germans were here looking for Jewish children. They've surrounded the whole woods with bloodhounds."

"Please have pity. Let me in. I'll hide in the stable. God will reward you."

"What's that on your arm?"

"A baby. My little brother."

"The child will give you away. He will start crying and be the death of all of us. Go away from here. The Germans are on the trail."

"Please, sir, help us." Iteleh stretched out her hand.

"Without the child I might have let you in. But as it is, you'd better get away. They'll be on your trail."

"But where can I go?"

"Drop the child and save yourself. Run to the nunnery. It's a mile and a half from here on the other side of the pond. They'll let you in."

"Drop the child? He's my little brother. My mother trusted him to me."

"Run away, little Jew. Here's a piece of bread."

And the shadow threw a piece of bread over the fence to her.

Iteleh left the bread lying there and went off with the baby. She stumbled farther among the trees, running from one tree to another. Her legs grew weaker and weaker. Her arms were breaking under Shlomoleh's weight. But the worst thing was that the child had been awakened by the dog's barking. He began to wail at the top of his voice, "Mama, Mama."

She sat down under the nearest tree and tried to quiet the child. The bottle had fallen out of his hands while she was running. She searched in her bag and found a nipple, which she tried to press into his mouth. The child sucked for a moment and then spat out the rubber nipple and began to howl.

Iteleh tried to cover his mouth with her hand, but this made him cry even louder. Iteleh's hair began to stand on end. Sweating with fear she couldn't think what to do. "Now I am lost," she thought, remembering the peasant's words, "The child will give you away." It seemed to her that the Germans were lying in wait with their hounds behind the trees, and the baby's crying was leading them to her. She could already hear the running of the dogs and their howling before the wind. She had to quiet the child. She had to. "Shlomo, I beg you, be quiet, be quiet. Shlomoleh," she kept repeating, although she knew her words could have no effect. Desperately, she tried to think of some way to hush the baby. Suddenly a thought came to her. She remembered what her mother used to do at times when Shlomoleh began to cry and would not let himself be stilled by any means whatever. Neither the bottle nor the nipple was of any use. Iteleh tore open her coat and took out her round little breast which had just begun to take form, like an unripe apple on a tree. And she put her breast into the baby's mouth.

"There, now, be still!" she repeated her mother's words. And the child was quiet. Surprised by the warmth that engulfed his little face, he nuzzled against her warm body and found the motherly comfort that quiets and relaxes all wailing children.

With his face nuzzled in her breast, the baby fell into a restful sleep. But not only the child was quieted. Without knowing how it came about, Iteleh herself felt a merciful peace settling down upon her. All at once the fearful thoughts and horrible imaginings were gone. No one was pursuing her any more. She no longer heard the dogs barking, and there was no more baby's crying. All around her everything was still, except for the hooting of the owls, invisible among the branches and leaves. They might have been creatures out of a strange world of fantasy. Yet even the howling of the owls faded to a cradle song, and Iteleh slipped down until her head rested on the dewy grass. And still holding her little brother warm and close against her breast she fell asleep, untroubled and un-afraid.

When she awoke from sleep, her fright returned. It was already full day. And here she sat with her little brother by the road. She had not noticed that she had instinctively followed the direction that the peasant had showed her during the night, around the pond toward Gombyn. All the danger of her position came over her. At any moment the Germans might pass by—a soldier, or a police-man—any German might come along and catch her. She had not the heart to return into the woods. It seemed to her that the woods was a trap surrounded by Germans, while their bloodhounds sneaked amongst the trees.

On the road before her was the nunnery. She had often seen it when riding with her mother to the market at Gombyn. The church was surrounded by a wall, and two large crosses stood out among the green trees on the other side of the high wall. She knew that if she took only a few steps out of the woods toward the road, she would see the crosses. And she tried to decide whether to go toward the crosses or back into the woods.

In the woods were the Germans and their bloodhounds, while under the crosses she might find safety for herself and her brother. But with the crosses came conversion. She would have to give up being a Jew and become a Gentile. And her little brother also would no longer be a Jew. No, she would not go toward the crosses, she would rather go into the woods. She would never become a Christian, and little Shlomo would never become a Christian. . . . But in the woods there were the German beasts. . . .

And in the meantime she sat there, with Shlomoleh in her arms. He was still asleep. His little face looked worn out, and he groaned with babyish groans. The Germans would take Shlomoleh and throw him into a fire. They would roast him in their ovens. But the nuns would take him and convert him. What would be better to do? And then she remembered what her mother had told her.

THE DUTY TO LIVE

"Iteleh, you must live, and see that Shlomoleh lives. Your greatest duty is to live."

Yes, she wanted to live, and she wanted her little brother to live. They had to live. So many Jewish children were dying. Everyone was killing them. And someone had to remain alive. But she would not become converted. She would somehow manage that they should remain Jews. They would never, never become Christians. She remembered the prayer that her mother had taught her to say every morning. *Oh, Lord, our Gracious King, bless and protect my little head.* And as though these words had been a last straw to grasp, she kept repeating over and over, *"Oh, Lord, our Gracious King, bless and protect my little head."* She would repeat this prayer every morning; she would repeat it with her brother. She would teach him this prayer, and through it, they would remain Jews. She looked at Shlomoleh. The child's eyes were now wide open, and he stared around him in wonder.

"Shlomoleh, Shlomoleh, repeat after me." The child stared at her and made a face as though he were about to cry.

"No, don't cry, just repeat after me, say Lord, Lord, Lord."

"Lord," the child repeated.

"Bless, Bless, Bless, say Bless."

"Bliss, blass, bliss, bee."

"Bless."

"Bless."

Armed with the prayer that the child had repeated after her, she got up from the ground, took Shlomoleh in her arms, and left the woods for the road. She could see the two crosses from afar surmounting the tall green wall that ringed the church. The crosses no longer stabbed her eyes as before.

When Iteleh with her little brother in her arms was brought before the Sister Superior, Iteleh made her declaration.

"Our mama told us to save our lives. She said that it was a

217

command of God that we should live. We escaped into the woods and we came here because people told us that you were kind and that you hid Jewish children so as to save their lives. But we are afraid of you because of one thing."

The aged gray Sister Superior studied the little mother with the child in her hands, saw her bare little feet torn and battered by brambles and stones, her hair undone and tumbling wildly over her frail back. She saw how the child stood quivering like a little green branch. The pallid maidenly face of the Sister Superior contracted into innumerable wrinkles. Her clear blue eyes became clouded under the gaze of the little mother who had fought her way through the woods and saved her baby brother from the German beasts. She took Iteleh by the hand, drew her closer to herself, and asked with tenderness, "Why are you afraid of us?"

"We are afraid that you might make us become Catholics. People say that you force Jewish children to become Catholics."

"We don't force anyone to become Catholics," the Sister Superior said. "Whoever doesn't want to, doesn't have to become a Catholic. But why are you afraid to become a Catholic? All of us here are Catholics, and you see we don't murder little children; instead, we save them."

"It's because we are Jews and want to remain Jews."

"That is very good of you, my child. You can remain a Jew, and your little brother can remain a Jew. No one will force you to do anything."

"Yes!" Iteleh cried out joyously. "And we can stay here with you? And you won't hand us over to the Germans, even if we remain Jews?"

"You can stay here with us. No one will betray you to the Germans, and you can remain Jews."

"Oh, that is wonderful!" the little girl cried happily. "But I would like to ask the Lady Superior one more thing."

"What is it, my child?"

"Every morning and every evening, I and my brother want to say the Jewish prayer. May we?"

"Of course you may, my child. It will please us for you and your brother to say the Jewish prayer every day. Does he know the Jewish ritual, young as he is?"

"I am teaching him. I began to teach him this morning in the woods when I was hiding from the Germans. He says every word after me. Would the Lady Superior like to hear how he says it? Shlomoleh, repeat after me, Lord."

"Lord."

"Bless."

"Bliss, Belis, Bess."

"Bless, Bless, Bless."

"Ba, Ba, Bess."

"Did you hear him, Lady? Did you hear how he says it after me? Oh, how happy my mother will be!"

"Come, Sister! Come here and behold the power of ancient Israel. Their God throws their children at the feet of the dogs, and from the very jaws of the beast their children praise the God of Israel," said the aged Sister Superior.

And the cloud over her clear blue eyes was dissolved in tears.

Jewish Eyes

DEDICATED TO THE MEMORY OF THE JEWISH CHILDREN
OF POLAND

FOR weeks Rivka Rabinowitz, the wife of a Hebrew teacher of Warsaw, succeeded in keeping her daughter Miraleh hidden in the concentration camp where the Germans had put her. Her husband had been taken away long ago, while they were still in Warsaw. So it was also with her eight-year-old son. She had no idea what had become of them but continued to deceive herself with the hope that they were alive somewhere in another concentration camp—the same hope, the same self-deception that was maintained by all the other women in the camp.

Frau Rabinowitz was in her prime—still in her thirties—a strong healthy woman with an energetic face; she was not at all bad looking. Her handsome black sparkling eyes were like two ripe cherries, well shaped, attractively set under the arch of her black brows.

At that time the Germans were in need of strong healthy workers to wash, clean, and repair the coats, dresses, shirts, and other garments that they removed from the men, women, and children they were sending off to death. For the clothes had to be properly prepared before being distributed among the German people. And that is how they came to spare Frau Rabinowitz's life; she was sent to a labor camp, where they could utilize her remaining strength before sending her off to share the fate of her husband and son and all her relatives—the gas chamber.

From the beginning, Frau Rabinowitz undertook a task no one would have believed possible. This task was to save her little girl from the hands of the devils. During the entire time she remained in the Warsaw Ghetto, she had kept the child from the eyes of the Germans by hiding her in a garret, where she could bring food to the little girl. For weeks and months, without a glimpse of sunlight, the child huddled behind a crate, until her hiding place had become like a normal home to her. When her mother came to her, she no longer cried as she had in the beginning. Young as she was, the child had realized her danger and co-operated with her mother to remain hidden from the executioners.

When Frau Rabinowitz had the good fortune to be selected for labor rather than for death, she decided to take the child with her to the concentration camp. After her year of education in conspiracy, Miraleh knew how to remain silent and motionless. Her mother simply hid the frail child against her own body, beneath her wraps. Thus she smuggled her into the boxcar that was packed with "selected" women, and later into the barracks of the concentration camp in Germany.

Eighty or ninety women were crowded into one long room, all Jews herded together from various lands. The number varied slightly as women arrived and women were sent away. Pressed close to one another, the women lay on wooden shelves on which a little straw had been spread. Most of them were mothers whose children had been taken from them; some had seen their children killed before their very eyes. They had constantly to watch themselves, had to concentrate with all their strength on suppressing the hysteria that arose in them when they thought of their children, for the slightest show of excitement was enough to have them sent to another camp from which no one ever returned.

Night was their time of crisis. For if a mother's longing rose in her, she might begin to scream, "Dovidele, my Dovidele, where are you?" and then all of the other women would have to fall on her, pressing her head into the straw, pushing her fist into her mouth, so that she would bite her fingers and become quiet, for she was endangering them all.

When Frau Rabinowitz brought her very own child, Miraieh, into the barracks, it seemed to the women that a miracle from heaven had happened. No, no, it was as though the skies themselves had opened, and a child had been returned to them from heaven, a child who would be a treasure and reminder of their own children. Miraleh was no longer the child of Frau Rabinowitz; she was the child of them all. In flesh and blood, Miraleh belonged to each one of them. It seemed to them as though God had taken all of the children that had been lost to them and put them all together into this one little body and given this little being the eyes of all Jewish children. And God had sent her to them in their pain and in their suffering. They had no special thoughts for Frau Rabinowitz. It never occurred to them that Miraleh was any one woman's child. Their maternal roots, so prematurely destroyed, now found fresh nourishment. All considered themselves to be Miraleh's mother, and all began to think of themselves again as mothers, and Miraleh was the child.

Miraleh accepted all their love. She was the typical child. She was too small and too thin for her age, for the year of hiding in a dark sunless garret, without proper nourishment, had stunted her growth. She was a miniature child; at five she looked like a child of three, with a meager little body, thin hands, narrow feet, contracted little face, a scrawny throat like that of a baby pigeon. But for all this her eyes compensated. One might have said that Miraleh lived, thought, breathed, moved, spoke, and dreamed only through her eyes. The life force had been sapped from the child's bones, and all that remained was concentrated in her eyes. They were not the ordinary eyes of a child. Set deeply under her high forehead, they appeared strange and large and scarcely of this world. Her small shrunken face was only a frame for Miraleh's eyes.

At times, the two round pools were like quiet water under the moonlight, but when the pools became agitated they took on the color of green jade, and there was movement in them, as of waves rising out of a stormy sea. Two large pupils floated in the pools of her eyes. It was difficult to say what color they were. They could take on all the colors of the rainbow. Sometimes they were black as ink, and at other times they were copper colored, and again they were transformed, becoming translucent as blue sapphires. It depended on what Miraleh wanted to say with her eyes.

For Miraleh knew how to speak with her eyes. Miraleh's eyes could express every nuance of feeling, from the unearthly elation of highest joy to the dumb appeal of animal helplessness. When she looked slowly away to one side, with her black-masked pupils peering out from under their pale white lids, one might have thought that the world was coming to an end. Her eyes could awaken infinite pity, for her glance was like a beam of light that slipped into one's very heart. Her eyes could lift one into a state of ecstasy in which all human suffering, pity, sorrow, anger, the most powerful love, and the most violent hatred were intermingled, until one felt one could move the world. Or, she had a way sometimes of lifting her eyes so that the pupils emerged from hiding, then those who looked into Miraleh's eyes felt an unbearable joy light up their hearts; they were happy without knowing why or wanting to know why.

It was agreed that all the women should watch over Miraleh, but during the day when they went out of the barracks, she had to remain hidden, in order that no evil eye might find her. When they returned in the evening, their first thought was for Miraleh. They saved food from their starvation rations for her. All their pent-up mother love was released upon little Miraleh; they hugged her, kissed her little fingers. Each wanted to comb and braid her hair; each one was half dead with longing for Miraleh to lie down beside her, even for a little while in the night.

Among the women there was a very young wife named Channa Silverberg, who was known in the camp as Little Cow. There was indeed something bovine about her. She was only eighteen or nineteen, the daughter of a wealthy Chassid of Galicia. Everything had been taken from her. The Germans had killed her husband and her father-in-law. They had taken away her only child and had sent her off to the labor camp. And she was herself still only a child. She didn't understand what was happening around her and didn't want to understand. She lived as though in a world of illusion. She performed her work because she was told to do it, and obscurely she knew that she had to do it. But the moment she came back into the barracks, she threw herself on the wooden planks, buried her blond young head in the straw, put her fingers in her dress, and began to play with her own breast. When her suckling child had been taken away from her, she had not lost her milk as had the other women. She kept up the flow by milking her overabundant breasts with her fingers. She continued to believe that a miracle would happen, and just as all this evil had come suddenly upon her, all would suddenly become well again. Then her six-week-old baby would be returned to her, and he would need her milk. Therefore she kept up the flow of milk in her breast, though all the women told her she had nothing more to wait for and that she had better let her breasts dry up, for otherwise she might injure herself.

From the moment Miraleh's mother brought her into the barracks, the Galician girl attached herself to the child. She simply stole Miraleh from her mother. With tears in her eyes, with heartrending pleas, she would beg Rivka Rabinowitz to let Miraleh sleep next to her at night. She would take care of her; she would watch over her. The mother, who seemed to have lost her rights over her own child, took pity on the Galician girl and granted her request. But scarcely had the young mother felt the child's body next to her own than she began to press her swollen nipple to Miraleh's lips.

"Please, Miraleh, suck a little."

Miraleh was five years old, of school age, and like every child she considered herself more grown up than she was. She felt ashamed and insulted by the young woman who wanted to treat her like a baby.

"Go away, go—I'm grown up." The child drew away.

"It will be good for you, Miraleh. You don't know how sweet it is. Milk from the breast is the sweetest of all. Taste a little, I beg you."

"Mother will be angry. Mother wouldn't want me to take milk from a woman's breast."

"Your mama will be glad. There isn't any milk or any sugar for you here, and a child of your age needs milk and sugar. It will do you good. Just taste a little."

And little by little she persuaded Miraleh, until at last in order to please her the child delicately took the young woman's breast between her lips.

Food was scarce in the concentration camp. It was months since the child had had a drop of milk. And though the first taste was so unpleasant to her that she spat it out, the freshness and the sweetness left on her lips drew her back, and she tasted it again. The second time the mother's milk tasted good to her.

In time, the women became aware of what the little Channa was doing with the child; the child's mother wanted to take her away, but the other women protested.

"After all, it's better this way. Mother's milk will put strength in her little bones. It can only do the child good. She has such thin little bones."

And so Rivka Rabinowitz gave in since it was for the child's good. She permitted Miraleh to suckle at the young woman's breast every night. The fact that the child was being suckled by one of them seemed to make her even more intimately the possession of all the interned women. They guarded Miraleh more carefully than ever. Although even during the day one or another of the women was left to clean and care for the barracks, there was always the danger that one of the SS or even one of the officers would come in for inspection and find the child. And so the women found a hiding place for Miraleh under the wooden beds, and they kept her there all day long. Miraleh accepted this as the way things had to be.

Day after day, the women labored at the task of sorting the coats, dresses, underwear that had been removed from the dead before their bodies had been shoved into the furnaces. More than once it had happened that some woman, while sorting the clothing, convinced herself that she recognized a garment that might have belonged to one of her own family. But people become used to anything; there is no limit to the human ability to adjust. The will to live is powerful enough to overcome all obstacles, and the will to live, the will to endure and to come out of this misery, had already overcome, in these women, every emotion that might have endangered their survival. The instinct for survival was like a thirsty sponge soaking up their every sentiment, every feeling, every nervous reaction, leaving them void of all human sensibility except what was directly needed to keep alive. Like long-experienced grave-diggers, they were used to death. And so they went on day after day, sorting the clothes that still had the warmth of life in them, cleaning the bloodstains with benzine, removing all that remained of the lives of the wearers. From the shirts, they washed out the sweat of anxiety that had soaked through the cloth at the moment when the imminence of death was realized. Mechanically, they piled up the funeral garments, the shirts, wraps, coats, the little children's frocks and underclothes, without a groan, without a tear, for the German supervisors were under orders instantly to remove from the sorting line any woman who showed a sign of hysteria or of uncontrolled nerves. Such women were shipped off to the gas chambers and the furnaces.

Once when the women were picking out items of clothing from a huge disorderly pile on the table, one of them picked up a child's coat, and a little doll dragged after it, having been tied to one of the buttons. Incidents of this kind were not rare, for many a child had clung to a favorite toy until the end. Such moments were extremely dangerous. For the women could scarcely control themselves; one or another might let out a spasmodic cry, and such an outbreak inevitably led to death. If a toy appeared, it was instantly dropped as though it were something lethal. But this time the woman who found the doll quickly hid it under her dress and carried it back to the barracks.

Later when they took Miraleh out from under the wooden beds, the woman gave her the doll. All of the women had found pleasure in making rag dolls for Miraleh from the bits of cloth that came off the clothes. They would give these dolls to the child, so that she would have something to play with in her hiding place.

But the doll that the woman brought home under her dress for Miraleh was a real doll, a doll from the time when there were children in the world, and when dolls were made for them, and when children could play openly and freely with their toys. This doll had real hair that could be braided, and great big eyes, like Miraleh's, that moved mechanically.

After Miraleh it was the doll that brought life into the barracks. The women sewed clothing for her, little skirts, scarves, aprons; they even made doll shoes. They were continually dressing the doll in new clothes and playing with her. The two supervisors, who frequently passed through the barracks on inspection, began to notice the doll dresses on the women's bunks, once or twice they saw a rag doll, and a few times they caught the women red-handed as they sewed clothes for the doll out of bits of cloth. The supervisors did not take any action themselves, but they notified headquarters that the Jewish women must be hiding something in their barracks.

One evening when the women had come back to their quarters and were undressing, the chief officer of the women's division of the concentration camp, Fräulein Gertrude, storm-troop leader of the Hitler women, marched into the barracks. Fräulein Gertrude was a pure Gretchen type, with long thick braids wound in a broad coil around her large round head. She wore a short khaki skirt that reached to her knees, a pair of elegant shining boots, a low-cut thin blouse with short sleeves half covering her fleshy arms. She carried a short whip in her hand. The handle was of deer-horn and the braided thongs were of thick cowhide. Two huge police dogs followed her closely. Behind them were two tall SS men in black uniforms, each wearing at his side the SS dagger in its black metal sheath, embossed with a swastika in red, black, and white. The women stood breathless, as though turned to stone beside their bunks.

For quite a while Fräulein Gertrude said nothing. She looked at the women with staring ice-blue eyes. She looked them through and through, slowly moving her eyes from one to another. There was an interval of silence that seemed to endure for an eternity; the silence was so palpable that one seemed to hear the movement of the angel of death creeping into the room and sliding along the walls. Then Fräulein Gertrude raised her bare arm and pointed to the doll, which she held in her other hand.

"Whose is this?" she asked calmly, while her eyes drilled through one woman after another.

The women were silent. They were pale as death. One heard only the beating of their hearts with the agitated movement of their breasts.

"Answer!" Fräulein Gertrude shouted, her voice rising a cat-like screech. And she brought her whip down with a whistling sweep upon the heads and breasts of the women. The howls of the dogs echoed the strokes of the whip.

"Please, Fräulein, it belongs to all of us. The women get amusement out of playing with the doll. It reminds them of their children," said the oldest woman, who no longer had anything to fear.

"So, it reminds them of their children to play with dolls. We'll see about that." She took the doll and put it under the noses of the dogs. After they had sniffed the doll, she motioned with her hand, "Search."

Whining and barking, the dogs crawled under the wooden bunks, and in a few moments the heartrending scream of a child was heard. And presently, both dogs dragged Miraleh out from under the bunks; they had their teeth in her legs. Perhaps the child was more frightened of the strange people she now saw than

231

of the wild dogs. She stopped screaming and did not even cry. She was quiet. But there was a flash of dark lightning in her eyes. Miraleh's glance met the eyes of Fräulein Gertrude, and it was as though something she knew of but had never before experienced touched the German woman. Miraleh's black lashes sank down to the horizon of the great liquid pools of her eyes, and from under the strained lids the pupils peeped out with heartbreaking appeal. The color of her pupils kept changing like the colors in a waterfall. Now they were deep as black midnight; now they changed and flashed with an orange reflection, and in another moment there was a violet shine in them, which became transformed into a deep blue, so that they looked like two large sapphires of the greatest clarity.

"What eyes!" Fräulein Gertrude could not help exclaiming to the two SS men who stood behind her.

And for a second even Fräulein Gertrude's expression changed. A line appeared on her smooth fat white-skinned cheek, near the corner of her mouth. Even her catlike eyes showed a flicker of light. The expression in Fräulein Gertrude's eyes, together with the line at the edge of her mouth, lit a spark of hope in the hearts of the women.

"Pure sapphires! I've never seen anything like them," remarked one of the Gestapo men.

"Ah, what a pair of earrings you could make out of them!" said the other.

"What?"

"From the Jewish eyes, naturally," the SS man repeated.

"Why, how is that?"

"If you can preserve animal's eyes, it must be possible to do the same with human eyes."

"Jewish eyes ... It's an idea!"

The conversation between Fräulein Gertrude and the SS men took only a moment. They carried on their talk quietly so that the women couldn't hear. Suddenly Fräulein Gertrude whirled and seized the little girl whom the dogs had dragged to her feet. She turned the child's head so that it faced her.

A scream as from a wild beast was heard from among the women. But the scream was quickly choked off. Several of the women had thrown the mother down on the bunk, smothering her by forcing her fists into her mouth.

In Weimar, the renowned city whose name is associated with that of the great poet Goethe, and in the celebrated city hall, which was named Schiller Hall after another noble German poet, there was a reception in honor of the great SS General von Wagner. The General had come to town to inspect a notorious concentration camp that was near the city. And after he had found the camp to be in perfect order, the town leaders, headed by their burgomaster, offered him an evening of entertainment as an expression of gratitude for the establishment of so notable a concentration camp in their vicinity. For the camp had become a symbol of fear throughout all Europe because of its renowned gas chambers, crematoria, and death factories. Into the brilliantly lighted grand ballroom where the notables of the town and their wives were assembled around the General, there entered the chief officer of the women's section of the camp. This time she was not wearing boots and military uniform. This was a civilian affair marked by the spirit of German *Gemütlichkeit,* in fact, even by a family spirit; the townsfolk had brought their wives and daughters, and there was to be a dance after the reception. Fräulein Gertrude had come dressed as Gretchen, thereby underlining the city's connection with Goethe, the poet. She wore a wide red woolen skirt cut after the style of the Middle Ages, with a girdle over her hips and a broad square opening in her tight blouse. From the opening rose her white thick throat upon which sat her fleshy white face. The two steel-blue eyes showed nothing. They were like dead stone eyes set into bare sockets without brows. But the most striking effect in her Gretchen costume was provided by her two heavy blond braids. This time the braids were not arranged in a coil around her large broad head, but hung down her back like the weighted pendants of a grandfather clock; the braids reached down to her knees. They were so heavy and so firmly twisted together that they made one think of two solid whips, the symbol and the mark of her occupation, rather than of a maiden's hair.

If her eyes sat as though frozen motionless under her browless forehead, showing not the slightest reflection of life, this was compensated for by the two large earrings she wore. They shone with human warmth. From the first moment the Fräulein entered the room, everyone's eyes were attracted by the ornaments in her delicate little ears. The earrings consisted of two large stones in the form of human eyes, set in white-gold rims, that hung by slender golden chains from the Fräulein's ears.

It must be admitted that the specialist who had undertaken to preserve Miraleh's eyes for Fräulein Gertrude's ears had done a perfect job. He had brought out all of the beauty of Miraleh's eyes, with the full magic of her glance. Just as in life, Miraleh's pupils were set in large sparkling white pools, but the master had been able to retain the whole delicate web of fine thin blood vessels that had spread over Miraleh's eyes at the moment when the Fräulein's operation had been carried out upon them.

In the irises themselves the master craftsman had had the opportunity to bring out, and permanently to embalm, the three elements of variegated color. First, a blue circle of the color of heaven ringed around the outside. The iris itself was pure golden brown in color. But in the golden-brown field there was a round black dot, and in that black center point there lay all the power of Miraleh's eyes. It was no larger than a pin point, yet it contained an entire unknown and unreachable world. It was as though the universe of human feeling were encompassed in that tiny point. It possessed a sensitivity that reacted to the slightest movement.

One might have thought that this black dot was continually in movement within the iris, changing its position, reacting to whatever glance fell upon it. It also possessed a magic attraction that forced everyone's gaze toward it, and no sooner had someone's glance lighted on this point than it was held and imprisoned. Even more, this tiny center sent out beams that seemed to steal into people's hearts and to kindle a warmth there that became a burning plea and a demand.

And it was this dark point in the irises of Fräulein Gertrude's earrings that drew everyone's gaze as she moved about among the respectable society that filled Schiller Hall. Wherever she went, the points of darkness shone from the strange and unusual stones in Fräulein Gertrude's earrings. Everyone's curiosity was awakened and excited. It was as though little Miraleh had come back to life and had settled herself in the little tower of her pupils. Her dark little doll face smiled to everyone with a childish smile. She greeted everyone; she was warm toward everyone. She seemed to be smiling and crying to everyone all at once, and in the same glance she made friends with them and pleaded with them.

And wherever the Fräulein went, at her every turn and movement, there seemed to be childish tears dropping from her, drawing everyone's attention toward her. A mournful childish tune seemed to echo about her earrings.

The SS General stood at the head of the hall, surrounded by his staff and by the leaders of the city, a few professors from the University, writers, musicians, and scholars, the burgomaster and highest Nazi elite. With their characteristic respect for Germanic authority, the townsfolk remained at a distance, gazing with adoring eyes and happy faces at their mighty ones, the Nazi leaders.

The General himself remained withdrawn. He smiled distantly, permitting himself to be admired. But even he finally noticed that something was happening in the hall. It would have been impossible for him not to notice the situation around Fräulein Gertrude.

He looked at the Gretchen with the long braids and the large earrings, who was attracting everyone's attention.

"Who is that?" he asked of his entourage.

"That is Fräulein Gertrude, the storm-troop leader of the Hitler women, and the commander of the women's section of the camp."

"Yes, I have inspected her section. She keeps it in perfect order. But what is it about her that attracts such attention?"

"Why, it's her earrings," was the answer.

At this, the General himself approached the Fräulein.

"What sort of stones are those in your earrings, that attract so much attention?" the General asked the Fräulein.

"Those are Jewish eyes in my earrings," answered the Fräulein.

"Jewish eyes!" repeated the General. "How interesting. May I examine them closely?"

Clicking her heels, she saluted and drew herself up before him. The great man carefully inspected Miraleh's eyes through his monocle.

"Perfectly preserved! Even the smallest blood vessels!" The General could not help admiring the craftsmanship.

"Not badly done," remarked a famous surgeon who had also been studying the Fräulein's earrings. "The entire net of nerves is intact. Who did it? It requires an expert knowledge of ophthalmology to preserve human eyes so perfectly."

"There is a master craftsman in this field in our city. He was always an expert in petrifying the eyes of animals. This was the first time he tried his process on human eyes, and he had good luck," said Fräulein Gertrude.

"Yes, he had good luck," agreed another one of the group around the General.

All the while that the General kept the Fräulein's ear under his interested gaze, and while the conversation was going on about Miraleh's eyes, the little girl lay in the tiny black center of her pupils and laughed with a childish laughter, warming the General's heart with her innocent playfulness and joy.

And so it went until the American Army spread over Germany. When they captured Weimar and the camp, a number of unusual possessions were found in the quarters of Fräulein Gertrude, commander of the women's section. There was a mattress stuffed with human hair upon which she slept, a lamp shade made of human skin by which she read, and there were Miraleh's eyes, arranged in little white gold frames as earrings.

"They're only Jewish eyes," the Fräulein explained casually, unable to understand the commotion her earrings had caused among the American military.

Miraleh's eyes were far too alive to be used as evidence at the trial. They were handed over to a Jewish chaplain who had come with the American troops. The chaplain carried Miraleh's eyes to a cemetery for Jewish soldiers, together with the remains of a Torah that had been found in a pile of miscellaneous souvenirs in a German house. He placed Miraleh's eyes in the grave of a Jewish soldier from the Bronx who had been killed during the taking of the city. As the chaplain stood by the grave of the Jewish soldier and spoke the prayer of the dead, he remembered Miraleh's eyes, and so he uttered a command to the soldier from the Bronx, "Take them to where they belong."

Meanwhile Miraleh was in heaven, in the palace of Mother Rachel, where she had come after her eyes had been torn out and she had died. She wandered about—a blind little angel among the pious women that were to be found in Mother Rachel's palace in heaven.

And the story was told that when Miraleh came into heaven, the On High decreed that Miraleh should remain blind for the time being, that is, until her eyes should be returned to heaven. For no other eyes could be given her, since hers were of a high and very unusual order, being the eyes of a child.

Meanwhile everything went as well as could be for Miraleh.

All the pious women in Rachel's palace occupied themselves with the blind little angel, for aside from the fact that Miraleh was blind, the child was an orphan. For, up there in heaven, children whose mothers are still in the world below are considered orphans. So the holy women made dolls and toys for Miraleh, out of the curtains of the Ark and the garments of the Torah.

And here it was not necessary to hide from guards all day long. Here she was free. There was always someone to take her by the hand and lead her to the green pastures by the still waters, as was written in the psalm. One time she would be led by a prophetess, and once by Hannah, the mother of seven sons; at other times it was Sara, or any one of the sainted women who had lately come into heaven in great numbers, to the palace of Mother Rachel. Miraleh even met some of the mothers she had known in the barracks in the camp, but these had no more time for her since their own children had been returned to them here. Even the little Galician woman who had fed her when she was in the barracks had received her own baby again here; she nursed it continuously.

Miraleh's mother had not yet come to heaven like the other mothers, and so Miraleh was dependent on the guidance of the sainted women, and they took the blind angel to their hearts.

The Jewish soldier from the Bronx carried out the chaplain's orders and brought Miraleh's eyes to the correct address that had been given him. Then a flaming little angel, a *sarafel* with rainbow-colored wings, placed Miraleh's eyes on a golden matzo plate that had come from the table of King Solomon and covered them with a sacramental bread cloth that had come from the table of a holy rabbi, and the *sarafel* flew swiftly, carrying Miraleh's eyes to the palace of Mother Rachel.

When Miraleh's eyes arrived at Mother Rachel's palace, there was great joy among the sainted women. But when they wanted to replace Miraleh's eyes in the holes cut in her face, she would not let them.

"I saw so much evil through these eyes—I don't want to see any more!" the child cried.

And then Mother Rachel wrapped herself in her black robe, with the Sabbath star set upon her brow and with a crown of sorrow on her head. Mother Rachel took Miraleh by her hand. In her other hand, the child carried her eyes, in a little prayer bag that a mother had sewn for her boy's confirmation after he was no longer alive.

And thus Mother Rachel brought Miraleh before the seat of the Most Holy. And Miraleh laid her eyes at the seat of the Eternal One. And God decreed. And Miraleh's eyes were imbedded in the Holy Throne, and there they shine with a clear pure light for the eyes of all the Jewish children whose light was extinguished.

Eretz Israel

IN the darkness of the night, at the sea's edge, in Israel, a small group of young men concealed themselves in the cleft of a ravine that gave on the Mediterranean. The heavy darkness lay like a great dead form upon the sea and on the shore. The sea was stormy, releasing its fury in high waves that beat upon rocks along the shore. Their backlash wet the cold shivering feet of the young people who waited there.

The immigration center had made contact with a ship filled with survivors from German concentration camps that had managed to get through the English blockade and was nearing the shore of Eretz Israel. They had sent out an advance guard to a point along the shore that was hidden and protected by high rocky cliffs. From there the land party would signal the ship's captain in code, instructing him where to land. And they would await the lifeboats filled with immigrants that would come from the ship.

A little farther inland, hidden in a thick orange grove, there were trucks waiting for the immigrants—trucks with armed guards ready to distribute the newcomers among various colonies in Israel.

The young people on the beach had been especially trained for this work. Among them were first-aid girls, whose equipment of medicines, blankets, and field cots lay hidden in the cleft of the ravine. They waited impatiently for the arrival of the lifeboats. Though they had purposely chosen this stormy night, they had not been prepared for the torrent of rain that came down upon them in full force. This would seriously interfere in their work. The fact that they themselves were soaked to the bone did not matter to

243

them. Their real worry was for the blankets and the cots, which were wet through. These had been prepared for the sick among the immigrants so that they might be cared for as soon as they reached the shore.

A light in a window of an isolated little house some distance inland guided the ship in its approach. But the disembarkment of the immigrants could take place only in lifeboats because of the perils of the rocky shore. The group on the beach was forbidden to use lights as signals. In the storm it would be impossible for them to hear the sound of the oars; they had no way to tell whether the boats were approaching, for in the pitch-dark night it was impossible to see more than a few feet. There was no choice but to try to pierce the darkness somehow, and to sharpen their ears in order to catch the signal of their lookout on the rocky point that projected into the sea. The lookout would try to direct the lifeboats to this landing place.

They waited and listened for hours on end. It was already far into the night. The damp cold congealed the marrow in their bones, and they had no way to warm themselves.

They were hungry for cigarettes but did not dare strike a light. Mostly young people who had been born in this land, they had only heard of the bitterness of exile without ever knowing its taste; they waited in silence. The only one who kept up a stream of talk from the very beginning of their watch was "Lady Hadassah." She was called Hadassah because she was in charge of the first-aid girls on these occasions. And she was called lady because she was a mature woman who had been one of the head nurses of the Hadassah Hospital. Also she seemed to them all a kind of symbol of the Hadassah. Whenever anyone thought of that great institution they thought also of Lady Hadassah.

Actually it was some time since she had been a nurse in the hospital. But wherever there was a misfortune, an accident, wherever an ambulance was needed, there Lady Hadassah was to be found. She was a chubby, homey woman with a bright motherly face, healthy red cheeks, and constantly smiling eyes. Young men said that one could tell she was an old maid, and there was a good deal of truth in this. There was something perennially healthy and serene in her face that was untouched by time; for, as sometimes happens with the faces of elderly spinsters who live under the mantle of their dreams, time seemed to have no effect upon her. On the face of Lady Hadassah, too, there was the romantic radiance of idealism.

If one did not look too closely to discover her age, one saw in her a young and energetic woman. Though there was no danger to which she would not expose herself, mostly she was to be found among the children of the Youth Aliyah. She was possessed of an extraordinary patience, which somehow had its effect on children who could not be controlled or quieted by anyone else. Whenever there were difficulties with the youthful immigrants in the various colonies, she was called, and with the magic of her motherly gift for harmony she would straighten out the difficulties.

Because of her gift with children she was made the leader of a group of Hadassah nurses whose task was to receive illegal immigrants, take care of the children, quiet them after their upsetting experiences, and make them feel at home in Israel. She it was who accompanied the immigrants in the trucks and wagons to the colonies. Yet she insisted on taking her place on the beach so as to be among the first to receive the newcomers. It was she who relieved the tired mothers of their crying children.

On this dark night she clambered over the jagged rocks, holding on against the heavy waves that might have washed her into the sea. Soaked through by the rain, she waited cheerfully with her comrades for the arrival of the little ships, keeping up a continual chatter and enlivening the spirits of the others with her talk.

"When we sit like this on the shore in the darkness waiting for the newcomers, there is no way of telling what sort of people will emerge from the sea. Sometimes it seems to me that a little boat will appear out of the darkness of the night, and from it will descend our fathers, Abraham, Isaac, and Jacob—to remain and live with us."

A chuckle was heard from the youngsters about her. The older generation, they seemed to say, the older generation and their romantic dreams!

"Why does it have to be Abraham, Isaac, and Jacob?" a young voice asked.

"Doesn't this sea remind you of the sea of Jewish sorrows, with its stormy waves howling over our pain and suffering, over martyrdom and pogroms? Then wouldn't it be fitting that out of this roaring sea and this black night a ship should approach our shore and that out of that ship should come our ancient patriarchs, returning to be with us as witnesses before the whole world that we are the true inheritors of this land that God promised us! Just imagine what sort of impression this would make upon the whole world, upon all of our enemies in the world, and upon our friends."

"An old maid's dream," one lad whispered to another.

"Not only the dream of an old maid, but the dream of an old generation, of the old world from which she comes," the other one answered. "They all go about with these dreams."

"If we really must dream about a little boat coming to us out of the night, sent by heaven, then I know something better it might bring, something that will have more effect on our enemies."

"What's that?"

"Let our father Moses send us that magic rod of his, by the little boat that will come to our shore out of the night."

This came from Ben Aryia, the leader of the group, whom the English had more than once dropped by parachute behind the German lines, into the Jewish ghettos, where he had organized resistance and partisan units.

"The rod of Moses?" some of them repeated, wonderingly.

"The rod that brought down the plagues on Pharaoh. We ought to have a rod like that for the new Pharaoh that spits out fire and dynamite and bombs. That's what the enemy will understand," someone added, in agreement with Ben Aryia.

"A rod has two ends. If it shoots fire out of one end, it might send back bombs out of the other. But if someone were really to drift toward us out of the night, from among our people in exile, then I have a more important wish—let the ship of Messiah himself come to us out of the darkness, not only for us but for the entire world which is on the point of death and longing for salvation—a little boat that will bring the sanctified spirit that we and the entire world are waiting for."

They all knew the voice of the orthodox worker, Aaronchik, who had been rescued from Hitler's hell by a series of miracles and wonders and whose faith had not been weakened but actually strengthened by all of the horrors through which he had passed. Since his recent arrival in Israel, he had volunteered to serve among those who went into every sort of danger in order to rescue whomever they could from Europe and bring them to the motherland. Tonight he had been sent on this mission, for it was thought that he would find others like himself among the immigrants, and because of their common experiences in the past, he would best be able to help them on their way to the new life.

"Another dreamer," his companions whispered among themselves.

"It's not to be wondered. He has nothing left but his faith. Hitler made a bachelor out of him," the leader said quietly to the others. He reminded them again to respect the religious sentiments of their comrade and not enter into disputes with him. And after this, the group became quiet.

But soon after they fell silent, the voice of the lookout was heard, "Ready! Be ready!"

As though sparked into action, they all leaped up, and four young men, one after another, jumped from the rocks into the sea, swimming through the angry waves. The others stood ready to catch the boat's line and drag it to the shore.

And then a tiny lifeboat appeared out of the stormy night. It was pulled and pushed by the youngsters, who guided it between the rocks. Silently, with practiced hands, they flung the line to the outstretched hands of their comrades on shore, and, all pulling in unison, dragged the little boat up on the rocky beach.

They stood as though turned into stone when, instead of a load of immigrants, they found only an aged, sick Jew lying on the bottom of the boat and, close to him, a crying child of about three.

"This is all they let down from the ship," said the Jewish sailor who was rowing the lifeboat. "The old man is nearly dead, so they had to get him ashore. And he wouldn't be separated from the child. Because of the storm, they are going to try to find another place along the shore where it will be easier to land the rest of the immigrants. Better take him now—I'm afraid he might be dead by now."

Lady Hadassah set to work. She put her ear against his chest. The old Jew was still alive; she could hear him gasping. "Eretz Israel?" he asked, with his last strength.

"Yes, you are in Eretz Israel," Lady Hadassah answered.

She tried to quiet him while bringing her flask of brandy to his lips. But the Jew's lips were closed. From between them his feeble voice came, "Now I can die. Father in heaven, I am thankful."

"You will live and not die. Here, take this in your lips," Hadassah insisted.

"I don't need anything any more. All that I wanted was to bring the child into Eretz Israel and fulfill my vow to his mother."

"From where have you come?"

"Do not ask. Take the child. I give him into your hands. I thank Thee, Lord of the world, that Thou hast permitted me to fulfill my vow." And the Jew closed his eyes and was silent.

Lady Hadassah took the child in her arms and said, "Even so has my dream been fulfilled. A ship came, bringing our forefathers to our shore."

"Not only her prayer, but mine, too, has been heard," remarked

248

the orthodox young man from Poland. "For the ship has brought Messiah to our shore."

"Our forefathers? Messiah?" the young people repeated wonderingly.

"Yes, our forefathers, and Messiah. Don't you realize, don't you understand? The past and the future lives in every child; the beginning and the end—our forefathers and the Messiah."

"Is that what you mean? Come, comrade, we have work waiting for us," said the leader.

And they carried onto the shore a dead Jew, and after him the living child.

Mama

AT last Dave came home, Dave Kalmanovitz, my friend, and the son of my friend Aaron Kalmanovitz, the widely respected community leader of our town.

We had waited five years for Dave's homecoming. Not we so much as his mother. For his mother steadfastly refused to believe that Dave had fallen in the Philippine jungles, with a Japanese sniper's bullet in him. The official communiqué, with its formal expression of sympathy, failed to convince her. Nor was she convinced by the letter from his commander, praising his heroism and his comradeliness and detailing his exceptional feats in the field of battle. Nor would she be convinced when his pack was returned home.

For his mother, Dave was still alive. She kept insisting that Dave was surely a prisoner somewhere in the hands of the Japanese or of the Germans, and that one fine day he would come to her; she would see him again, just as he had been the last time he was here with us on leave—young, and full of laughter; she would see his broad laughing face just as we had all seen him when he took the chubby figure of his mother in his arms and looked into her sad, worried face. "Come, smile, Mama! That's it! Isn't she the sweetest girl of all!" he exclaimed to the houseful of girls, that farewell afternoon in his father's house. They were dancing to victrola music, and he made his mother dance with him.

That was how his mother saw him and that was how we all saw him when we took him to the station. He gave his mother a last hug and threw a last kiss to her from the window as he called out, "Cheer up, old girl!"

253

And that was how his mother saw him until the train arrived at our station platform, puffing heavily, moving slowly, like an old woman. The car behind the locomotive halted at the spot where we all stood with the Legion delegation and the flags. Now we saw a box being carried out of the car—a box draped in an American flag. There were other boxes remaining in the car, and all were draped in American flags, and they would be distributed among the other stations along our railway line.

The box was loaded on a little wagon and rolled in front of the mother and father. A young lieutenant, with a sad, sympathetic face, carried out his unhappy mission. He approached the parents, with a document in his hands, and asked, "Are you the parents of Sergeant Dave Kalmanovitz?"

"Yes," answered the father.

The young lieutenant offered them the document to sign. A receipt for their son. He inclined his head deeply to them, stammered a few embarrassed words, and mounted the baggage car where the other coffins, covered in their American flags, rested side by side. It was only then that the black-robed mother fell with her face on the coffin, clinging to it, clawing with both hands. She uttered a sound like the cry of a beast who feels in her very belly the woe of her wounded offspring. "Dave, Dave, Dave, my Davie, Dave!" she cried.

The father remained manly and brave through all this; his tall figure was stiff and upright. His pain was visible in his deep-sunk eyes. But while the mother hugged the coffin and kept crying, "Dave, Dave," I noticed that my friend, Aaron Kalmanovitz, suddenly ran toward a pale blond young soldier who had descended from the train that brought David's body home. I was just able to see how the pallid face of the old Jew buried itself against the soldier's throat, and then I heard the Jew sobbing against the shoulder of the Christian lad.

"Who is that?" I asked of a friend who was standing nearby.

"Don't you know? That's Pat Evans, Dave's closest friend at the front. Do you know what that Irishman did? He named his son after Dave. David Mosheh. Can you imagine the furor that there was in his family? A Catholic child with a Jewish name! That's a rare friendship between a Jew and a Catholic."

"They say that in the Army on the battlefields it wasn't so rare."

"But this is an exception. There never was one like this. He's not only named his child after a Jew, but he wants to circumcise the boy and raise him as a Jew—just as if he were the son of a Jew."

"What are you saying?"

"Didn't you know about it? He came here to see old Kalmanovitz to ask him to adopt his son. He even went to the rabbi. Kalmanovitz was scarcely able to talk him out of it. Something must have happened between them."

"Between whom?"

"Between the Christian and the Jew, there on the battlefield."

Patrick sat in the Kalmanovitz house. His thin lips were drawn in resentment, his blue eyes flashed with a steely glint under pale blond brows. To all of my questions, no matter how carefully and tactfully they were put, he answered steadily with the same reply, "It's no one's affair but ours." At last the old Kalmanovitz said to him, "Patrick, it's all right to talk to him. He's a good friend of Dave's. Dave himself would have told him." And Patrick carried out Kalmanovitz's request, just as a son carries out an order from his father.

We retired into another room and Patrick Melvin Evans told me the story.

It was difficult for him to get going. He didn't know where to begin. He rubbed his hand a few times over his temples. He let out a few incomprehensible murmurs and a few meaningless words.

255

"I don't know if you will understand, and there is really nothing to tell." But finally he found his tongue and set off.

"Our friendship—I mean what there was between Dave and me—had nothing to do with the war, and there is nothing in it to be proud about. On the contrary. And yet I don't know if someone who wasn't in the war, I mean someone who wasn't right in the middle of danger and who never saw death staring him in the eye, will be able to understand. Because there was quite a background between Dave and myself.

"I'll tell you the truth—I never liked Jews. That's how I was brought up. And I didn't like that smart Jew, I mean Dave, because that's what I used to call him in those days. He used to stick his nose in everybody's business. And he had a way of talking to the boys that drew their most intimate, hidden feelings out of them. They used to talk to him, entrust him with things that they had never told anybody. They used to listen to his advice—you would almost have thought he was their chaplain. Well, there *was* something of a chaplain in Dave. I didn't like him. Him, and his whole race—as we used to say in those days.

"Actually, our friendship began with a quarrel. It would even have come to a fight if the boys hadn't pulled us apart.

"We were in a training camp in the Arizona desert. They trained us under live fire; they kept us out twelve hours under the burning sun. We crawled over mountains; we crawled with our noses in the sand. We tore our skins on brambles and cactus. If a man just raised his head, a bullet went over him. Some of us were actually wounded, and there were even some who were killed.

"The camp was too far for visitors to come to see us, or for us to run home on leave, like some of the boys who were in camps nearer to home. So you can understand that when we got back into the barracks we had nothing better to do than to brag about our experiences; we talked about the girls at home, about the dates we had had, and we showed each other photographs of our sweethearts.

"Once when a couple of boys in our corner were bragging about their girls, a voice behind us began singing a bit of the Piccadilly song—'My girl is the sweetest girl I know!' I looked around and saw that it was the God-damned Jew sticking his nose in among us.

" 'Do you want to see her?' he asked me with a wink.

" 'Yeah, let's see her.'

"So he took a photograph out of his wallet and showed it to us.

"Mel Walker, the boy from Georgia, took hold of it first and glanced at it. I saw that he wanted to burst out laughing, but in the last second he managed to put a smile of surprise on his face, and he handed me the photograph with a warning wink as though to say 'watch out.' I saw the face of an old Jewish woman, full of wrinkles. She reminded me right away of the Jewish women in our own town. I can't say that I had much sympathy for them. The sadness in their faces never touched me. Instead they irritated me —those Yiddish mamas with their weeping faces. You always hear sentimental songs about them on the radio and in vaudeville. My Yiddish mama—just as though a mother didn't exist among any other people except the Jews. So I handed him back the photograph, remarking, 'A real Yiddish mama.'

" 'Doesn't that suit you?' Dave asked, getting red.

" 'What's it got to do with whether it suits me or not? All I said is, a real Yiddish mama.'

" 'Yes, she is a Yiddish mama. The sweetest Yiddish mama, and I am proud of her.'

" 'Who says you shouldn't be?' I answered.

" 'I see that she's not good enough for you,' said Dave, getting a little excited.

"Knowing how sensitive the Jews are about family matters, especially when it came to their mothers, I kept control of myself, so as not to excite him. Still, I couldn't keep myself from saying, 'Would it bother you if from now on I called you Mama?'

" 'I told you I was proud of her,' Dave answered.

" 'It's settled then. From now on we'll call him Mama. Mama, Mama.'

" 'I don't mind if all of you call me Mama. I am proud of her. Everyone here can call me by that name except you, Evans.'

" 'Why?'

" 'Because you wanted to insult me with it.'

"And for the first time we saw Dave when he was furious. His eyes were fiery, and anyone could see that Dave was ready to fight.

" 'But he didn't mean anything bad by it, Dave. Really he didn't, Dave,' one of the boys said. 'Pat said that, thinking he was giving you pleasure.'

" 'Let him say so himself,' Dave demanded.

" 'Tell it to him, Pat.'

" 'I've got nothing to tell him,' I answered stubbornly.

" 'Let it go, I don't need him to say it. You boys call me Mama as much as you like. I like it. But I don't want to hear it from him.' And he put the photograph back into his wallet, and left us.

"From then on we avoided each other. We didn't speak to each other even later when we had to step all over each other's feet, in the landing craft on our way to a Philippine shore. We bumped our noses together once when a flaming shell flew over our heads and we both threw ourselves to the ground. And it was like that until we found ourselves in a foxhole at the edge of the jungle. That place was a hell—it was worse than hell. And I don't want to make us out to be heroes. There are no heroes in a war. It's only discipline, and faithfulness, and luck, and the belief that you alone will survive. Outside of that, there is only human weakness, and the will to live until everything is over with. Fear is often one of the most valuable things in war. Our captain used to tell us this himself every night when we crawled out of our hiding places in the jungle. 'Don't expose yourselves to fire, and don't try to be heroes.' In the beginning when we had just arrived on the island and were green, we lost a number of our boys even before we had seen a Jap. The jungle was full of Japanese snipers. Death peered at us from every tree, from every bush, from every bit of growth. Soon enough we learned how to crawl on all fours like dogs, how to keep our heads close to the ground, how to keep in touch with each other through our chain of foxholes, and all the rest of it.

"But the real hell began in the evening as soon as it got dark. We couldn't see the enemy. But we could hear him when he began to call to us from the jungle in that high singsong, 'Americans get ready, you die. Death is waiting for you,' and all sorts of things like that. Then there would be a whistle over our heads like a wind passing. We couldn't tell how or from where it came. Sometimes it would dig itself into the ground, making a big hole right at our feet. And sometimes it would burst, burying some of our boys alive.

"There was shrapnel all around us. We couldn't silence their batteries. Our artillery was helpless—when we had tried to set it up we were greeted by a thick rain of shells from two sides from hidden snipers, and we lost so many men that we had to give up the job.

"We could only hang onto our positions by lying in our foxholes and holding off the enemy with automatic fire.

"The enemy was afraid to show himself during the day. The real hell always began at night. If we came out of our hiding places in the woods at night and tried to drive the enemy out of his holes, we were simply walking into sure death. We knew that half of us would be left in those holes. The order was to hold the position under all circumstances until the arrival of reinforcements. We expected reinforcements every day.

"We had no chaplain with us, neither we Catholics, nor the Protestants, nor the Jewish soldiers. And even if there had been a chaplain with us, the idea that he would pray for us when we asked couldn't have helped us. So, without talking, we just used to press the hands of those nearest to us when we crawled out to our holes.

"It was the fifth night that I was lying in my hole, and on each night I had had a different man next to me. Three had been killed; two had been taken off to the hospital. On the sixth night, I got a new partner in the foxhole—Davie. I must confess that I was not very happy about this. Not that I had anything against him. That incident between us had long been forgotten, wiped out by the fear of death that we had shared. But I felt uncomfortable because the Jew might recognize my cowardliness and fear. The truth is, when the shells began to fly overhead, I used to fall with my face to the ground and cry, 'Jesus, save me!' And I was ashamed to do this before Dave, because I didn't want to show my fright before a Jew. . . . I used to pray a lot in the foxhole. And now I was ashamed to take out my cross and kneel, as I always used to do.

"We greeted each other as though there was nothing wrong, naturally. I called out, 'Hello, Dave,' catching myself just as I was about to say Mama. I swallowed the word just in time because I didn't want to excite him. He said, 'Hello, Pat.' We both began to dig, so as to deepen our foxhole. We fixed the barbed wire around us, and we dug out places for our heads in the walls of the hole. We worked silently for a while. Then we got ourselves into position, watching our heads. We placed our automatics facing the jungle, ready for the enemy. Over our heads there was a starry night, but we paid no attention. Our eyes strained into the black night that lay before us, into the thick blackness of the jungle.

" 'Your first night in the foxhole?' I asked him.

" 'No, third night. They've regrouped us. My position was smashed up last night!'

" 'Any dead?'

" 'Koslovisky was killed; Anderson the Swede got a piece of shrapnel in his head.'

" 'You were lucky,' I said.

" 'Yeah, but for how long?'

260

MAMA

" 'Are you afraid, Dave?' I asked arrogantly.

" 'What else? Aren't you afraid?' he answered.

"I thought over my reply. The fact is, I wanted to brag a bit before the Jew. I wanted to tell him, 'No, I'm not afraid.' But, something better and more honest got the upper hand in me, and I answered him, 'Yes, I'm afraid too.'

" 'Anyone who says he's not afraid is either a liar, or he's bragging, or he's an idiot.'

" 'I think you're right, Dave. We're all afraid.'

"For a moment we were quiet. Then I heard Dave mumbling something in a language I didn't understand. He was holding a little book in his hand that he had taken out of his rucksack, and he was murmuring words to himself that were strange to me.

" 'What are you doing, Dave?'

" 'Can't you see? I am praying to God.' He seemed annoyed at my interruption. Then I was no longer ashamed of my own religion in front of him. I took out my little crucifix, put it to my lips, and also began to murmur a prayer in the silence. And so we stood next to each other with our automatics in our hands and we prayed, each to our own God. Each of us was murmuring to himself the prayer that he had learned as a child and that he remembered by heart. Suddenly there was a commotion as though a tornado had struck our hole. The blast of air threw us to the ground. We stuck our heads into the holes in the wall. A flaming shell whirled over us and came down with a devilish impact, slamming into the earth just alongside our hole. The hole was covered with a cloud of dirt, sand, twigs, and branches of jungle plants, all mingled with sparks of fire. Everything came pouring down on our heads and our skins until we thought that we were buried alive. It was quite a while before I heard Dave's voice. It seems that I had been deafened. I didn't hear anything or feel anything in the darkness. I didn't even feel his hand as he passed his fingers over my body.

261

" 'Pat, are you wounded? Pat, Pat!' I heard as I recovered my senses.

" 'I think not. Nothing hurts. How about you?'

" 'The same with me.'

"And suddenly I heard Dave's voice again. He was speaking out loud, no longer in a quiet murmur. He was calling out in prayer, 'Father in Heaven, have pity on us, save us! Save us!'

"And suddenly I found myself on my knees praying out loud. 'Jesus, save us! Holy Mary, pray for us!'

"In those first moments, we didn't realize that we were no longer saying the prayers that we had learned by heart as children. Before he had prayed to his God and I to mine. Now we were praying to the same God, and not each for himself, but for both of us. And we didn't even realize that we had our arms around each other and were crying out together in one voice. I repeated his words and he repeated my words, and together we cried, 'Lord God, have pity on us!'

"I don't know how long we stood there holding on to each other and praying to God. Perhaps it lasted a moment and perhaps it lasted an eternity. I only know that in that moment something happened to me. I can describe it only in the words of Paul, 'My old self died in me and a new self was born.' But I was not reborn alone. I was born with a brother and perhaps with many brothers."

Patrick broke off the thread of his story and became quiet. I let him rest a while and after a time I asked him, "Well, and what happened?"

Patrick started up as though I had jarred him from sleep.

"Nothing happened. What should have happened? We became close friends. We didn't make any compact between us. We didn't speak of anything. The fact is, we were silent the rest of the night, except for a few words. He gave me a drink from his flask, and he took a long pull for himself. Then he asked me if I felt better. 'Yes, I feel fine!' I answered.

"Then Dave began laughing. You know how he could laugh. And I began laughing too. After that we brushed off our automatics and put them back in place and stood watching for the enemy."

"And the shelling stopped?"

"What stopped?"

"I mean the fire, from the jungle?"

"From the Japs? Why should it stop? It kept coming over us in short bursts. There was one grenade fell so close that we both got all confused again. But our fear of death was gone. Not because we really believed that we would be saved that night. Perhaps in our hearts we did believe that our prayers would be heard. But it was rather the certainty that death could no longer hurt us. Death was no longer a beast of which we were afraid. Good, let it come. We had nothing more to fear, for both of us possessed the belief of life after death, stronger than ever. I know that Dave died with this belief, just as I live with this belief. I know that the dead are born into a new life, a higher, a nobler, a more beautiful life than this, and there we shall meet and be friends, as we were here on earth."

We were silent for a long while in order to erase the solemnity of his last words, which had affected us both very strongly. I said in jest, "And there was no more talk of Mama?"

"Yes," he said with a smile. "I even thought about it all night long, wondering whether I should tell him that I was sorry about the incident with his mother's photograph, and whether I should ask his pardon or not. But then I thought, after what's happened between us, Dave understands. Still, in the morning when we got back to our base, I said to him, 'Please Dave, let me call you the way everybody calls you.'

" 'Mama?' he smiled. 'Sure, call me Mama all you want. I like it.'

"And so I called him Mama. The word got to have a new mean-

263

ing for both of us. For in that word I saw not only his mother; I began to see the face of my own mother. And I began to understand that in the wrinkles of a mother's face there are engraved all the worry and love that a mother possesses for her own child. In the thoughtful eyes of his mother, I saw my own mother's eyes, and I remembered the long nights that she had watched over me, and her hopes and her fears for me. And I, idiot that I am, had not understood this before and had made fun of his mother's anxious face."

Patrick again halted his recital, becoming absorbed in his memories.

"And how did his last and greatest act of heroism come about?"

"You mean how did Dave die?"

"Yes, tell me, I beg you."

"But you know all that from the regular report."

"The report is so short. I would like to hear it from you, from someone who was with him at his last moment. Please—tell me."

"I myself know less about it than almost anybody. Of course, you know Dave fell while he was helping me when I was wounded. I can't remember anything. I don't know anything at all of what happened in that moment to me or to him."

"But how did it come about? Please—tell me."

"Very simply. There was nothing special or heroic about it. There were dozens of actions like that every day, and many lives were lost in them. I've told you that the entire jungle was planted with Japanese snipers. We had to clean them out before we could set up our own artillery. The engineers had selected a spot where we were to set up one of our big guns. We thought this spot was cleaned out, because a scouting party had been sent out, and they had cleaned out this spot not without losses on our side. But when our detail brought up the gun, we were greeted with fire from a lone sniper who apparently had succeeded in hiding himself while he waited. The artillerymen got panicky and made a quick retreat.

Dave, who was by then a top sergeant, got angry. He called for volunteers and asked me if I would go with him.

"I answered 'Sure.' The two of us crawled on all fours as far as the tree where we figured we would find the sniper. But before we got to the trunk, a bullet tore through my helmet and embedded itself in my head. What happened from then on I don't know on my own account, but only from what I read in the report after I was operated on in the hospital. They found Dave's body riddled with bullets. I also knew that he had covered me with his own body, protecting me from the sniper's bullets after I had been hit. And that's all I know of the incident."

Patrick had ended his recital. He got up immediately, and went into the other room, where Dave's parents were sitting.

After she had felt Dave's coffin with her own hands and seen him buried with military honors in his home-town cemetery, his mother finally came to accept the fact that Dave had died. This brought her a noticeable peace. She had cried herself out and thereby drained off a great part of the bitterness that had gathered and been locked in her heart. Her wrinkled face became even more wrinkled. Her eyes sank even deeper into their dark sockets. Nevertheless the hopeless look of sorrow and despair that had darkened her face through the entire time when she believed that Dave was alive was gone. A long-suffering peace had come to her. The light returned to her eyes and illuminated her entire face. Like a child after a long crying spell she kept on sighing and groaning for a time, but her groans were now only a release from pain and sorrow. She sat with a kind of a peaceful sadness and held her worn-out wrinkled fingers folded together.

Patrick quietly slipped into the room and sat down on the footstool near her. He took her old hands in his and looked lovingly into her eyes, just as though she were his own mother.

"Do you feel better?"

"Yes, I feel better, my boy," said the mother.

"May I call you Mama?" Patrick asked with a smiling face.

"Of course you may, my son," the mother answered. And for the first time in years a restful, translucent smile softened her tight lips.

The Finger

I MUST admit that when I was invited to their wedding, I went with an apprehensive heart and an uneasy mind. I knew that the bride was a refugee who had been only miraculously spared from Hitler's furnaces. I knew, too, that the young man who was in love with her had been born and raised in America. He had met her while he was serving with the Army overseas. He had managed to get her out of the concentration camp after it became a DP camp and had brought her here to marry her.

After all that she had lived through under the brutal and pitiless hands of the Nazis in her years of slavery in the concentration camps, surely, I imagined, the bride would forever carry traces of her enslavement on her face, and she would forever carry memories that remained like nails hammered into her soul. This was scarcely a suitable girl for a young man in his best years, with an athletic build and a likable face, a young man raised in America, a lad who had grown up under the warm rays of American freedom. I was afraid that the young man had made his decision in an hour of pity when, strongly affected by the plight of the survivors, he saw something of what they had gone through and realized the suffering of his people under Hitler's regime. I thought he was impelled toward the marriage more through the need to make a gesture of self-sacrifice than through burning love.

I had never seen the bride until she came down the stairs into the wedding hall, walking to the music of Mendelssohn's *Wedding March* on the arm of her American father-in-law. My heart began to beat violently. I had to force myself to keep in mind the thought that this was a girl who had lived for five years under the shadow of death, that at every instant her life had been less secure than the life of a beast in the woods. For more than a year, they had told me, this girl had lived with her cellmates enclosed between narrow prison walls, buried alive. She had had to carry out her natural functions before the eyes of others. For more than a year and a half she had lived in a stable as a bondservant to crude and ignorant peasants. For two years she had lived in an extermination slave camp under the lash of human beasts. During the days, she and the other slave girls had to carry heavy burdens; each night she was exposed to every whim of the vicious guards. Every moment there was danger of death, and always there were insults and humiliation. They had been as helpless as birds. They were considered as spewed-out refuse. Street sweepings were more highly valued and better cared for.

But down the stairs there came a bride of Israel, a princess of Judea.

No daughter of good family, guarded under her mother's eye from the day of her birth to her wedding day, no child protected by a mother's hand, neither my own daughter nor your own daughter, was ever more perfect to behold. Untouched innocence, childish purity, and unblemished virtue, mingled with the bridal charm that is fitting in a daughter of Israel, shone from this girl who had only recently been snatched from Hitler's hell. She was twenty years old, and each of her years seemed to be a blessing of God. Her face glowed like a summer's day; one could measure her youth in her fragrant cheeks. There was a rhythmic movement in her limbs, light and athletic, that sang out like a sweet melody. There was a dancing innocence in her very walk. Her figure, completely enveloped in spotless white, was like an untapped spring, and upon it there still seemed to rest the seal of untouched virginity. Her face was white as chalk; she had the look of a half-frightened gazelle that is suddenly uncovered amongst the shrubbery, but her skin had the delicacy of ivory, shining through her pallor. Her features were most delicate; the lines were straight and pure, and she had a firm, rosy, fresh little mouth and large cherry-black eyes that looked out warmly from under their thick well-formed brows.

I shut my eyes. I tried to see her with the eyes of my spirit, for it still seemed to me that I was dreaming or that this was something utterly extraordinary, something in the way of a miracle.

And truly there was a miracle before me. I beheld the miracle; I felt it and understood it, for this bride that approached, this maiden was a symbol for all the Jewish brides who had been taken and turned into living sacrifices in the furnaces. I saw the hundreds and thousands of Jewish daughters, the blameless children, the terrified mothers, the trembling old men, on their way to death; and I saw still more: I saw in this bride the living symbol of Israel.

For five years Israel was helpless in the hands of a human beast, yet she had emerged unsullied, untouched, clean, and holy as this bride in Israel.

Later, at the wedding feast, I sat next to the bride. I happened to glance at her hands, and in the bride's hands I witnessed the meaning of five years of death agony under Hitler. No cosmetic could disguise or hide or heal what was in her hands. There I came to understand the deadly anxiety through which she must have lived during every moment. The entire five years of Jewish helplessness, the unrelenting strain of an existence that stood at every instant in the face of death, lay in these hands. Two finger-nails were missing; a third finger was split and grown over with a red lump. Her contorted thickly veined fingers were the terrible witnesses she had brought with her out of that time of night. But it was her middle finger that seemed to speak most eloquently and to tell me of all she had been through—the finger upon which she now wore her wedding ring. This finger was stiff and atrophied. It could not be moved. It protruded from her hand, and it was conspicuous not only because of its deadly stiffness, but also because of its deadly white color. And it was upon this finger that she wore her wedding ring.

Then I saw the meaning in this. In the sacred wedding ring on her dead finger I saw the symbol of the marriage between us, the living, and the dead. With this ring, the young man had sanctified for himself, and for us through him, the suffering of the tortured ones. I bent my head, and, with a sense of performing an act of religious observance, I lifted the dead finger with its wedding ring to my lips.

The bride did not say a word; she made no effort to mask or to hide her dead finger. She looked into my eyes; at first her look was solemn and cold, but afterward she smiled.